Praise for Peter Geye's
Safe from the Sea

"A **rich, satisfying novel** about family members who make amends after a lifetime of estrangement." —*The Minneapolis Star Tribune*

"*Safe from the Sea* is small in scope but substantial, on all levels, in its impact. **It is a thing of beauty; a lesson in the ineffable power of story to take us out of ourselves and bring us to a place we never knew but recognize all the same.**" —*Bookslut*

"In this deeply moving, powerfully realized debut novel, an estranged father and son find reconciliation in the final week of the father's life ... Geye tackles the subjects of death, dying, and living with admirable insight and courage ... Geye engages the complexities of family dynamics skillfully and handles especially well the kind of family grudges and misunderstandings that can cripple relationships for decades, as they do here. **Inspiring, wise, and enthusiastically recommended for all readers.** —*Library Journal*

"**A reader can just about feel the cold spray of Lake Superior and taste the softness of the lefse.**...What we expect from a man vs. nature story is not that man will win, but that man will be wise and valiant, and give it everything he has. Olaf's account of the wreck **lives up to the great tradition of adventure storytelling**. His pain about the shipwreck is not only survivor's angst, but also specific guilt about a lost shipmate that he has never shared before.... Olaf's last wish presents Noah with a watery physical challenge of his own, and gives the back end of the novel **a touch of fairy tale, *a la* late John Cheever.**" —*The Milwaukee Journal Sentinel*

"A finely crafted first novel ... **Give this book to readers of David Guterson and Robert Olmstead**, who will be captured by the themes of approaching death and the pain and solace provided by nature." —*Booklist*

"**A lyric story of familial strife and reconciliation** ... Geye excels at capturing the importance of life's seemingly small moments and at cataloging their beauty ... Geye shows how relationships—however flawed the participants—can be salvaged and strengthened when people strive to make things work through understanding and the search for and sharing of the truth." —*ForeWord Magazine*

"Geye is a skilled and subtle observer. Throughout the book, readers are given an affectionate and perceptive view of roughhewn northern Minnesota, not only its Waldenesque lakes and forests, but also its thrifty and honest people ... **Geye is a gifted storyteller ... He also excels in creating characters who are ordinary and exceptional at the same time**—high praise for any author ... there are no heroes or villains in the book, just good people working through tough issues with grace and good humor." —*The New York Journal of Books*

"**My suggestion to you? Read it, read it, read it.** Grab a blanket and a comfy chair and turn in for an early night filled with vibrant people and an intriguing story. You won't want to miss this one." **—*Duluth Budgeteer News***

"**Beautifully written . . . when I find myself reading passages from the story aloud, I know the writing has truly captured me** . . . some scenes made me laugh out loud, while others were so moving that I had to take a moment away from the pages." **—*A Curious Reader***

"*Safe From the Sea* **grabbed me from the start and will stick with me. It is a finely crafted character driven saga.** Sure there have been stories done about father and son relationships before, but not like this. Peter Geye captures the relationship as well as the beautiful Lake Superior landscape with pitch perfect ease. In my opinion, it is **a must read!**" **—*So Many Precious Books, So Little Time***

"**There are just so many amazing things about this novel**—the writing, the characters, the story and even the setting . . . Not only did I find the setting of the Great Lakes to be an integral part of the novel, but I loved how the author incorporated so much about the Norwegian immigrant culture into the story as well as the shipping industry . . . *Safe from the Sea* **would make an excellent discussion book for book clubs**" **—*bookingmama.com***

"Everything about the novel was captivating to me, from the father-son dynamics to the running of the freighters. And the theme of events, certainly catastrophic events but also simple ones, that forever change lives and relationships is monumental and artfully handled. **I can't say it enough: read this book and revel in its beauty.**" **—*booknaround***

"**Geye writes with exquisite tenderness** . . . Revealing the heartrending connections between a father and his son and between a husband and his wife, the author beautifully infuses a man's love for the sea with hope and trust. The result is **a gorgeously melancholy journey of forgiveness mixed with an endless capacity for love.**" **—*Curled Up with a Good Book***

"**Stunning and gorgeously written** . . . spell-binding . . . an unforgettable novel of a father and son who come to recognize that what connects them is stronger than what has divided them . . . one of the best books I've read this year. Literary fiction lovers who also appreciate great adventure stories will love this novel." **—*caribousmom***

"I can't remember the last book that brought me to tears. This one did . . . twice. . . . **A most impressive debut.**" **—*litandlife***

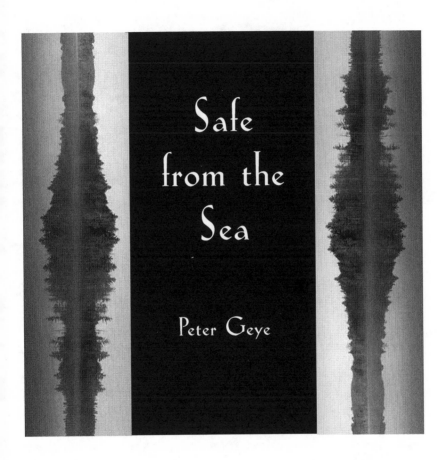

Safe from the Sea

Peter Geye

UNBRIDLED BOOKS

Unbridled Books

Copyright © 2010 by Peter Geye

First paperback edition, 2011
Unbridled Books trade paperback ISBN 978-1-609530-57-0

The Library of Congress has cataloged the hardcover edition as follows:

Geye, Peter.
Safe from the sea / Peter Geye.
p. cm.
ISBN 978-1-60953-008-2
1. Fathers and sons—Fiction.   2. Prodigal son (Parable)—Fiction.
3. Minnesota—Fiction.   4. Domestic fiction.   I. Title.

PS3607.E925S24 2010
813'.6—dc22
2010023074

3   5   7   9   10   8   6   4   2

BOOK DESIGN BY SH · CV

Second Printing

For Dana, of course.

And for

F.A.

C.D.

E.M.

Safe
from the
Sea

PROLOGUE

The officer stood the midnight watch, his hand easy on the wooden wheel. He was steering the ore boat *Ragnarøk*, five hours outside Duluth harbor and downbound for the Superior Steel Works in Detroit.

"Jacobsen," he called.

"Sir?" The wheelsman stepped to the helm.

"Bear northeast, Jacobsen. And never mind this." He tapped the binnacle dome. "Steer for Polaris." He pointed up at the firmament. "The top of the dipper." Their load of taconite had sent the compass dithering.

"Yes, sir."

The officer stepped to the chart. He withdrew his tobacco and papers from the inside pocket of his coat and rolled a cigarette. In the weary light of a twenty-watt bulb he studied their course. They were some twenty nautical miles north of the Keweenaw Peninsula in water a hundred and fifty fathoms deep. He marked their position. It was a passage plotted ages ago, one he knew by rote. He stood there because he was a prudent man, strict in his habits and in his discipline.

An upholder of protocol. Consulting the charts was written into his duties.

He stepped outside, rounded the pilothouse decking. With his feet astride the keel line he lit his smoke. There was the sky to the north. The aurora borealis. Coronas the color of ice, the color of fire. This man was no philosopher, but neither was he blind. He could see what lay before him.

When his smoke was down to its nub he flicked it over the deck railing. He tucked his chin into his coat and again rounded the decking.

Back in the pilothouse he said, "Jacobsen, do you have children?"

"No, sir."

"My first child was born nine days ago. A son. Nine days ago, and here I am bound for the Soo. Can you beat that?"

"What's his name, sir?"

"My wife named him Noah."

A weather report warning of snow squalls off the Keweenaw crackled over marine radio. This sent both men's eyes back to the north.

"Look at that sky, Jacobsen. Have you ever seen anything like it?"

"It's something."

"If only my son could see it."

"Someday, sir."

This pacified the officer. "Someday," he echoed.

The officer settled into his loneliness, thinking of his son and wife. The feeling was specifically sad and beautiful. The colors in the sky vanished, were replaced with the brightness of stars.

By the time they cleared the Keweenaw the sky was indeed squally. A chop had come up with the wind. The officer checked his pocket watch against the sky.

I.

Red, Right,
Returning

ONE

That morning Noah boarded a plane for Duluth. By seven o'clock he was driving a rental car down Mesaba Avenue. Between the intermittent swoosh of the windshield wipers he recognized the city he harbored in his memory. It lay below him smothered in fog, the downtown lights wheezing in mist. Though he could not see the lake in the distance, he knew it rested beyond the pall. Soon he pulled onto Superior Street. The manholes blowing steam might have been freeing ghosts.

It had been his plan to drive up to Misquah, but he'd been delayed during a Minneapolis layover and decided it was too late. Instead he drove onto Lake Avenue, parked, and stepped out into the evening. Now he could see the lake, a dark and undulating line that rolled onto the shore. The concussions were met with a hiss as the water sieved back through the pebbled beach. The fog had a crystalline sharpness, and he could feel on his cheeks the drizzle carried by the wind. It all felt so familiar, and he thought, *I resemble this place*. And then, *My father, he was inhabited by it*.

But Duluth had also changed. Where now T-shirt and antique shops kept address, dive bars and pawnshops and shoe-repair shops had once done a dismal business. More than a few of Noah's boyhood friends had ordered their first steins of beer in the slop shops that were now coffeehouses and art galleries. As a kid Noah had seen grown men stumble from doorways, drawing knives as they fell, ready to fight. Now he saw squalling kids and husbands and wives bickering over where to have dinner. The hotels had once offered hourly rates, now half-a-dozen national chains were staked in Canal Park. There were book-shops, ice-cream parlors, wilderness outfitters, toy stores, even a popcorn and cotton-candy cart, all lining the street like a Vermont ski town.

There did remain two stalwarts: the Tallahassee and the Freighter. The former, though it advertised JAZZ! ON SATURDAYS, was a topless bar with filthy taffeta curtains bunched in the windows. The latter was where Noah had ordered his first beer more than twenty years ago. It had also been his father's hideaway of choice. They were next door to each other, laggards from a vanished time.

For all its squalor, the Freighter was a landmark, a bare-knuckle place that had not given way to slumming conventioneers or frater-nity brothers down from the colleges. Dark, greasy air thick with smoke and blue neon hung like the fog as Noah stepped in for a draft and something to eat. A gauzy linoleum floor curled up from rotten floorboards, and a cobwebbed fishing net hung from the ceiling. Be-hind the bar, above the bottles of cheap booze, a series of photo-graphs of ore boats in teakwood frames were nailed into the wall. A few tipplers sat at the bar, and behind the pull-tab counter a silver-haired churchgoer did a crossword puzzle. The sign above her head announced a meat raffle on Wednesdays.

Noah took a seat at the bar and swiveled around. Other than the murmuring of the drinkers and tinkling of pint glasses, the only sound came from an ancient television on the end of the bar broadcasting the local news.

"You look familiar," the barman said, "but you aren't from around here." An old man with a ruddy face and drooping eyes, he looked familiar to Noah, too.

"I haven't been here in years," Noah said. "But my old man used to call this place home."

"Who was your old man?"

"Olaf Torr."

"Oh, Christ," the man said, wiping his hands on a rag before reaching under the counter for a bottle of Wiser's. "If you're Torr's boy, this is on me."

Before Noah could decline, two shots of whiskey sat on the bar.

"I can't drink this," Noah said.

The barman drained the shot he'd poured for himself and smacked his lips. "You ain't Torr's boy if that's true." He poured another drink for himself. "Your pop's dead?"

"Jesus, no," Noah said. Then added, "Not yet."

"He still living up around Misquah?"

"Unbelievably, he is."

The barkeeper had not taken his eyes from Noah. He shook his head thoughtfully. "We used to fall on over to the Tallahassee every odd day of the week, your pops and me. Watch them girls shake tail."

"You corrupted him, then."

"Sure, he needed corrupting." His father's old crony sipped the second ounce of Wiser's. "What brings you home?"

"I'm headed up to see him."

"You tell that son of a bitch Mel says hello."

"I'll do that," Noah said.

"You hungry?" Mel asked.

Noah ordered a burger basket and a pint of beer to help with the whiskey.

. . .

THE LAST TIME he had been in the Freighter was almost six years ago, on the morning after the wedding of a childhood friend. Before heading back to Boston he'd met his father for breakfast. On the mismatched barstools half-a-dozen gray-haired men sat like barnacles. When the door creaked shut behind Noah they turned in unison to sneer at the schoolteacher in pressed khaki trousers standing in the doorway. Olaf stood up, last in line and farthest from the door, looked down at Noah over the top of his glasses, and pulled out the barstool next to his own. "Hello, boy," he said across the room as he pushed two empty Bloody Mary glasses into the bar gutter and crushed out a cigarette. "Come here. Have a seat. What do you know?"

As Noah approached, he took inventory of the old man: A baggy chambray work shirt frayed at the collar and cuffs and a pair of dungarees cinched with a canvas belt brought attention to how thin he had become; his hair and beard were both completely white now and even more unkempt than Noah remembered; his black boots were untied. As Olaf extended his hand, Noah saw evidence of the arthritis his sister had warned him of, but when he took the old man's hand, the strength of the grip surprised him.

"Hi, Dad."

Olaf pulled the barstool out further. When Noah sat, his father stepped back, sizing up Noah in his own manner. "Penny loafers, huh?"

Noah shrugged and held his hands up in a gesture of deference.

"What'll you drink?" Olaf said.

"Orange juice. It's ten o'clock in the morning."

"Orange juice for the boy, Mel!"

Whereas the other patrons had newspapers or each other for

company, Olaf had been sitting alone, with only his drink before him. When he rejoined Noah at the bar, he resumed the posture of a loner, looking straight ahead at the bar back and rolling another cigarette.

Their talk over the next hour could hardly have passed for conversation. Between bites of runny eggs and greasy hash browns, Olaf asked Noah about his job and his girlfriend. Noah asked after the old man's health and the state of the cabin up on Lake Forsone, where Olaf had recently moved after selling their house on High Street. Olaf drank two more Bloody Marys with Grain Belt snits. Occasionally his voice surged and the other men in the bar set their drinks down to look at him. Everyone knew who he was, of course, and there seemed to be dueling sympathies in their attention. On the one hand, they must have admired his tragedy, and on the other, pitied his churlishness.

In a lull during their breakfast Noah said, "I'm getting married."

"That's what your sister tells me." Olaf shifted his gaze from the bar back to the ceiling and blew a stream of smoke. "Getting hitched," he continued under his breath.

Noah slid his plate forward and swiveled to face his father. "In October. I hope you'll be there."

Instead of answering, Olaf summoned Mel. "The boy's settling down, partner," he announced. "Tying the knot."

"The slipknot?"

"That's the one," Olaf said.

"God help him," Mel replied.

"I'd offer to buy you a drink," Olaf said, turning his attention back to Noah, "but you've already got your juice." Instead he motioned for another Bloody Mary. Mel set about making it. "A slipknot, it's like a noose," Olaf explained. "It's a joke, boy."

"A good one, too."

Noah remembered looking his father in the eye and seeing nothing but a boozy vacancy. The old man's drunkenness had always struck Noah as cumulative. Olaf had not spent nights in the hoosegow, he'd not crashed the family car into light poles or missed mortgage payments because his paycheck had been squandered here at the Freighter. Despite this, the years had surely added up to something, to some soggy history that diminished the old man. Noah had an impulse to scold him but did not. Instead he rose to leave. "I've got a flight," he explained. "I hope you'll make the wedding." He put his hand on his father's shoulder in a gesture that should have been reversed. "Take care of yourself, okay?"

Olaf looked again over the top of his glasses. "I'll see you in October."

"YOU READY FOR another beer?" The bartender's voice came as if from that morning years ago. He cleared the empty basket, took measure of Noah's shot glass on the bar.

"No, thanks."

"I swear, if you weren't the spitting image of that old cuss, I'd suspect you of lying." He pointed at the whiskey.

"Sorry," Noah said. "I appreciate the thought. I've just never been able to stomach the stuff."

"No harm," he said, then placed the tab on the bar.

"Are there any boats tonight?" Noah asked.

Mel looked at the clock on the wall. "*Erindring*'s outbound in an hour. Load of coal for the good people of Stockholm."

Noah laid payment on the tab. "Does he ever come down here anymore? You ever see him?"

"Your old man? Nah. I haven't seen him in what, five years? Maybe longer."

"I'll tell him you said hello. Thanks for everything."

"Anytime, now. Good-night."

AT THE BREAKWATER he listened to the canal water lapping against the wall. Herring gulls squawked and rolled and dove on invisible currents above the aerial bridge. Every couple of minutes one would pull up on the breakwater and hop toward Noah with a cocked head. They appeared famished and well fed at the same time. Their iridescent eyes glistened in the lamplight. He had always loved watching the gulls and thought there was something majestic about them up here, something very different from the scavenger gulls back in Boston. Here the gulls fished first and begged only after the smelt had gone out.

He looked over the breakwater wall, caught his shadowy reflection in the waves, and wondered how many times during the last twenty-four hours he'd tried to remember his father's aged face. Even as Noah had replayed the memories of that morning years ago in the Freighter, he had not quite been able to summon it.

The last of the gulls flew into the harbor, and he turned to head back. A light rain now mixed with the fog, and the temperature seemed to be falling. Not fifty paces to his left the foyer of the maritime museum was still lit. He approached the entrance and saw that it was open for another half hour. Inside, the split-level entryway was covered with posters and artifacts representing the Great Lakes shipping industry. He took the ramp up, which led into a large room with windows overlooking the canal. But for the person sitting behind the information desk, Noah was alone in the museum.

A crumpled lifeboat hung suspended from the ceiling on the edge of the main room. Next to it one of the anterooms advertised itself as the RAGNARØK EXHIBIT. Noah ventured in. A montage of photographs hung on the wall, and his father's image glared back from two. The first took Noah's breath away. It was an eighteen-by-twelve-inch black-and-white of the crew of the *Rag*. They huddled dockside in front of the black-hulled freighter during a late-winter snow squall. Taken in March 1967, the day of her first cruise that shipping season, it reminded Noah of countless other departures. Most of the thirty faces in the photograph were blurred in the snow or hidden by the wool collars of the crew's standard-issue peacoats, but the image of his father's gaze—unblemished by the snow and unhidden by his collar—was clear. The placard beside the photo said: THE CREW OF THE ILL-FATED SUPERIOR STEEL SHIP SS *RAGNARØK*, MARCH 1967. THE SHIP IS AT BERTH AT THE SUPERIOR STEEL DOCKS IN DULUTH HARBOR. THE *RAG* WOULD FOUNDER IN A GALE OFF ISLE ROYALE EIGHT MONTHS LATER. TWENTY-SEVEN OF HER THIRTY HANDS WERE LOST. It also listed, in parentheses, each of the men, from left to right, front to back.

Noah recognized the second photograph, taken of the three survivors. Luke Lifthrasir lay on a four-handled gurney being carried up the glazed boulder beach, his gauze-wrapped arm raised triumphantly in a frostbitten fist. Two men in Coast Guard uniforms tended to Bjorn Vifte, who sat huddled under a wool blanket. Noah's father sat in the edge of the picture, alone, his shoulders slumped over his knees, the small of his back resting against an ancient cedar tree that grew from a cleft in the bedrock. Blood frozen in parallel lines stained his cheek. In the background, a photographer aimed his camera at the same wrecked lifeboat that hung on display from the ceiling in the next room. The second placard read: THE THREE SURVIVORS OF THE WRECK

OF THE SS *RAGNARØK*, ASHORE AT LAST, HAT POINT, WAUSWAUGONING BAY, LAKE SUPERIOR. NOVEMBER 6TH, 1967.

Noah toured the rest of the museum like a somnambulist. A collection of ship models and more photographs chronicling the nautical history of Lake Superior filled one room. Recovered relics from Great Lake shipwrecks—forks, lanterns, life vests, a teakettle, a sextant, a compass, an oil can, a coal shovel, a brass bell—lined the glass cases that circled another exhibit. A row of small rooms replicated the cabins of different ships, a sort of timeline of living conditions aboard Great Lakes freighters. A steam-turbine tugboat engine, circa 1925, twenty feet tall, rose between the split-level entry. And the museum's centerpiece, a model pilothouse complete with an antique wooden wheel, a chart room, and a brass Chadburn set to full steam, sat in the middle of the main hall.

From behind the wheel Noah looked out onto the lake. Although it was dark, he could see through the bare branches of a maple tree. Beyond the canal breakwaters and the channel lights the lake disappeared into an even deeper darkness. To his left, he knew, the hills stretched above town, shrouded in a chrysalis of late-autumn mizzle. And behind him the aerial bridge loomed like a skeleton.

Back outside, he resumed his spot at the breakwater. He heard the *Erindring* before he saw it. The ship blasted its horn, giving notice to the bridge-keeper. One long blow, like a cello's moan, followed by two short blows was responded to in kind. The warning arms dropped on either side of the bridge, and it rose. A couple minutes later and the freighter was in full view, pushing through the pewter lake fog and faint harbor lights. It moved slowly, almost imperceptibly, and Noah marveled—as he had maybe a thousand times before—at the original notion of a million pounds of floating steel.

A faint hum accompanied the steaming ship under the bridge as it eased its way through the channel, past Noah, who had walked out to the end of the breakwater. The muted drone and eerie slapping of water against the hull accentuated a silence that seemed to grow as the ship inched its way nearer the end of the pier. When the first quarter of the bow passed, it was quiet enough that he could hear two men standing on the pilothouse deck, speaking a language he didn't recognize. One of the men tossed his cigarette into the lake and nodded at Noah. In another few seconds the stern was even with the end of the breakwater and the hum replaced by water gurgling up from the prop. For five minutes Noah watched the ship until it disappeared into the eventide.

NOAH STOOD AT the breakwater thinking of Natalie long after the *Erindring* had passed into the darkness. After he had hung up with his father the day before, he sat on the edge of the bed in dumb disbelief. He heard his wife come into the bedroom, and when he looked up she was leaning against the door frame in the oversized Dartmouth sweatshirt she wore around the house.

"Who was that?" she asked.

"My father."

She stepped fully into the bedroom and stood before Noah. "What's wrong?"

"He's sick." Noah looked back down. "I told him I'd come home."

"Are you sure that's a good idea?"

"No." He stood and put the phone back in the bedside cradle. "It's probably not a very good idea. But why would he call? I have to go, don't I?"

"Noah, you haven't seen him since our wedding." There was a tone of incrimination in her voice.

"He's old, Nat, and this sounded serious."

"If you think you should go, then I guess you will." With those cryptic words she walked down to the basement for her treadmill workout. Noah was too stunned—both by Natalie's reaction and his conversation with his father—to follow her.

Later, as Noah packed, Natalie lay in bed with her laptop open and files spread around her. She hadn't said much all night, and the weight of her silence was troubling. "Want to tell me what's on your mind?" he said.

She clapped her laptop shut and gathered her files. The look she gave him could have cut glass. "You don't know."

"Don't know what?"

"There are other things now, Noah."

He looked at her, confused.

"Never mind," she said, leaning over to turn out her lamp. "If your father's ill, you should go. I hope it's not serious."

"Tell me what's going on."

"It's nothing. Forget it."

"Hey," he persisted, going around to her side of the bed, "why aren't you talking to me?"

"I said it's nothing," she said and pulled the covers over her head.

Noah knew her dismissals to be final, so he let her go to sleep. It was only later, while he lay in bed himself, unable to sleep, that he understood her chagrin: It was time to try to get pregnant again.

Natalie was a woman wholly given to her convictions. Because just about everything in her life had gone according to plan—by virtue of some good luck but more hard work—their inability to have a child had become, for her, less a thing to puzzle over than proof that she had exhausted all her good fortune. Her fatalism drove Noah crazy, and he had recently become apathetic about their travails. Though he resented their childlessness, he simply did not see it as a reason to cease with the rest of his life. Oftentimes, it seemed, she did.

He tossed and turned, weighing his father's phone call and all that it portended against his wife's sorrow. He thought of waking her, of telling her that he understood why she was so sad but that he had to brave this homecoming. He thought of taking her in his arms, hoping his embrace would prove his devotion.

But he didn't wake or embrace her. He lay awake nearly all night, falling asleep only after the first hints of light had filtered into the bedroom. When he woke a couple of hours later she had already left for work.

NOW HE WALKED back to his car and drove up Superior Street to the Olde Hotel, where he checked into a lakeview room. Natalie had never visited Duluth, and he was glad of her absence now. It seemed not only right to be alone but a relief.

He dropped his bag on the settee and walked over to the window and spread the curtains. He knew he should call her. She would expect a call.

He called Ed instead. Three years ago Noah had quit teaching history at a Brookline prep school and bought an antiquarian map business he'd seen advertised in the back of *Harper's*. His single employee was a retired marine colonel. Ed was dependable to a fault and was looking after the store while Noah was away. Over the phone he reassured Noah that he needn't worry, said he'd call if he had questions, and told Noah firmly to go take care of his ailing father.

Outside, the rain had stiffened and was washing away the fog. Noah kept his eyes on the lake while he dialed home.

"Hey," he said, "it's me."

"It's you," she said, the sound of her voice taut with disappointment.

"I'm in Duluth. I got here about three hours ago, too late to drive up to Misquah. I hope I didn't wake you."

"You didn't."

"I got a hotel room. I'll drive up there in the morning."

He noticed a light gathering form out on the lake.

"Okay," she said. "How are you?"

"I'm fine. Listen, Nat, I'm sorry about how I left."

"It's not how you left, Noah. It's *that* you left." She took a deep breath. "But I think you know that."

It was his turn to take a deep breath. What could he say to appease her? "I said I was sorry."

"There's no need to apologize." He heard the refrigerator crunching out ice, her glass of water before bed.

"I didn't plan this, Nat."

"You haven't seen your father in more than five years, Noah. You've hardly talked to him."

Noah thought of the pictures in the museum. He thought of his father's distant voice on the phone just yesterday. "He's sick."

"I know." The strain in her voice lessened. "The timing is terrible, that's all. It's incredible."

"You're right about that," he said.

Noah watched the rain strengthen, saw sheet lightning up over Minnesota Point. He knew that the root of her terseness lay in her overwhelming sadness, one that consumed her often. He feared that his coming here was unforgivable as far as she was concerned, but he also knew that when he'd told his father he was coming, he'd had about as much sway over his own words as he now had over the thunderstorm outside.

"Just call me again after you get there. It's late and I have an early morning," she finally said.

"I'll call tomorrow."

"I have an appointment with Dr. Baker tomorrow, in case you forgot."

"I didn't forget, Nat."

A meaningful silence passed, as though both had more to say but neither could articulate their thoughts. Finally Noah said, "Good-night, then. I love you."

Natalie said, "Good-night."

Noah remained at the window. When finally the rain let up the light he'd been watching out on the lake came into focus. A freighter, her deck lights radiant with caution, lay at anchor. It was a fitting view for his faraway feelings.

NOAH THOUGHT OF the map of the north shore he had framed above his desk at home, a lithograph of the Minnesota arrowhead circa 1874. There were no roads then—either on the map or in reality—but the Lake Superior shore was dotted with towns, most of them now gone or renamed. Whenever he found himself sitting back in his desk chair, looking up at the map, he was reminded of passing along this shore as a child.

Highway 61 was as forlorn in those predawn hours as it had re-mained in his memory. The potholes and seasons-old frost heaves yet pocked the blacktop, the dilapidated wooden storefronts and signs warning of deer crossings and dangerous curves still marked the roadside, the countless rivers and streams rushed under the highway bridges as they had for ages. But the two deadliest curves—curves that had once pinned cars on sheer cliff tops—had been replaced with quarter-mile tunnels burrowed through the bedrock.

He had left Duluth an hour ago, sleep starved and anxious, and now was toying with the radio. A disc jockey from a station in Marquette announced the time, seven twenty-five, and an old country-music song. The first few chords of a steel guitar moaned before fading to static. He turned the radio off and settled into the hum of the tires on the pavement. Occasionally the road curved to the right and the trees dispersed and the brown rocks and the brown water of the lake came into view. The lake was unusually still, especially in contrast to his memories of it tonguing up onto the stone beaches. They were a child's memory, though, the water all froth and fury.

Just clear of Taconite Harbor and the Two Islands he saw the sun rise over the water, remembering the adage about a red sky in morning. It was red—the sky over the lake—and lowering. It reminded him of the late-season gales that had been the curse of his mother, the curse of all the ore men's wives. He never knew what to think about the storms but that they were spectacular. There was one stewing in the distance.

He passed the Temperance River and pulled the directions from his shirt pocket. His father had called just two days ago, his voice hoarse and whispery.

"Hello, boy," he said, the heavy pause between words freighted with circumspection. Without waiting for Noah to respond, Olaf continued, "I may need a bit of help getting the place ready for winter."

"Help?" Noah said. *Help?* he thought. He almost said, *Who is this?*

"The woodpiles, some work around the house."

"Why?"

His father took a deep and raspy breath. "I'm sick, Noah."

It wasn't what his father said as much as it was the fact of hearing him speak at all that alarmed Noah. The silence between them had become unconditional. Noah couldn't have said whether the estrangement—from his point of view—had evolved into forgetting or forsaking, but when he said to his father, "I'll come, I can leave tomorrow," he was alarmed again, this time by his own impulse. "I'll fly into Duluth. But I'm not sure I remember how to get to the cabin." Now, approaching Misquah, he began to feel uneasy. He'd traveled this road a thousand times, but not since he was in high school.

The directions Olaf gave were those of a man who knew where he was and where he was going unconsciously: *Up in Misquah you'll see the Landing there—it's got a red sign. You'll recognize it. Past the Landing the county road goes into the hills. You'll see a stand of firs burnt red from this summer—it was a warm summer—look for those trees. Twenty minutes into the hills you'll come on Lake Forsone Road. There's clover still flaming in the ditch on the right. When I first saw it, I thought it was a goddamn brushfire. Turn and follow the road around the lake. You'll remember when you get here. Anyway, it's simple now that I think about it: Just keep the red on the right, like the harbor buoys—red, right, returning.*

Among the red markers his father had mentioned, only the gas station was plain to see. He spotted no stand of red-burnt firs, no flaming clover. The county road was tucked behind a rock outcropping at a bend on the highway. He'd been expecting gravel, but it was paved now. The trees his father had mentioned were barely distinct in the forest of millions. The burnt red his father had described was an almost indiscernible rouge they wore among their green, green boughs. The road ascended quickly and narrowed into the deep timber.

Ten minutes later it veered sharply to the left and in the middle of the curve, on the right, a dirt road tunneled into the trees. At the wooden marker Noah stopped to watch a whitetail deer and her fawn breakfasting on the tall grass. They were so lithe and alert. Noah moved ahead slowly, taking a last look out the passenger-side window. There in the grass he saw a patch of red clover.

Despite his father's suggestion that it would all look familiar, Noah had no memory of where the house might be. He followed the road left, to the north, past the public access and over a culvert. The road continued to curve away from the lake, so it surprised him when he saw a mailbox, barely attached to a rotted post, with his father's name faded to the edge of invisibility. He stopped again, opened the mailbox, and found mail postmarked as long as three weeks ago: supermarket flyers, real estate offerings, magazines, and a handful of envelopes from the Superior Steel Company. He took it all with him.

Noah turned onto the trail. Long grass grew between the tire tracks, and overgrown trees brushed the top of his car. For a quarter mile he crept toward the lake under the shade of the trees. Then the road widened and began to go downhill. Rain runoff channels a foot deep grooved the hill, and what little gravel remained on the trail was unpacked. After three sharp turns, the cabin appeared before him.

He parked beside the rusted Suburban that his father had bought the year Noah went to college. Noah's Grandpa Torr had been a meticulous man and had kept the house shipshape. The woodpiles—like bunkers along two sides of the house and in the middle of the yard— had always been expertly stacked. His grandpa used to boast that they could withstand a tornado. He kept the trees trimmed, too, and the small lawn mowed. His Grandpa Torr's fastidiousness was redoubled in Noah's own father, so the disrepair of the house shocked Noah.

The rough-sawn cedar siding had taken on a green-gray hue, and the grainy, knotted siding had been weathered smooth. The roof bowed and had bunches of moss and spry grass growing between the shingles. Either his father had become a different man or he'd not been well enough to maintain the place for years.

Not knowing whether to knock or just walk in, Noah hesitated before pushing the screen door open and stepping into the house. "Dad?" he said. "Dad," he called again, waiting for his eyes to adjust to the dim light. No one answered. After looking in each of the two bedrooms he stepped back out and walked to the shed at the edge of the yard. With its fieldstone foundation sinking into the earth, cracked windows, and peeling paint, the shed looked as bad as the house. A padlock secured the door, and curtains covered the windows inside. He turned, stood for a minute watching the privy up the trail, and when his father didn't appear, he started toward the lake.

As he walked down the footworn path he recalled countless days when as a child he'd followed his father up this same trail. He could picture his father's broad shoulders, the stringer of lake trout hanging from his thumb, the purposeful stride. Noah could never keep up with him and was always out of breath when he reached the top of the hill. There he'd find his father standing over a tree stump on the edge of the yard, his fillet knife ready. Noah would pause every time, watching from a short distance the man he hoped someday to become. Those memories were coming back to him sadly now, and as he neared the shore he stopped suddenly.

Was that man really his father? He had a rod in the water, fishing in the shallows alongshore. His spine was bowed and knobby. His stark white hair framed his head. He cut a lonely silhouette against the lake, so lonely in fact that the steely resolve Noah expected of himself gave immediately over to sadness. Noah stood there for a moment, then coughed and said, "Hello, Dad." He took a step in his father's direction.

Olaf turned and looked up. "Ah, he's here."

Olaf reeled in his line and set the rod in the bottom of the boat. The rusted and bent dock poles evidenced the many winters it must have spent in the water. The missing planks were more confirmation of the sad state of the place. The dock swayed with his father's clumsy steps as he came ashore.

Olaf stood before him for a long moment. He had become so slight that Noah was able to look squarely into his eyes. Finally Olaf said, "How was the trip?"

"Okay. Fine."

"All right."

"How are they biting?" Noah pointed at the fishing rod.

Olaf turned to the lake. "There's fish out there, just none for me. You eat breakfast?"

"Not yet."

"I've got some oatmeal."

"I'd eat oatmeal."

Olaf looked up the hill, took a deep breath, and combed his beard with his hand.

"How are you feeling?" Noah said.

Olaf looked at him as though he were surprised by the question. "Like a hundred goddamn bucks."

"That's good."

And Olaf started up the hill.

Noah trailed him, watching his father's slumped shoulders, listening to his heavy breathing. The old man could barely lift his feet. When they stopped midway and Olaf rested against a boulder Noah said, "You sure you're okay?"

"It's a long goddamn walk nowadays," Olaf said and then started up again.

When they reached the top of the hill Olaf leaned on the corner of the house. His flannel shirt hung on him like a drape, his pants sagged. The deep wrinkles around his eyes lent them a hollow aspect and accentuated the look of fatigue on his face.

"I can make breakfast," Noah offered.

Olaf stood up. "Come on inside," he said.

Olaf put a kettle of water on the potbellied stove, which stood along the wall between the two bedroom doors. He stoked the fire and walked back to the kitchen. The box of steel-cut oats sat on a shelf over the sink. Olaf filled two bowls and placed a spoon in each.

"Can I help?" Noah asked.

"You just sit."

After the water began to boil, Olaf carried it to the kitchen with a grubby mitt, poured it over the oats, and then asked Noah if he wanted coffee.

"Whatever you're having."

"You want nuts? Raisins?"

"Sure," Noah said.

Olaf stored the nuts and raisins in Mason jars. The almonds were sitting on top of a bookcase, and Olaf went into his bedroom for the raisins. He mixed the bowls of oatmeal as if they were filled with cement, carried them one at a time to the table. Finally he brought two mugs of coffee over.

"You want anything else?"

"No. Thanks. This looks great."

"Well, then, come on while everything's still warm."

They ate silently at first, blowing on spoonfuls of steaming oats and sipping their coffee. Neither had much flavor, and the raisins and nuts were hard as stones. Olaf thumbed through the mail Noah had set on the table, taking measured bites, determined to show that whatever ailed him hadn't gotten too far along yet. Noah couldn't bring it up, not yet, so instead he said, "You've been doing your reading." Two bookcases in the dark corner of the cabin teemed with paperbacks. "Since when are you such a bookworm?"

"What else have I got to do up here?"

"Looks like you've been fishing," Noah said.

Olaf paused over a spoonful of oats. He looked at Noah. "Fishing? Sit on the dock and catch a perch and call it fishing?" He put the oats in his mouth. "I haven't fished the steps all year. I thought we could go over there after breakfast."

"It's been a while. But fishing the steps sounds good."

Olaf said, "All right, then. We'll go fishing."

NOAH OPENED THE cabinet and saw half-a-dozen rods hung carefully on the inside of the door. Among the collection he recognized his old fly rod—the one he had used as a high school kid almost every summer day—and his favorite Shakespeare spin caster with the cork handle. He had seldom used the spin caster after he'd discovered fly fishing.

"My god," Noah said as he stepped out of the house. "This is the same rod and reel I had as a kid."

"That's a good setup. I just changed the line and oiled the reel. It's all ready."

Noah imagined his father's huge, bumbling hands, arthritic and pained, putting a new line on the reel. He must have spent a full afternoon on it. "So we're all set, then?" Noah asked.

"And we better get moving. By sunset it'll be raining like the end of days."

They descended the hill and climbed into the boat, Olaf straddling the forward thwart, leaving Noah to row. Noah untied the stern line from the dock and pushed out into the shallows. The oarlocks shrieked as he made his first stroke. With each stroke after, they quieted until he turned the boat north and the oarlocks quit complaining altogether.

Lake Forsone was cut from an ancient batholith, the last above-water remnants of which rose in a sharp palisade of iron-streaked granite on the far northern shore. Fifty feet tall and a quarter mile long, the cliff dominated the landscape. On the western edge of the escarpment the Sawtooth Creek emptied into the lake. It was here that the late-season trout would be gathered on what the Torrs had named the first step. The water beneath the palisade descended in four broad steps to a depth of more than a hundred and fifty feet. There were almost a thousand lakes in the county, Forsone was the deepest.

The southern quarter of the lake was much shallower, and the rock outcroppings that dominated the northern shore gave way to a muskeg thick with black spruce and fen. The muskeg drained into Tristhet Creek, a fishless stream that trickled all the way to Lake Superior. Noah watched as a barred owl rose from its hollow tree in the bog land, its wings flapping in slow motion. A breeze rose with the bird.

By the time they reached the shadowy water beneath the palisade, Noah felt well primed. It had taken him nearly half an hour of constant rowing. He reached over the gunwale, cupped his hand, and brought a scoop of water up to splash his face. It was ice cold and clear as glass.

When he turned to his father the old man was already tying a bucktail jig onto Noah's line. "It's still enough we won't drift much," Olaf said, handing him the rod. "Cast up against the cliff, let it sink, crank her in. The water's cold enough the lakers are out of the depths. They're spawning now."

Noah took the rod, thinking, *You could be dying, but still you're baiting my line? I know how to bait a line, I remember.* He stared at his father, who cast his own line up the shore. It hissed in the otherwise silent morning and then splashed as the jig hit the water. The old man rubbed his nose and combed his beard with his fingers again, looking past Noah and out over the still black water.

"We're poachers now. Trout season ended more than a month ago. And you with no license on top of it all," Olaf said softly, working the jig with quick jerks of his rod. "I hope the DNR is busy with the bow hunters."

Noah could not take his eyes off him. For the first time since he had arrived that morning he really looked at the old man. The gaze must have made Olaf uncomfortable because he glanced away, hurried his line in, and cast again.

"Well, it won't be long," Olaf said.

"What's that?"

Olaf shifted his weight, picked something from his teeth, and shrugged. "The fish. We've got to be quiet if we want to catch fish." He looked at Noah. "They aren't stupid. They can hear us."

Hear us, Noah thought, suddenly overcome by the significance of being there, by the sickness practically radiating from the old man. He leaned toward his father and whispered, "Who cares about the fish?"

"No fish, no dinner."

"Dinner is easy enough to come by. I can get in the car and be back in half an hour with dinner."

"Chrissakes, you want potato chips and bologna sandwiches, why'd you come all the way up here?"

"I came because you're sick. I came to figure out what we're going to do. I came to give you a hand."

"Well, right now the best thing you could do for me would be to shush. I want to catch some of the fish swimming around down there. Maybe spare me your bologna sandwich. What do you say? How about you bring us back in a little closer?"

Okay, Noah thought, *we can fish today.* He put the oars in the water for two pulls toward the palisade. He cast his jig onto the placid water, ripples widening in perfect circles as he waited for the lure to reach its depth. As he made the first crank on his reel he heard the hiss of his father's drag. He looked over, saw the old man's rod arcing from his hand. His face looked serene.

Olaf caught three lake trout—the first was as long as Olaf's forearm—enough fish for dinner that night and three meals stored in the freezer. Noah didn't catch a thing.

"That's just rotten luck," Olaf said as they rowed back toward the cabin.

Noah pulled harder on the oars and felt the skin on his hands toughen.

AFTER THEIR FOUR o'clock dinner of cracker-crusted trout, instant mashed potatoes, and creamed corn, they sat at the table and talked for an hour about the things Noah could help with around the house. Olaf was most concerned about his woodpile, a concern Noah could not comprehend given the bounty of split boles stacked, seemingly, everywhere. Olaf mentioned that the hearth needed some mortar work, that the eaves trough spanning the roofline on the front of the house required repair, that there were shingles missing on the shed. He also said he wanted to get the dock out of the water this winter. Noah insisted, despite his misgivings and certainty that he would be unable to repair any of it, that anything Olaf needed, he would do.

Noah got up and cleared the table. Standing at the kitchen counter he said, "We've got our chores lined up, now what about you?"

"What about me?"

"You said you were sick."

Plainly, Olaf said, "I'm dying."

Noah felt the word—*dying*—like a punch in the gut. He returned to the table and sat down. "What? How do you know? What have the doctors told you?"

"I haven't been to the doctor."

A guarded hope entered Noah's mind: *How could his father know he was dying?* "How do you know what's wrong?"

"I've done my research."

Noah looked at him, puzzled. "Research?"

"At the library. Up in Gunflint."

"The library? Dad, if you're sick enough to die, you've got to go see someone. You've got to get help."

Olaf put his hands palm down on the table and cleared his throat. "I want you to listen to me," he said patiently. "I know what I'm doing. I know what I want. I'm not going to the doctor and the reasons are simple: I'm sick, I'm going to die. Whether it's tomorrow or six months from now hardly seems important. What is important is that I don't prolong my misery, don't hold on and end up in a nursing home with a bunch of old ladies reeking of Listerine and playing goddamn bingo. This is going to happen on my terms, understand?"

Noah buried his face in his hands. "Who said anything about a nursing home? All I'm saying is you need to see a doctor. You're in no position to diagnose yourself, even if you've read every book in the library. Is there still a hospital up in Gunflint?"

Olaf stood heavily and looked Noah squarely in the eyes. "I will say it one more time—I am not going to the doctor. It's final. Now, I'd like nothing better than to have you help me get the place ready for winter, but I will not be lectured."

He lumbered into his bedroom, closing the door behind him.

Noah's first impulse was to anger. But as he sat there alone, the seriousness of his father's health now a certainty, his anger subsided, was replaced instead with an unnatural calm. There was a new light cast on his being there, one that complicated even as it made clearer.

Noah walked to the door and looked out into the yard, now being swallowed by the gloaming. Thinking to call Natalie, he took his cell phone from his pocket. But there was no signal, there hadn't been since he was twenty minutes north of Duluth.

So now what? he thought as rain began to fall.

Two

The next morning Noah woke early and headed toward the lake. The overgrown trees dripped rainwater. The giant bedrock boulders shouldering the path were covered with feathermoss and skirted with bunchberry bushes. Mushrooms and reindeer lichen grew among the duff and deadfall on the trailside.

At the lake Noah turned left and walked along the water's edge. A hundred feet up the beach he came to the clearing in the woods, a clearing he'd all but forgotten in the many years since he'd last seen it.

When Noah turned five years old his father and grandfather built a ski jump on the top of the hill just east of the house. They cleared a landing hill on the slope that flattened at the beach. Back in Norway Noah's Grandpa Torr had been a promising young skier. He had even competed at the Holmenkollen. When he immigrated to the States, he became a Duluth ski-club booster and helped build the jump at Chester Bowl, where Olaf himself twice won the junior championship.

Each Christmas Eve morning Noah's grandpa and father would boot-pack the snow on the landing hill and scaffold before grooming it with garden rakes. On Christmas morning they would sidestep the landing hill with their own skis and set tracks for Noah. Olaf would stick pine boughs in the landing hill every ten feet after eighty, and by the time Noah turned nine he was jumping beyond the last of them, a hundred twenty or a hundred twenty-five feet.

Looking up at the jump he remembered the cold on his cheeks, his fingers forever numb, his toes, too, the exultation of the speed and flight. And his skis, the navy-blue Kongsberg, their camber and their yellow bases and the bindings his grandfather mail-ordered from a friend still in Bergen. They were the first skis his father bought for him, the first not handed down. He remembered the way his sweater smelled when wet and the way it made his wrists itch in that inch of flesh between the end of his mittens and the turtleneck he wore underneath it.

But most of all he remembered the camaraderie and the lessons and the pride felt by each of them—son, father, and grandfather—in the knowledge of a lesson well learned. Even after his father had washed up on the rocks the morning after the wreck there had sometimes been a sort of reprieve from Olaf's drunken vitriol in that isolated week between Christmas and New Year's. Now the landing hill had grown trees again, and the bramble and deadfall made it almost indistinguishable from the rest of the hillside. Even so, at the top of the hill he could still see the scaffold and the deck standing at the side of the takeoff where his father or grandfather had stood for hours at a time, coaching and encouraging him.

"You remember this thing?" his father asked, out of breath.

Noah turned, startled, "Of course I do."

"You can hardly see it up there."

"I can see it."

They were both looking at the landing hill with their hands in their pockets. The temperature was dropping, but the sky was clearing. "I used to wonder about you when it came to this thing." Olaf gestured up at the jump. "You were a pretty good jumper, but that attention span."

Noah smiled. "I was easily distracted." He thought, *Whatever happened to those days?*

As if intercepting Noah's thoughts, Olaf said, "Chrissakes those were fine, fine mornings."

"They sure were."

"You should have stuck with it."

"I often think that. Guess I wanted to get away, out of Duluth."

"Duluth was so bad?"

Noah shrugged.

Olaf nodded. "Maybe it wasn't Duluth you wanted to get away from."

"Maybe not."

Olaf looked at him charily. "Come with me, I want to show you something."

THE TRUCK SMELLED of cigars, and the inside of the windows dripped with condensation. The plastic upholstery covering the enormous front seat was split and cracked from corner to corner, and mustard-colored foam padding burst through the tear. A speedometer, fuel gauge, and heater control sat derelict on the dashboard, and beneath it, where a radio should have been, three wires dangled, clipped, with copper frizz flowering from each.

Noah felt like he was in an airplane, seated so high, and he marked the contrast his father's truck cut against his own Toyota back in Boston. His car got fifty miles to the gallon. He'd have bet that the truck got less than ten. Still, he derived a definite satisfaction from sitting there in the passenger seat. He thought he'd like to drive it.

Olaf put the key in the ignition, pumped the gas pedal four or five times, and turned the key. The truck shook and grumbled but did not start. He tapped the gas pedal a couple more times and tried again. This time it groaned but finally started. He revved the accelerator, and white smoke blossomed from the tailpipe. Inside, the cab filled with the smell of old gasoline.

"Carburetor," Olaf said, grinning. He reached under the seat and pulled out two cigars wrapped in plastic, gave one to Noah, unwrapped and bit the end off his own, and finally lit it with a kitchen match. Noah rolled his between his thumb and forefinger.

"We can take the rental car," Noah said.

"Don't worry about the truck."

"I can't believe you still drive it."

"It's got almost four hundred thousand miles on it."

"That's amazing. I lease a new car every couple years so I never have to worry about repairs. I haven't had a car in the shop since I started leasing."

"This thing's never been in the shop, either."

Olaf pulled a stiff rag from beneath his seat and wiped the condensation from his side of the windshield. He rolled his window down, too. "Crack your window, would you? Let's get some air in here."

Noah cranked his window down. "Where are we headed?"

"Thought it would be nice to get down to the big water."

Olaf navigated the truck up under the low-hanging trees and onto the county road. Cool air streamed through the open windows.

"It's getting colder," Noah said.

"But the pressure's rising, which means it'll be clearing up. This wind, though, it's going to blow the high pressure right through."

When they reached Highway 61, Olaf turned left, away from town, and drove slowly in the middle of the road. After a few miles the lake unfolded before them. "Look at all that water," Olaf said.

"Those waves are huge. It looks like the ocean," Noah said. "It's been a long time since I've seen this. The water was practically still yesterday."

Olaf stared out at the lake. The deep creases around his eyes and in the slack of his chin and neck seemed flexed all the time. His lips and nose crinkled in a constant grimace, and his mouth parted as he alternated between slow breaths and puffs on his cigar. Noah watched his father's hands, too, one on the steering wheel with quivering white-haired knuckles, the other sitting on his leg as if helping to keep the accelerator constant. He drove thirty miles per hour.

At the Cutface Creek wayside Olaf pulled into the lot and left the truck idling in one of the dozen parking spots.

After a few quiet minutes Noah asked, "How far is it from, say, Silver Bay across the lake to Marquette?"

"Well, I'd say it's about a hundred and seventy-five miles as the gull flies. There're eighty nautical miles—plus or minus a piece—from Silver Bay to the middle of the Keweenaw Peninsula, which makes it, what, ninety miles or so. Beyond that my best guess is another eighty or eighty-five miles, most of that across the Keweenaw, over the Huron Mountains, and only another ten or twenty nautical miles across Keweenaw Bay. Farther, of course, if you were getting there by ship. Why do you ask?"

"On my way here yesterday I picked up a radio station from Marquette. It surprised me, that's all."

By now they had gotten out, moved around to the front of the truck, and were leaning against the rusty bumper. Four-foot waves curled up onto the rocky shore in white explosions. They were facing the sharp wind that brought a delicate spray of lake water with it. Olaf said, "For some reason the big breakers always remind me of my mother."

"I wish I could remember her better."

"My mother was the single kindest person I ever knew. A saint she was. Never hit me once, never even raised her voice," Olaf said, taking a long, satisfying puff on his cigar.

"That's how Mom was, too."

Olaf glared out at the water, toward a horizon resting somewhere in the middle of the lake. "My mother, she was faithful. She loved my father, God knows why. She was patient."

Noah interpreted his father's words as a challenge, knew that if he wanted to he could have a fight. Enough forbidden history surrounded Noah's mother to keep him and Olaf fighting for a while. Noah pictured Phil Hember—their neighbor across the street from the old house on High Street—his mother's lover during Noah's high school years. *There* was some forbidden history. Noah resisted the temptation to bring it up. They watched the lake churning.

Olaf finally cleared his throat, spit, and stubbed out his cigar. "Solveig tells me you sell maps out in Boston."

Caught off guard by the change in topics, Noah stammered. "That's right. Antique maps."

Olaf looked suspect. "Who needs an antique map?"

Noah described the maps as works of art. He told his father how he'd come to own the shop.

"What about teaching?" Olaf asked.

"I wasn't a very happy teacher. Not a very good one, either."

Olaf teased Noah about all those wasted semesters of college. Noah heard the good-natured timbre of the old man's needling, so he spoke more of his own crash course in learning the business and of its strange and unexpected growth thanks to the Internet. He wondered whether his father knew what the Internet was. Noah told him about Ed, and of how the colonel reminded him of Olaf himself, of how when the mood to lecture struck him the colonel could not be stopped. Finally he said, "I have Natalie to thank. She's the one who reviewed the prospectus and lease—she even negotiated the purchase. She's got a mind for details I don't have myself."

"So how are you making it go?"

"I guess I have a mind for the maps."

And because Olaf seemed interested, Noah elaborated. Some of the maps were three or four hundred years old and from as far away as the Horn of Africa. He described the beautiful Latin and French words he had such trouble translating, the beautiful script they were written in.

Olaf, looking even more dubious, said, "Say I wanted to buy one of these maps, what would it set me back?"

"You could spend a hundred bucks, you could spend ten or twenty thousand."

"For an old map that couldn't get me out the front door?"

So Noah explained again how they were less maps than collectibles, or, he repeated, works of art. Not to be used, as his father said, for getting out the front door but for admiring on the wall in your billiard room, to ogle with your country-club friends over twenty-year-old scotch.

Olaf said, "I'll take my atlas and gazetteer."

"When was the last time you needed an atlas?" Noah said, remembering his father's instructions for finding the house.

"Let's just say one won't be necessary to find lunch. You hungry?"

OUTSIDE THE MANITOU Lodge hay bales and cornstalks and pumpkins had been set out for Halloween. There were a dozen pumpkins, all half eaten, a feast for the deer; their tracks were all over the mud. Three cars were parked in the lot, but inside, the dining room was deserted.

It was a moderately sized room with grand ambitions. The walls were paneled with dark, stained wood, and the vaulted ceiling supported four chandeliers that aspired to some kind of elegance but failed. A rippling, knotted pine floor glimmered, polished to a shoeshine brown. Along one wall a colossal fireplace with a mantel as big as a canoe loomed over the deep hearth. Hanging over the mantel a moose head and antlers spanning four feet surveyed the room with glass eyes. On either side of the fireplace black-bear skins hung like paintings. Above the wall of windows that faced the highway, a dozen fish—chinook and brown salmon, steelhead, northern pike, walleye—hung mounted on elaborately carved and lacquered pieces of wood. The tables were sturdy and unvarnished and covered with paper place mats and lusterless silverware. The three waitresses wore black skirts and white blouses. One of them directed Olaf and Noah to a table by the window and gave them menus.

"Our soup of the day is Lake Superior chowder," she said, filling their water glasses. She switched a peppermint from one cheek to the other and asked if they had questions.

Olaf said, "Give me the chowder. And coffee."

Noah smiled and asked, more politely, for the same. The waitress put her pencil behind her ear, collected their menus, and walked toward the kitchen.

"Once upon a time you would have ordered a bottle of suds with your chowder," Noah said.

"A bottle of suds? Times you're talking about I'd have skipped the chowder altogether, ordered four boilermakers over the noon hour, and called that lunch."

"No more boilermakers?"

"No more cigarettes, either."

"Since when?"

Olaf ran his hand through his beard. He appeared reluctant to speak. "On the way back from your wedding I stopped in the Freighter for a pair of bourbons before finishing my drive up here. Twenty straight hours I'd been behind the wheel, thought I deserved a nip." He paused, ran his hand through his beard again. "Met a couple of the old boys. We had a high time of it. A high time.

"The next morning I woke up in the truck. Couldn't see a thing, the windows were all rimed from a night of snoring. I mean, they were completely fogged over. I had no idea where I was until I stepped out of the truck." He smiled, looked almost as if a punch line were in the offing. "I was parked in front of the old house up on High Street. Hadn't lived there in what, three years?" His smile vanished. He paused to look Noah in the eyes. "One of my bright shining moments. Enough was enough."

"Just like that?" he said.

"Never a drop since."

"I didn't know people could quit drinking like that."

Olaf merely raised his shoulder to his ear and closed his eyes for a moment. "I guess they can," he finally said. "At least I did."

"Do you miss it?"

"Not the booze, but I'd smoke a hundred cigarettes a day if they weren't such hell on me."

"What's that?" Noah asked, pointing at an envelope on the table.

Without a word Olaf slid its contents onto the table. There were two dozen or more photographs sheathed in plastic. Olaf took one of the photos from the pile, set it down on the place mat, and wiped an imaginary layer of dust from it. He looked at Noah from over the top of his glasses—big, black-rimmed bifocals that he'd pulled from the pocket of his flannel shirt. "I guess this is what I wanted to show you."

The waitress interrupted them with their soup. Noah thanked her.

At the same moment, as if they were one man in a mirror, they moved their soup aside. Olaf said, "Anyway."

Noah sat dumb as his father took one and then another of the photographs from their plastic wraps. The first, a black-and-white snapshot of five men standing on the main deck of the *Ragnarøk* and two others suspended over the side, one in a bosun's chair, the other on a rope ladder, looked like something out of a *Life* magazine pictorial. Printed on heavy Kodak paper, it had faded to sepia. Of the seven men Noah recognized three: his father, Jan Vat, and Luke Lifthrasir. They all wore scowls on their faces and looked identical in dress, wearing black wool caps, three-quarter-length peacoats unbuttoned to the waist, gray trousers cuffed at the ankle, and thick-soled black boots. The ship's bowline was attached to a harbor cleat, sagging heavily under the weight of icicles. The ship, as the unmistakable block letters of his father's handwriting on the back of the photograph said, was wintering up.

On the deck behind the men, the riveted hatch coamings and covers and the hatch crane were glazed with ice. The two men hanging over the side of the ship chiseled at a layer of ice. The men on deck all wore that expression so fixed in Noah's memory—they looked caught between humor and tragedy, as though they were thinking, simultaneously, that they were elated to be home but craved leaving again, too.

In the steely background of the picture, a million shades of gray blended into the harborscape: the cone-shaped piles of taconite and limestone, the enormous cranes and rail tracks, the rail cars steaming with coal heaps. Fences, barbed wire, wooden pallets. The crisscrossing power lines and ten-story-tall grain and cement silos. A squat tug steaming through snow flurries. Ice. And, enveloping all of it, smoke from a thousand stacks and steam whistles.

Noah looked up from the picture and saw his father staring out the restaurant window. Noah thought of saying something but looked back down at the picture instead. In the background he recognized a big part of his boyhood. Driving into downtown Duluth just two days earlier he'd felt similarly transported in time. In his exhaustion he'd chalked it up to the depressive autumn mood that seemed to have settled on the city like the fog. But now, seeing the same place and thing in a different time and in different hues, he knew that he had mistaken fatigue for the nature of the city, not autumn's coming on.

He thought back to his boyhood and the ships, his father's ship especially—his third, actually, the storied *Rag*. The Superior Steel Company had a fleet of fourteen ore boats, and though there were many distinctions in their size and capacity, in their age and shape, each of the ships was distinctly *superior*—as they were known across the lakes—as well. Just as the Pittsburgh Steamships wore their tin or silver stacks, so the Superiors wore their black hulls and white decking. And emblazoned on the stern and port side of each ship's nose the diamond and S.S.C. logo of the fleet looked like an opened serpent's mouth. Though any ship from any fleet or port of call stirred something like awe in Noah—even now but especially as a boy—the ominous, serpentine Superiors ruled his imagination.

And the *Rag*, of course, ruled most, both in Noah's boyish imagination and in the collective imagination of the people of Duluth. Although flagship honors fell on the newer, bigger SS *Odin Asgaard*, the *Rag* remained—until her foundering—the secret darling of the Superior Steel Company brass. Her officers' crew all hailed from Duluth, a fact that alone would have made her revered, but she had a mystique, too, one whispered about in the sailors' bars and church basements. Though exaggerated, an ounce of truth pervaded the legend. She was tenacious in wicked seas, as she proved over and over again in the November gales. She'd withstood ice, the shoals, the concrete piers jutting out into the lakes from Duluth to Ashtabula, and even, allegedly, a tornado in the middle of Lake Huron. She possessed the belly of a whale, too, exceeding her load limit from one trip to the next. Though the *Asgaard* was one hundred feet longer and made to carry three thousand tons more ore than the *Rag*, though the *Asgaard* and her type eventually replaced the ships in the *Rag*'s class, during the last few years of her life the *Rag* performed—categorically—on an almost equal annual footing with the flagship. She was the mother of the Superiors, even if not her majesty.

Noah knew all this because when the subjects of ski jumping, what was for dinner, or the goddamn unions weren't being discussed at home, the *Ragnarøk* was. He knew her statistics like some kids knew the batting averages of their favorite ballplayers. He could still remember them.

Olaf's voice seemed to whistle at him. "That's the *Rag*."

Noah looked up from the picture and saw his father's nub pinky—the one that had been amputated at the second knuckle because of frostbite—pointing at the picture. "I know."

"And those are the Bulldogs there, the Bulldogs and a couple hands working on the hull." "Bulldogs" was the moniker given to the all-Duluth officer crew of the *Rag* in honor of their tenacity but also because it was the namesake of the local state college. "That kid in the chair is Bjorn Vifte. You knew Bjorn. Seventeen years old there. That's me, of course, that's Jan, that's Joe, that's Luke—you knew him, too—and that's Danny Oppvaskkum, the engineer. This picture was taken a few days after Christmas the year before she went down."

"Who's this?" Noah asked, pointing to the kid on the ladder.

"Ed Krebs, one of the deckhands."

"And who's Joe?"

"Joe was second mate. Joe Schlichtenberg. He hung around when you were a kid. Joe probably froze to death. Or drowned. Danny O. was in charge of the engine room. He probably burned to death."

Noah had always longed to hear—from his father—the story of what had happened the night the *Rag* went down, and even a hint of it got his pulse thrumming. "The ship here, she's at Fraser shipyards?"

"Four or five ships from our fleet wintered up there every year. In '66 and '67 the *Rag* got her new engine, a diesel. They did it at Fraser."

"You guys all look the same."

"We were."

They sat in the dining room of the Manitou Lodge for a couple hours, talking about each photograph as if it were a wonder. The pictures dated as far back as the spring of 1938, Olaf's first year on the lakes, when he had shipped as a deckhand on the two-hundred-fifty-three-foot *Harold Loki*, a ship named for the original chief executive of Superior Steel. Olaf was a baby-faced kid in one of the pictures, his shirtsleeves rolled to the elbows, a cigarette dangling from his lips while a buddy's hand stuck him with a fake jab to the ribs. Along both sides of the main deck of the ship in the background, a procession of fresh-air vents loomed like a marching band of tuba players, and the smokestack in the stern coughed up its coal smoke in pitch-black plumes.

Olaf couldn't remember the other deckhand's name, but he told Noah about a whole crew's worth of sixteen- and eighteen-year-old kids shipping out in order to avoid abusive fathers or college. Some of the boys, he said, were just cut from the lonely cloth and wanted to get lost. He told him about Tony Ragu, a kid from Muskegon who worked on the *Loki* for the first three months of the shipping season that year before being picked up by the Duluth Lumberjacks, a minor league baseball team that wanted his ninety-five-mile-per-hour fastball. He remembered Cliff Gornick, a Chicago guy who put himself through Northwestern Law School by working Superior Steel boats in the summer and who eventually became a famous Chicago newscaster. Russ Jackson was the first black guy he saw on the boats, second cook on the *Loki*. A potbellied, middle-aged man with a receding hairline and a wife and seven kids in Detroit, he cooked the best beef brisket north of New Orleans. Olaf smiled when he talked about the Cejka brothers—one of whose sons was later a watchman on the *Rag*—thick-shouldered shovelers who worked in the engine room of the *Loki* moving coal. If not for the whites of their eyes and their ungloved white hands, Noah might not have known there were any people in the picture at all.

There were pictures of the aerial bridge at the entrance to Duluth harbor, cloaked in fog, a cat's cradle of steel; of the *Loki*, the *Valkyrie*—his father's second ship—and the *Rag* all scuttling through the locks at Sault Sainte Marie; of the Mackinac bridge spanning the straits between Lakes Huron and Michigan; of the loading and unloading complexes in Gary and Conneaut; of crewmates, some anonymous or forgotten, others so well remembered it seemed as if Olaf expected them to walk into the dining room any minute and join them; and of Olaf, standing in front of the offices of Superior Steel in the LaCroix Building on East Second Street in downtown Duluth, an ear-to-ear grin on his twenty-eight-year-old face the afternoon he passed his Coast Guard exam to become an officer, and standing behind the wheel in the pilothouse of the *Valkyrie*.

Noah looked up and down between the pictures and his father, and what struck him was how much he himself resembled the man in the photographs and how little the man sitting across from him now did. Three days ago he might have overlooked his father in a crowd, now he felt like he was him. Noah wondered, as his father reconstructed more than thirty years of his life with the help of the photographs, how it had felt to *be* him then, in the spring of 1938, and how it felt to be him now, with the burden of all that had happened and all that he'd suffered, suffering who knew what illness. More than anything Noah wondered what it would be like to sit across the table from a son, imagined a whole lifetime of moments like this: spooning baby food, helping with homework, explaining the birds and the bees, sharing a beer over a cribbage board.

By the time the waitress announced that the dining room was closing for the afternoon, they'd finished with the photographs and had been sitting in a reverential silence. "Listen, Dad," Noah said, "why don't you pack these up? I have to call Nat before we head back to the house."

Olaf said, "Sure, sure." And with the care of a surgeon, he placed each of the photographs back into their sheaths and then into the manila envelope.

"We'll be out of your hair in a minute," he assured the waitress behind the cash register at the Manitou Lodge. She nodded and turned her attention back to painting her nails as Noah dialed the pay phone.

"Hey," he said, "I didn't think I'd catch you." The phone at Natalie's office had rung five times before she'd picked up.

"I was starting to think you'd forgotten me. I left messages on your cell."

"I don't have cell reception up here. Sorry. I was going to call last night."

"It doesn't matter. I worked late last night anyway. New clients." She was a management consultant and never discussed clients by name. The late nights were a job hazard. "How's your father? How's everything going?"

Noah looked out the window at the galloping lake, he glanced at his father. "It's hard to say. We went fishing yesterday," he said as though it were the strangest thing. He paused. "What about you?"

Her voice turned grave. "Now that you're in the middle of the woods, I'm finally going to ovulate again. Of course."

He could hear her crying and felt an impulse to hang up the phone, not because he didn't want to hear what she said but because he knew that whatever he replied would be monumentally wrong.

"Okay," he began cautiously. "I know the timing is terrible, I know it stinks, and I wish I were there—"

"But you're not," she interrupted. "I thought this would be the month. I wish you were here."

"I know, me, too. But we might have to wait until next time."

"What if there isn't a next time?"

A next time. Since their most recent failure, an ectopic pregnancy that had taken Natalie months to recover from, she had come to suspect that the reason things weren't working—the reason their efforts had yielded nothing but endless fretting, thousands of dollars in fertility-clinic bills, and a terminal attitude—was that they hadn't been doing everything together. "You go to the clinic at eight in the morning to drop off your sperm, and I go at noon to be inseminated between a tuna-fish sandwich and a conference call—I mean, how *could* we expect anything? It's just unnatural," she had said, ignoring the fact that their course of action couldn't be anything but unnatural. So they'd decided they would make their clinic visits together, sure that the *next time* things would be different. The next time was now.

He tried again. "I know this hasn't been easy."

"Hasn't been easy? Noah, they had an easier time putting a man on the moon than they've had getting me pregnant. Keeping me pregnant anyway." She blew her nose. "Maybe you could over-night it."

He could practically see her, sitting behind her desk at work, looking out the fourteenth-story window. The tears, he'd not often seen them for any other reason.

"There's an OB/GYN at St. Mary's hospital in Duluth. You'd have to go down there, but I bet we could make arrangements. They could still inseminate me tomorrow."

Inseminate, the sort of word that had become stock in the parlance of their infertility. All the words—*prescription, ovulation, suppository, uterus, fallopian, cervix, endometriosis, laparoscopy, motility*—made the whole thing feel like a science project.

"I'm sure I could make an appointment."

"So we could overnight it? Nat, honest to God."

"What?"

"Let's be reasonable."

"Injecting myself with a syringe full of fertility drugs every night *is* reasonable?"

"Is it the end of the world if we have to wait another month?"

"What if you're there for three months, what happens then?"

This startled him, and he looked across the dining room at his father, whose chin was on his chest. He must have been sleeping. "I'm not going to be here for three months. Listen, I just got here. I can't very well leave tomorrow. My father needs me right now. He's not well, remember?" Across the dining room Olaf twitched, his head bobbed up, and he looked around the restaurant, confused. "He can hardly get his feet off the ground."

"What's wrong with him? Where is he now?"

"He's sitting across the dinning room here at the lodge."

"You're out to lunch? You went fishing?"

"It's hard to explain."

"I've made a list," she continued, the tone of her voice suddenly businesslike, "trips to the doctor's office for fertility- or pregnancy-related visits: fifty-two. Number of prescriptions filled for fertility- or pregnancy-related drugs: no fewer than thirty. Number of injections: roughly two hundred. Cumulative full days missed at work: fifteen. Number of times you've had to jack off over some dirty magazine in the doctor's office: eight. Number of miscarriages: three.

Number of ectopic pregnancies: one. Number of dead fetusus: five." She paused. "Number of hours spent in paralysis, bawling my pathetic eyes out: a million. Do you get the idea, Noah? I need you to come home. If it doesn't work this time, I can't go through it again. This is it."

Noah looked at his father. He squeezed his eyes shut and pictured the old man laboring up the hill from the lake.

"Are you listening to me, Noah? I have a scar on my arm from where they've drawn blood the last three years. I have permanent bruises on my thighs from the injections."

"My father is dying. He lives alone in the woods. He has to drive eight miles just to use the nearest pay phone."

"He's dying?"

"That's what he says."

"What does the doctor say?"

"He won't go to the doctor."

"But he can go fishing?"

"I know. I said it's hard to explain."

"Would leaving for one day matter?" she persisted, though clearly she was less emphatic.

The truth was, he *did* think one day was going to matter. He thought an hour mattered now. But he didn't say anything.

"Then I'll come there," she said after a moment.

"You'll what?"

"I'll get a flight on Friday. I'm in meetings the rest of today. I have to go."

"You're coming here?"

"On Friday."

"It's not an easy place to find," he said.

"I'll MapQuest it." And before he could protest she hung up.

He stood there in stark amazement, the idea of her coming to Misquah sinking in slowly. This sort of impulsiveness was not one of her character traits—though conviction of this magnitude was—and he realized again how single-minded she had become. He tried to imagine her sitting in his father's cabin but could not see it.

Before he went back to the table, he called his sister. When she did not answer, he hung up, realizing any news of his being at their father's house would alarm Solveig.

As they made the slow drive back to the house Olaf looked at Noah and said, "You always did wear it around on your sleeve."

Noah had been studying the roadside. "What's that?"

"Whatever's troubling you."

Noah turned to his father. "I hope you don't mind more company."

"What do you mean?"

"Natalie's coming."

"She is?"

Noah turned his attention back to the woods. "It's hard to explain. It's ridiculous, really. And embarrassing."

"Out with it already."

"Well, she's ovulating."

"Ovulating?"

"Like now's the time she could get pregnant."

Olaf slowed the truck, pulled over, and stopped. "She's coming here to get pregnant." A smile spread across his slack mouth. "You're a lucky man."

"We've been trying for years."

"That's one of the best parts of marriage," Olaf said, persisting with his sailor's wit.

Noah thought to turn the conversation but realized his father was trying to make things easier for him. It was a gesture of simple kindness. Now a smile spread across Noah's face. "I guess you're right about that."

THREE

The blunt head of the splitting maul, stuck in the oak stump, looked like clay. Noah had his hand on the smooth ash handle.

"I'm falling behind," Olaf said, sweeping the back of his hand lazily toward a pile of sawn oak.

"How much more do you need?" Noah asked, looking around at what seemed an unending supply of wood.

"It needs time to cure. That pile there"—Olaf pointed at a four-foot-tall by eight-foot-deep pile of split wood as long as Noah's rental car sitting beside the shed—"it won't be ready until next year."

"It won't burn?"

"Of course it'll burn, just not very well."

Noah jerked the maul free of the stump. He swung it up onto his shoulder.

"There are a couple of trees down in the gulch. They blew over this spring. One's an oak, the last on the lot, I think. I'd like to get them up here before it snows."

"We can do that."

Noah measured the distance between the log on the block and

the head of the maul in his extended arms, swung the handle over his right shoulder, and let the steel head fall square on the balanced log. The wood split with a clap, and the two pieces landed four feet away on either side of the stump.

"We'll get the city boy out of you yet," Olaf said.

"That felt good," Noah said, still feeling the reverberations in his shoulders.

"Let's get at that oak," Olaf said.

"All right."

They emptied the wheelbarrow in the yard, and Olaf fetched a chainsaw, a gas can, and two pairs of gloves from the shed. They started toward the gulch, Noah in front and pushing the wheelbarrow.

"I called Solveig," Noah said over his shoulder. The wheelbarrow bounced over the roots and pine saplings that had overrun the path. "I left her a message."

"What are you talking about?"

"I mean, she ought to know what's going on."

"Aaah," Olaf grumbled. "What does she need to hear about it for?"

"Maybe," Noah said, setting the wheelbarrow down and turning to face him, "she just deserves to know. Maybe she would want to know because you're her father, after all, and people tend to worry when their father is sick."

"Do me a favor and don't call her again. She doesn't want to see me like this."

Noah took a deep breath and rolled his neck over his shoulders. He turned back for the wheelbarrow.

They followed the path slowly for another five minutes before they reached the oak, which had fallen across the whole expanse of an old creek bed so that it formed a kind of bridge between the two sides. The sinewy roots hung like dead willow branches on the other side of the ravine.

"Must have been some wind," Noah said.

Olaf agreed. He explained the chainsaw, said it'd be easiest to work on the branches first, that he should approach the job as if he were whittling a stick. He warned Noah about how, when cutting off a particularly large branch—and he pointed out half-a-dozen examples—he had to be careful because the tree's balance might shift. Finally he pulled the cord and the saw fired up. He handed it to Noah. Olaf sat down with his long legs hanging over the edge of the gulch and pointed at Noah to get going.

The saw whined with the first squeeze of the trigger, pulling Noah toward the tree. He trimmed the first branches, the finer tree-top limbs still thick with dried leaves. He ripped through them, moving quickly, the branches falling into the gulch, until he had worked halfway down to the thicker limbs. After fifteen minutes he looked back at the pile of branches lying on the bank of the gulch. The air smelled of sawdust, and his ears rang from the shrill saw.

He kept at it until the only thing left was the spotted trunk spanning the two sides of the creek bed. Olaf sat there, his shoulders draped over his chest, his hands folded on his lap, like a child. Noah flipped the power switch and the saw choked off. The muscles in his arms and back stung and twitched.

"Oh-hohh!" Noah hollered. The air had gone silent when he turned off the saw, but his ears still buzzed. "That's work!"

Olaf smiled.

"Now what, just start on the trunk?"

"We'll leave that for tomorrow. It's getting dark." Olaf turned his attention to the sky. "The days are so goddamn short this time of year," he said.

Noah looked back at the tree, wanted to continue but said, "You know best."

They left the wheelbarrow and started back for the house.

They were almost to the cabin when Noah saw something moving close to the ground in the yard. It had crawled out from under the truck. Noah flinched, dropped the saw on a pathside rock, and froze. "What the hell is that?" he whispered.

"What?" Olaf said, startled himself by the thud of the saw on the stone.

"That," Noah whispered again, pointing at the bushy shadow. "Is that a wolf?" he asked. He bent down and picked up the saw. *"Is that a goddamn wolf?"* he asked again, this time in a louder whisper, turning his head but not taking his eyes off the shadow in the yard.

"What are you talking about?" Olaf said.

"There. Sitting right there, by the firepit."

"That's not a wolf," Olaf said, elbowing Noah aside. "That's my dog. That's Vikar—come here, Vikar." And he whistled. The dog came bounding around the truck and ran a circle around them.

"Jesus Christ," Noah said, all of his held breath coming out in one relieved rasp. "Jesus," he said again, watching the huge dog roll on his back as Olaf scratched its stomach. "Where has he been?"

"Wandering around the woods, I'd guess. Comes home when he wants. Must've heard the chainsaw."

The dog was enormous, a malamute or husky a hundred and fifty pounds or more. It had long, coarse hair and ears and forepaws the size of Noah's own hands. "He scared the shit out of me," Noah said. "I thought it was a wolf."

"That's what you said."

Noah let the dog sniff his hand.

"How long have you had him?" They were standing in front of

the house now, the dog jumping and twisting under Olaf's snapping fingers.

"Couple years."

Noah sat on the step and the dog came up to him, eye level, ears submissively fallen, to be petted. "Any more surprises?" he asked, scratching the dog behind its ears.

"Surprises?" Olaf replied. He stepped behind Noah, onto the porch, took the top off a tin garbage can, and filled an empty ice-cream bucket with dog food. He put it down beside the steps and the dog set to eating.

"Do you remember your mother playing the piano?" They sat in the rusted steel lawn chairs on the grassy beach, an oar's length from the lapping water, darkness cascading down the sky. Vikar lay at Olaf's feet, his legs outstretched, a stream of groans muttering from his black lips.

"Of course I do," Noah said.

"She played beautifully."

"It used to drive me nuts."

"Why?" Olaf asked, his chin on his shoulder, his long white beard pointing out toward the lake.

"Because I could never listen to my records."

She used to play the Acrosonic upright for hours at a time, in summer especially, when her long evenings alone went on endlessly. Mendelssohn, Beethoven, and Grieg were always drifting through the house on High Street while Noah and his buddies pitched pennies outside against the garage door. Solveig played, too, in her mother's style but without any of her elegance.

Olaf was teasing a sprig of brown grass. He sighed, cleared his throat, and put the grass between his lips. "She always wanted to play at your wedding."

"My wedding," Noah said, stiffening at the mere mention of it. "I'm surprised you'd bring it up."

"That was a long time ago, Noah."

"Five years now," Noah said, feeling his anger rising. His father's worst performance ever had come on the eve of Noah's wedding. He hated to remember it. And here was talk of his mother again, Noah's sacred subject.

"You know, I was on my way home when she died," Olaf said, seemingly oblivious.

"I remember when she died," Noah said, wondering now if his father really was looking for a fight.

"That's the only time I've ever been on a plane in my life. I had to leave my boat in Toledo, take a bus to Detroit and get the plane. It cost a hundred bucks."

"A regular hero."

Olaf turned away, set his chin back on his chest. The sky sparkled with stars, lightening and darkening simultaneously as it got later and the moon rose.

"Your mother wanted you to play the piano," Olaf said.

Noah sneered incredulously, nearly stood up to leave.

"She did," Olaf said.

"What difference did it make who played the piano?"

"None," Olaf said. "I'm just trying to remember."

"Why are you doing this? You can't even face it now, can you?"

"Chrissakes, Noah."

Noah had to clench his teeth to keep from saying more.

When, one night early in their relationship, Natalie had asked Noah how his mother had died—they were eating oysters and drinking Pimm's at a place out on Marblehead Beach—Noah had said loosely but with conviction, "Of a broken heart."

His mother had, in fact, died of heart failure, of a heart attack brought on, Noah always imagined, by an excess of longing.

"They called you on Saturday. You got to port on Sunday morning. You didn't get back to Duluth until *Thursday*. For four days you knew how sick she was, and still you didn't get home? And somehow you were a hero for getting on a plane?"

"It's not that simple," Olaf said.

"She was *dying*."

"We didn't know that then."

"Are you kidding me?" Noah stood up, walked to the edge of the water, picked up a rock, and threw it out into the lake.

"I didn't expect her to die, Noah."

"What did you expect, huh?" He threw another rock into the lake and turned to face his father. "We were fucking kids."

"Your mother and I, we were hardly speaking to each other by then."

"You had two kids, too. Did you forget about us?"

"I didn't forget about anything."

"You know what?" Noah said, stepping back toward his father. "That only makes it worse. We needed you and you weren't there. You were never there."

"The story is a lot more complicated than you remember," Olaf said.

Noah dropped back into the chair and ran his hands through his hair. "What part of the story am I forgetting, Dad? All we wanted was for you to come home and tell us that the world hadn't ended, that's all you would have had to do."

"The world ended long before that night," Olaf said.

Noah heard a note of resignation in his voice, a pitiful, sad, thoughtful timbre that he'd never heard before but that he didn't quite believe. "Don't you get it? Mom had just died. Whatever tragedy you suffered shouldn't have mattered. It still doesn't matter. You had a responsibility, and you blew it."

"Do you think I'm sitting here ignorant?"

"I think you've always believed that what happened to you was more tragic and more meaningful than anything that ever happened to anyone else. And that's wrong. You just couldn't shake it, that's all, you lugged it around like a yoke and nothing else mattered. That's what I think."

"You're dead wrong about all of that. Dead goddamn wrong."

"Then tell me why you weren't there. Tell me why you disappeared. Tell me why Mom never had a funeral."

Olaf looked squarely at Noah, a face full of regret if Noah judged right. "I still have her ashes," he said.

"What?"

"They're in the shed. They're stowed away."

Noah was dumbstruck.

"I can't tell you why I wasn't there, Noah. I can't tell you why I disappeared or why your mother never had a funeral. I can't tell you because I don't know."

"They're in the shed?"

"I never knew what to do with them. What are you supposed to do with your wife's ashes?"

Noah had no idea.

They sat quietly for a long time. The night was stunning, cooling, the sky bursting with stars. Noah watched his father doze off, his chin on his chest. Twice Vikar stood and went to the shore to drink, and twice he came back to Olaf's feet.

Eventually he thought of Natalie. He imagined her at home, curled up on the couch in the den. She was coming here. A fact Noah found hard to imagine. Sometimes, at home, before they fell asleep, they'd lie in bed conjuring up their fantasy child—a baby boy—whose ascendance into the nighttime world of forgiveness and fantasy was like religion for them. The boy would be a prodigy, of course, but a prodigy of ordinariness. This meant a Little League career that included errors and strikeouts galore but also a zest for the game straight from the little guy's good nature. It meant a seventh grade girlfriend and questions about her. It meant high school and the prom and ski trips up to Sugarloaf with the boy and a couple of his pals. It meant college at Dartmouth, Nat's insistence, and law school and a job in downtown Boston where the two of them—Noah and his son—could get together for lunch on Fridays. There were no dislocations in this fantasy, no shipwrecks. And certainly no ashes stowed in the shed.

"Winter's in that wind," Olaf said, turning the collar of his shirt up.

His voice startled Noah from his reverie. He hadn't noticed the outright chill in the air but felt it the moment his father mentioned it.

"You fell asleep."

"It's awfully damn late for me."

Noah turned his attention back to the lake and the rippling water. Steadier now, the waves lapped gently against the dock posts and onto the beach. "Two weeks ago that sky would've been a circus with northern lights," Olaf said, pointing upward. "It's a goddamn sight."

"My first year on the *Loki* I used to sit watch from midnight until four. Ninety percent of the time this meant just staying awake. Sometimes I'd be up in the pilothouse, sometimes down on deck, depending on the weather and where we were. It was a boring job, boring as hell to tell the truth, but my captain that first year was a German guy named Wolfgang, a hell of a guy, smart as anyone I ever knew. He introduced me to the stars, so to speak." Olaf nodded up at the sky. "He taught me some things about navigating. Just basic stuff, but I was hooked. He said that a true seaman could sail around the world without anything more than a watch and a sextant and the sky to guide him. I didn't even know what a sextant was, just figured you knew where to go if you were in charge of one of those boats. I never reckoned there was any science to it. Wolf taught me how to take sun sights, how to chart our course, how to estimate our position using dead reckoning when the sky was cloudy and the shore out of sight." He paused, cleared his throat. "Now it's just a bunch of satellites telling you where you are and where to go. Back then it was still something beautiful to steer a ship."

Olaf stopped talking, looked up at the sky, and pointed to different clusters of stars, marking the air with fingertips. Noah, in all his life, had never heard his father say so much at one time. He'd never heard him say half as much.

"What are you pointing at?"

Olaf looked down. "Nothing," he said. "There was a lot of downtime on the ship, especially as a kid when I didn't have any responsibilities outside my watch. On clear nights I used to stand on the stern deck looking out at the wake. There're a lot of things to see in the night sky, especially on Superior. And there were a lot of reasons to be lonely, especially if you were the new kid onboard. But when you're aching to get away, which I was, even the worst loneliness doesn't sound too bad.

"Anyway, I got interested in what the captain was teaching me. I used to watch him take his sights, consult our charts, mark our position, do the math. After a couple seasons I had a real sense for this stuff. I could keep time in my head. I knew where we were all the time. I got good at it.

"You see there?" he asked Noah, pointing nearly straight up at a cluster of bright stars. "That's Andromeda, you can tell by the spiraling cloudiness of it. It'll be lower in the sky in the next month. That's Cassiopeia to the left there. That's Auriga there, and that's Capella, that bright star right on the edge of that cluster. You can't see Orion or Betelgeuse now because they're too low on the horizon. Jesus, those stars are a long ways away. I can hardly even think about it now. But I'll tell you what"—he coughed to clear his throat and nodded affirmatively—"I used to sail by their light—I used to sail by Andromeda's light—and I got around just fine."

A long silence ensued, Olaf still calculating some impossible star equation with the tip of his finger, still conducting, Noah thought it looked like, some star symphony.

"The galley would start serving breakfast at six o'clock on every ship I ever sailed. Those first couple seasons I'd sit on deck until right before chowtime, take my morning sight, then head to the galley and eat breakfast like it was meant to be eaten." He smacked his lips. "Buttermilk pancakes drowning in syrup, eggs, hash browns, bacon and sausage, coffee, juice, fruit. Sometimes we'd even have chops or steaks. We all ate like that, all the time. It was one of the perks for living on those boats. I still remember what it felt like to be that full. I'd go back to my cabin, slide off my boots, and lie down on my bunk." He sighed. "Didn't have a goddamn thing to worry about in that sleep. Nothing."

"But later," Noah said.

"I've never been a good sleeper, but those mornings were pretty damn fine. After your mother and I got hitched and you came along, the sleep got a little bit tougher. I was ten years into my career when I met your mother, though. There was nothing else I could do."

Olaf stood and stretched. "It all blends together for me now, everything before the *Rag*. Each of the ships and each of the years have turned out to be the same thing unless I've got pictures to remind me. But I'll tell you what, my life was split the night she sank."

FOUR

Olaf had adjourned to bed with only a nod. So many old feelings had been uncorked down on the beach, not least of which were the ones Noah had been expecting most, the anger and reproach years in the making, stirred up by the mere mention of his mother and her wanting to play piano at his wedding.

Noah had sent his father a wedding invitation as if he were a distant relative. The reply had come by way of his sister, who had told Noah their father intended to make the drive east by himself. Noah did not believe he would, but on the night before his wedding, Olaf showed up.

They held the rehearsal dinner at Natalie's parents' Swampscott home, a beautiful place with huge oak trees in the front yard, a deck overlooking Foster Pond in the back, and a red-brick chimney set against the clapboard siding. When Olaf stepped from his old Suburban and looked up at the three-story house, Noah felt heartsick. In order to quell the sadness he doubted his father deserved, he summoned his anger instead, put it on as if it were a coat of arms. From the window of the foyer he could see that the old man looked presentable if rustic. His beard and hair were longer than they'd been, but they were also more kempt. The corduroy pants and rumpled chamois shirt were at least clean. Instead of boots he wore a pair of chocolate-brown, size fourteen loafers. It wouldn't have surprised Noah to find the box they'd come in on the floor of the truck.

They met at the front door, shaking hands as they had before breakfast at the Freighter. Noah said, "Nice shoes."

The look of smug satisfaction on the old man's face said all Noah needed to know.

Grudgingly, Noah said, "Come on, I'll introduce you."

Having been cautioned about the impending and inevitable debacle, Natalie graciously ignored Noah's warnings. She treated Olaf like her own father from the start. When she introduced him to her parents, Olaf offered them a gift.

Natalie's mother sold real estate and presented the agent's facade that everything was always fantastic. In fact, she was a whip-smart pessimist with a master's degree in art history. Mr. Maier had served as an Essex County public defender for thirty years before retiring that summer. As they leaned against the granite countertops of their newly remodeled kitchen, sporting their Ralph Lauren garb, each with a long-stemmed glass of chardonnay, Noah knew the cut of their jib would not sit well with his father. In fact, he knew his father hated people like them, people who had no discernible faults, no tragedy in their lives.

"What *is* it?" Mrs. Maier said, withdrawing a brown bottle from the paper sack.

"This is aquavit, Linie aquavit, to be precise. Comes from Norway. I have a friend, captain's a salty running Minnesota wheat to South Africa, he brings me a case each year."

"This is very thoughtful, Mr. Torr."

"This stuff has been across the equator twice. There's caraway in it, and in order to blend the flavors, it needs the roll and pitch of the ocean waves. This bottle started out in Norway, crossed the Atlantic, come up the St. Lawrence, went back down the St. Lawrence, spent a week bound for Cape Town, then back again to Duluth. Now here it is. Won't work for taking paint off the house, but enough of it will put the feeling fine in you."

"Should we open it?" Natalie asked.

"Save it for a special night," Olaf said. "There must be something else to drink around here."

Noah led his father to the study, where two guys in tuxedos manned the bar. Olaf ordered a drink and turned his attention to the room.

"What is all this shit?" he said. "It looks like some kid's bedroom."

"Mr. Maier is a huge Red Sox fan. This is his memorabilia. You don't even have to ask and he'll tell you Johnny Pesky grew up right down the street."

They stood silently for a few minutes while Olaf looked over the autographed baseballs and jerseys, the framed ticket stubs and bobble heads. "Well, it beats the hell out of me. To each his own, I guess."

"Listen, he's a really good guy. They're all good folks. Take it easy on them."

Olaf had already turned back to one of the bartenders and signaled for another. "Take it easy on them? What am I, a lout? Chrissakes, I'm here. I brought them a gift."

"That was thoughtful," Noah admitted.

Olaf quaffed the first third of his cocktail in a single, effortless pull. "Anyway, I don't need a goddamn babysitter."

"I know."

"Then go mingle with your friends."

At the end of the rehearsal dinner Olaf stood at the curb with a half-drunk beer in his paw. He had his eyes on the night sky. Noah stepped from the front door and walked down the brick footpath to say good-night.

"There isn't a cloud in the sky and still hardly a star to be seen," Olaf said. "But you can goddamn smell the ocean." His words were slightly slurred. "Funny, all that time on a boat and I never saw the ocean."

"How about I take you back to the hotel?" Noah said.

"I'm okay to get back to the hotel."

"Really," Noah insisted. "I can show you the town. Solveig can drive you to the wedding tomorrow."

Olaf relented.

The silence on their short trip was broken only by the din of traffic. When they pulled up under the hotel marquee, Olaf drummed his fingers on the dash. "Why don't you come in for a nightcap? The least I can do is buy my son a drink the night before his wedding."

"I don't need a drink."

"Didn't say you did. We'll call it old time's sake."

Noah looked at his watch, thought of many reasons not to have a drink with the old man, and pulled up to have the valet park the car.

In the bar Olaf ordered twelve-year-old bourbon from the top shelf. Noah asked for beer, trying to estimate the number of cocktails the old man had put down. It didn't seem possible a man could drink so much and still be coherent. The drinks arrived, and Olaf twirled his slowly. Tea candles flickered in small bowls of water beside ramekins of cashews on the mahogany bar. Through the curtained windows they looked onto a harbor with sailboats still in their slips.

"Natalie's a nice gal," Olaf said. "How she came out of that brood I can't imagine."

"I told you they're decent people."

"That is what you said."

A piano concerto that both men knew filtered through the faint conversations taking place around them. Occasionally Noah could hear the halyard lines ringing on the masts of the boats in the harbor. Olaf finished the last of his drink and signaled for another.

After it arrived Olaf said, "Marriage, it humiliates a man."

"What?" Noah said. He had not been expecting this.

"Makes a man less of what he is."

Noah shook his head in complete awe of the old man's audacity. He looked at the jigger of bourbon set before his father and said, "It's not marriage that makes him less of what he is."

"I've got firsthand proof, boy. I know what a lifetime of marriage can do to a man."

"What do you know about a lifetime of anything but coming and going, huh? You were always *gone*. I'm really supposed to sit here and listen to life lessons from you?"

"I'm doing you the favor my old man should've done me."

Noah faced him. "Do you have any idea what you're saying? Can you not see how insulting this is? To Mom. To me. To Natalie."

"I don't mean to insult anyone."

The calm in his father's voice only made Noah more upset. "What bullshit. It's *exactly* what you mean to do."

Olaf didn't waver. "Someday you'll—"

"For god's sake, spare me the rest of the lesson. I won't hear it," Noah interrupted.

"You will hear it, goddamnit," Olaf boomed, loud enough that people turned to look. "Marriage dogs a man his whole life. Your mother dogged me. Natalie will dog you. Mark it down."

Noah took a minute to memorize his disdain. When it was burned in his mind, he dropped a twenty-dollar bill on the bar and stood to face his father. "What happened to you?" he said. He wanted to continue, but his loss of words overwhelmed him, and he left without saying another.

The next afternoon Olaf showed up in his rented tuxedo. He had trimmed his beard and combed his rim of white hair. He sat there easily during the ceremony, kissed Natalie on the cheek while they danced at the reception, even offered Noah a wink from across the ballroom.

That had been the last time they'd seen each other.

OLAF WAS SITTING in the great room with a cup of coffee when Noah woke the next morning. Noah was still smarting from their talk on the beach the night before, but he said good-morning and poured himself a cup and sat down.

Without pleasantries Olaf said, "You mind running into town for me?"

"Not at all."

"I need a length of chain. Forty feet. Polyurethane coated. Go to the hardware store. Knut will help you."

"I'll go after this." He held up the coffee. "You mind if I take your truck?" Noah wanted to see what it felt like to be behind the wheel of that thing.

"The keys are hanging by the door."

"Anything else you need?"

Olaf shook his head. An awkward moment passed while Noah sipped his coffee. Before it was a quarter gone, he got up to leave.

By the time he got to Misquah he'd made a short list of things to do himself, and as he dialed his sister's number on the pay phone outside the Landing, snow flurries began to blow across the parking lot. Solveig answered on the first ring, singing hello and asking how he was. They exchanged pleasantries, but the conversation became as dismal as the weather the moment he announced his whereabouts. She had managed, through her own adult years and despite the fact that her childhood had been just as fatherless as Noah's, to forgive the old man most of his disgraces. Perhaps this was because Noah had borne most of Olaf's brutishness. Solveig still dutifully visited the old man each Christmas, still invited him to her summer home each Fourth of July. Though Noah had never understood her devotion, he was glad for it.

She of course knew that only extraordinary circumstances would have brought Noah to Misquah, so she asked plainly what he was doing there. Noah filled her in, sparing no detail. When he neared the end of his recounting, he told her how feeble and sickly their father appeared. It was as if Noah had forgotten his audience altogether.

Solveig paused before commencing her litany of questions and concerns: She begged for clarification, asked Noah to repeat his story and elaborate on what he meant by sickly and feeble, instructed Noah on their father's habits and proclivities, spit out her husband's trial docket—he was an attorney in Fargo, where they lived—and her kids' hectic schedules. Noah could practically hear the machinations of her distraught mind. Finally she told Noah she would get there as soon as possible, though she admitted she had no idea when that would be.

It was only after he had hung up that Noah realized he hoped her arrival would be delayed, realized that he wanted some time alone with the old man, come what may.

THERE WAS AN agate and smoked-fish shop on the northern edge of town. He'd seen it on the day before. When he walked in, a synthesized loon call startled him from above the door. On the left a refrigerated deli case—an antique thing that hummed and clinked and dripped—was filled with smoked fish. There were sockeye salmon, ciscoes, lake and rainbow trout, whitefish and smelt, all whole, all golden, desiccated, and eyeless. On the right another glass case full of agate jewelry sat under canned lights. A counter spanned the two cases, and an antique cash register sat in the middle of it.

"How do?" a man said from behind the fish counter. Thin and long-fingered, he offered his hand. The two sides of his gray goatee were unevenly trimmed. "Rocks or fish?" he said as Noah shook his hand.

"Agates," Noah said. "I'm looking for something for my wife."

"Normally it's my own wife who handles the rocks, but she's visiting our daughter out in Portland." He wiped his hands on a dirty apron as he circled behind the counter to the agate case. "I can help you, though. What're you looking for? A nice necklace? Maybe a bracelet?"

The only piece of jewelry he'd ever bought Natalie was the half-carat diamond ring he'd given her when he proposed. "A necklace maybe. Something simple, not too gaudy."

"What color eyes has she got?"

"Green-gray."

"You like the green or the gray better?"

"The green, I guess."

"Then you want a green agate." He fumbled with the latch on the case. There were hundreds of pieces of agate jewelry on display, arranged without any regard for appearances. Gold- and silver-chained bracelets and necklaces lay heaped and tangled together, earrings and rings were dumped in ceramic bowls. There was even a tiara on a Styrofoam bust.

The first couple of necklaces he pulled out of the case had agates the size of Ping-Pong balls attached to thick gold chains. Noah asked if he had anything with a smaller agate, something on a silver chain perhaps. As he said it the absurdity of buying her an *agate* hit him. Just as he thought it, though, the man behind the counter pulled out a pearl-sized, emerald-green agate attached to a very thin, very pretty silver chain. "This one's actually a real Superior agate," he said, putting on a pair of glasses and reading from the little tag. "An Agate Beach agate. Not all of them are." He winked.

"How much is it?"

He checked the tag again. "Says here thirty-five dollars."

Noah would have paid ten times the amount. "I'll take it," he said. "And while you're at it, how about a pound of that salmon over there?"

II.

The *Rag* Is Burning

FIVE

I t wasn't until Noah got back to the house that he remembered the chain, and he might not have remembered it then if not for the padlock on the shed. The shake shingles and cedar siding that had been so inconspicuous at first—sitting under the overgrown trees, among the overgrown grass and bunchberry bushes—had taken on a new significance with the knowledge that the shack was doubling as his mother's tomb.

The smoke coughing from the tin chimney on the house smelled wintry. It was a good smell, clean and faint. As it rose and dispersed into the flurries, Noah forgot about his mother's ashes and felt an urge to hunker down and spend his afternoon with a big book—a book of myths or the biography of a king. The thought of bundling up and heading back to the gulch to finish with the oak seemed not only arduous but a waste of time. There was no way his father would live to burn a tenth of the wood that was already split and stacked around the house.

Inside, Noah kicked off his boots, set them on a braided rug beside the door, and hung his coat on a peg. He put the smoked fish in the refrigerator.

"He's back," Olaf said, setting a magazine on his lap.

"Hey. How are you doing?"

"Fine, fine."

The fire was searing, he could tell, not only from the heat pouring out of the stove but from the faint whine and pinging of its cast-iron flanks. Noah took off his turtleneck and tossed it into the spare bedroom.

"Have any trouble with the truck?"

"No. But I forgot the chain. Sorry."

"I'm going to need that chain. And soon."

Noah sensed more than heard agitation in his father's voice. "I can go back and get it."

"Next time you're in town. You've been there more in the last handful of days than I have in the last handful of months."

Noah sat across from his father. "I talked to Solveig today. She's going to come as soon as she can."

"I asked you not to call her."

"I can't leave her in the dark even if you can. She's worried about you and she loves you and she wants to help."

"I guess that's her prerogative. Though I don't see why it's necessary. She's got a busy life."

"We've all got busy lives."

"I guess between your wife and your sister coming, we'll just be a regular meeting place."

"I guess we will."

Olaf set the magazine he'd been reading on the coffee table and settled back into the sofa.

"What's that?" Noah said.

"Magazine article Luke gave me. You remember Luke?"

"Your partner in survival. Who could forget Luke?"

"He's a good man." Olaf held the magazine up. "Anyway, it's about shipwreck property. Can't make the first bit of sense of it."

"You thinking about diving for the booty left on the *Rag*?"

Olaf declared, "Rest assured of this, nobody's ever salvaging the *Rag*. She's too deep."

"You know, I always wanted to hear the story from you. About the *Rag*, I mean."

Olaf looked down into his coffee. "I wouldn't know how to tell it."

"Start in Two Harbors."

"It's a long story, Noah."

"And we're sitting in the middle of the woods. It's snowing. We've got nowhere to go."

"It was a long time ago."

"It was snowing then, too," Noah coaxed.

Olaf took a deep breath and looked squarely at Noah. "We took twelve tons of taconite," he began. "It was the first mate's job to oversee loading, but you knew that."

Noah nodded.

"Well, it snowed like a son of a bitch, and before we could start with the hatch covers we had to shovel her clear. We got started, but before even one of them was clear, Jan called us off."

"It was the fuel line, right?" Noah asked, knowing perfectly well that it was.

"On the trip up, we noticed a leak. It wasn't too bad at a glance, and we managed to get from Toledo to Two Harbors without any trouble, but after we unloaded the coal and were refueling, the bilge started to fill with diesel. That's when Jan got jittery.

"I wasn't ever a spook, but something in the back of my mind got a little itchy when they told us to replace the fuel line. I remember thinking it was strange that the higher-ups okayed a repair like that so late in the season. I mean, their priority was always bottom-line tonnage." He paused, scratching the back of his head. "I chalked it up to the engine being new and the brass just not knowing how reckless they could be. But I was still uneasy about it.

"Twenty-two hours we sat there while a contractor put the new line in. We gave the crew fourteen hours' leave and watched them all hump into Two Harbors."

"I bet they did their best to hump once they got there, too."

Olaf smiled. "They usually did."

"In Two Harbors, though?"

"You'd be surprised." Olaf smiled again, shook his head, and then turned more serious. "Some of those boys lived up there. Bjorn did. He had a baby girl and a sweet little wife. I'll tell you what, he was off that goddamn boat in five minutes.

"The boys who didn't live there got pissed in the bars up on Willow Street. I'd venture to guess that more than one or two of those fellas had a pretty good time that night." Olaf smiled again, as if to admit that despite his age, the memories of those little Great Lake ports, the run-down pubs that filled them, and the sailor-loving girls who knew the ship schedules like their multiplication tables hadn't escaped him even now.

"The next morning, when they came back aboard, it was like watching a zombie parade. I remember the days before I met your mother, before I became an officer, too, and the shit we used to get ourselves into." He smiled again. "Those boys knew how to dig it up. They were all red-eyed and pale, sweating in spite of the weather. Goddamn.

"The boys who lived up there, though, they all looked happy as clams. Walking lightly, you know," he said and winked. "But not Bjorn.

I didn't know him well, but he looked like two different people at once. You could see he was happy—must have been thinking of his little girl and wife—but he also looked resentful as hell, probably about shipping out again. He was one of those guys who got tricked into his life on the boats. He was just dumb enough not to be able to do something else and just smart enough to hate what he did. There were a lot of guys like that on the Lakes."

Noah scanned his memory for the men he knew from his father's trade. Having had it put so simply, he could recognize the split in many of them. Some of the men, like Luke, stood out. They were single-minded types, gruff and bigger than life. But the majority of the men he remembered—men from his childhood cruises on the boats with his father and from his time slumming down in Canal Park with his high school buddies—were just ordinary guys.

"I'll bet you put them right to work," Noah said.

"Of course. We had to get the deck cleared and only had a short window of time to do it."

"Because of the weather?"

"One front had already passed—the one that left a foot and a half of snow on our deck—and another one was coming, a nor'easter. We knew the seas would be rough and that it'd be cold as hell, so we wanted to get loaded and in front of the weather. It was no fun to be out there latching the hatches when it got below zero."

"Didn't the forecast warrant sitting tight for a few hours?" Noah asked.

"We could see it coming, we could feel it, too, but we never would've backed down on the basis of the weather reports we were getting."

"Were they wrong?"

"Not wrong," Olaf said. "When the wind turned around and the flurries started out of the northeast, we all got that sinking feeling. When the lake started crashing over the breakwater and the harbor water got choppy, we knew it was going to be a mean day, but it would've taken more than we saw to keep us in port.

"Anyway, we knew we could hug the lee of the Minnesota shore if we had to. There were also three ships ahead of us, a French freighter full of lumber . . ."

"The *Lachete*," Noah said.

Olaf looked at Noah sideways. "Yeah, the *Lachete*. There was also one of our boats out there, the *Heldig*, and one of the boats from the Cleveland Cliffs fleet." He tapped his bushy lip, thinking.

"The *Prudence*," Noah said.

"Was it you there or me?" Olaf asked.

Noah grinned.

"All three of those ships were updating us on the weather."

"And each of them talked about seeking shelter from the time they left port. What did they tell you that made you think getting started was a good idea?"

"It didn't matter what *they* told us. We were going to go or not go on the basis of Jan's gut, not on what some goddamn Frenchman had to say about the wind."

"What about the *Heldig*? Didn't you have any confidence in her?"

"You see, it was never a question of the confidence we had in the reports the other boats were sending. They were instruments, that's it. It was always just a simple question: Did we feel like the *Rag* could handle what the lake was giving? If the answer was no for the *Heldig* or the *Prudence* or any of the other boats out on the Lakes, it didn't necessarily mean it was no for us." There was no vanity, no posturing, in what his father said. Noah knew this as simply as he knew the story itself.

Olaf gazed over his shoulder at the stove.

"Don't tell me you're cold."

"No, no," Olaf said, looking up at him. "I was just thinking about how it felt to be on that ship," he said. "Standing on the bridge, even in the worst weather, it was easy to stick your chest out—to puff it up—because we knew that no matter what was in front of us, the *Rag* was behind us.

"She was six hundred and ten feet long. Sixty-two feet abeam. The hull alone—hull number 768—weighed five thousand tons. Loaded as she was, there were more than eighteen thousand tons— *eighteen thousand tons*—of steel lugging it up that lake under two thousand horsepower," Olaf said, raising an eyebrow. "The bridge was forty feet above the surface of the lake, and still we had to keep the wipers going in order to see out the damn window. Despite all this we were making better than seven knots. Under normal conditions and with a normal load we would've made twelve knots, thirteen on a good day. But seven was a hell of a pull, all things considered."

"Seven knots makes for a long day up Superior," Noah said.

"Better than sixteen hours to Rock of Ages light."

"As opposed to?"

"Ah, nine or ten," Olaf said with a wave of the hand. "The point is she wasn't normal."

"What do you mean?"

"I mean she shouldn't have been making that time. The other ships were thirty or forty miles ahead of us and they weren't making a third of the time we were." Again he shook his head. "But that's just how the *Rag* was—above the weather, above the seas, those things just didn't bother her, they didn't stop her."

"Why?"

Without a touch of embarrassment Olaf said, "She was a goddess, I guess.

"I remember storms she weathered that would've sunk other ships in a second. On Erie we sailed through the worst lightning storm I ever saw. Took two bolts right on deck. Lost one coaming thirty miles from safe harbor. The pumps were working that night.

"Another time we hit a real beast coming out of Whitefish Bay, heading up to Marquette. When we got to the Soo they were all set to close her down until it blew over, but when they saw we were next in line to pass, they let us up. Eight or ten boats had to wait out a twelve-hour blow in the St. Mary's River while we chugged out onto the lake. Now *that* was a storm we might've sat out.

"I remember eating dinner that night. We had pork chops and applesauce—that's it. Nothing that had to be cooked on the stovetop because we were rolling too goddamn much. The guy that did the baking was named Ed Butterfield—we called him Butter—used to put together this delicious rye bread. When the weather got rough, we'd soak thick slices of it in water and stick them under our plates to keep them from sliding around. It was an old trick. The next morning, when things calmed down a bit, I remember watching the porters hacking it off with hammers and spatulas."

"Did you ever wait on the weather?"

"Sure we did, just not as often as other boats. Once or twice every couple of years we'd sit one out, but it took some kind of hell for that."

"Should you have sat it out the night she wrecked?"

Olaf guffawed. "The winds were supposed to shift more to the east. If they had, we knew we wouldn't want to face the middle of the lake. But we also knew we wouldn't have to, see? We knew that if push came to shove we could take shelter in the lee of Isle Royale." He was snaking his arm—as if it were the ship—into the imaginary estuary between the Canadian shore and the long finger of Isle Royale. "It was an uncommon course but one we'd taken before. And even if the wind shifted sooner rather than later, we knew we could muscle our way to safety.

"By the time we passed Rock of Ages light we'd been at it with that goddamn lake for almost seventeen hours. It was two o'clock in the afternoon and snowing so hard we couldn't see the railing around the pilothouse deck.

"And Jan hated to be blind," Olaf continued. "I mean, we knew exactly where we were and where we were heading, but when you can't see your hand in front of your face and you're putting up with the hell we were, you have a tendency to get a little hot. At least Jan did.

"He had a guy at every position every minute of that cruise—a man at the wheel, a man at the radar, a man at the compass, a man on the charts—it was like watching an orchestra. Jan would say, 'My heading?' and the watchman at the gyrocompass would say, 'Four five, sir,' and Jan would say, 'Speed?' and a voice would say, 'Eight knots steady, sir,' and Jan would boom again, 'Is it clear?' and the wheelsman at the radar would say, 'Clear, sir,' and Jan, 'Position?' and the wheelsman at the chart, 'Captain, we are at such and such latitude and longitude, sir,' and Jan, 'How much water have I got between me and that goddamn island?' and the wheelsman at the radar would say, 'Sir, Isle Royale six point zero seven nautical miles bearing one hundred and forty-one degrees,' and the wheelsman at the chart would settle it all, 'Six point zero nautical miles to shoal water, sir.'" Olaf related the whole pilothouse episode as if he were a conductor himself, raising and wagging his fingers.

Noah, his heart actually beating a little faster, was sitting on the edge of the sofa. "And the water is coming over your deck and it's snowing like the end of the world . . ."

"And in the middle of it all, roaming from the charts to the compass to the wheel, Jan would take each piece of information and plug it into his internal calculator and come up with some goddamn equation the sum of which dictated every move he made. And despite his aggravation at being blind, despite that *goddamn* lake and the wind like a hurricane, he still managed it all without a hitch. I don't think he ever even spilled any of his coffee."

Noah stood up and stretched his arms above his head. He felt boyish, nearly giddy in the thrall of the story. "What about the rest of the crew?"

This question seemed to sober Olaf. "The crew? They were just a bunch of anybodies. With the exception of guys like Jan and Luke, they were just men and boys."

For the first time since Noah had arrived at his father's house, he called up the picture in the museum, the one of the whole crew dockside with the *Rag* in the background. Although he could not summon a single face clearly, he could recall the apathy he'd felt looking at them. He remembered chalking it up to some kind of ambivalence toward his father, but in retrospect it was an ambivalence borne by the unconscious knowledge that what his father had just said was—and always had been—the truth. Twice already he'd alluded to the commonness of the crew, and twice now Noah had paused at the realization of this deflating fact: They weren't gods and giants sunk on that ship, they were men and boys.

"That takes some of the starch out of the story, don't you think?" Noah asked.

"What do you mean?"

"Isn't it more fantastic to think of the guys who died as a little bit heroic, as swashbuckling sailors? As something more than a bunch of yokels from Great Lakes port towns?"

"I don't think so," Olaf said, pausing to consider it seriously. "It's real life. In real life there're boys from port towns.

"There's one picture of them that I've never been able to get out of my mind," Olaf continued. "After we'd cleared the southwestern tip of the island, must've been around suppertime, I went down into the crew's quarters for a fresh thermos of coffee and something to eat. You remember that the top two decks on the bow of the *Rag* didn't have any interior passageways, don't you?"

Noah nodded.

"Well, that walk usually took, what, twenty seconds? Two flights of stairs, maybe thirty steps altogether? There were eighteen hours of snow and ice coating those stairs and that railing. You put that together with the wind and rolling of the boat and that walk was the hairiest time of my life. Until then anyway.

"The temperature couldn't have been above zero, and I was out there without my mittens, without a hat, gripping that goddamn railing for dear life. In twenty seconds my fingers were burning cold. I was slipping all over the place helter-skelter. And I couldn't see three feet in front of me. I remember sitting down for a second, wrapping my arms around the railing with my hands tucked up inside my coat, and hugging that goddamn thing like I was a child.

"The sound of that storm," Olaf continued, shaking his head as he closed his eyes for a long moment, "it should have been my first warning. I could hear the lake washing over the deck. I could hear the wind roaring. And I sure as hell could feel that wind coming from every direction." He looked hard at Noah, his eyes colorless in the cabin light. "For maybe three seconds while I was sitting there, everything went quiet, though, and I could hear her bending."

"Bending?" Noah said, sitting up and combing his sweat-damp hair back with both his hands.

"I sat on that icy step for a couple of minutes. I don't know what in the hell I was waiting for, but I couldn't move. The ruckus was out of this world, howling and drumming all over the place. But then it just stopped, went quiet, and I heard it: a slow, high-pitched cry. I knew it was the *Rag* under the weight of all that ice and water. It sounded human."

Noah dropped back onto the couch. "Those boats don't bend."

"Sure they do," Olaf countered. "Like skyscrapers give a little in the wind."

"What did you do?"

"I finally got down into the crew's quarters. And that's when I saw them—this is what I was getting at—all bleary-eyed and miserable, sitting around the common table playing euchre. Most of those boys were still drunk when they came back on board in Two Harbors, and when you put the weather and seas like we had on top of what they must have been feeling to begin with, well, they might as well have been dead already.

"Tell you what, I never saw a card game on that ship without a pile of money in the middle of it. Hell, those boys found ways to gamble over Crazy 8s, but not that night. They were just trying to keep their cards on the table.

"There were thirty men on that boat, the lesser part of half of them on the bow—wheelsmen, watchmen, deckhands, the mates—and the rest on the stern—the engineers and oilers and firemen and wipers. The galley crew. The boys on the back had their berths in eight small cabins above the engine room in some goddamn cold and clammy quarters. Steel bunks with lumpy mattresses attached to the low overheads. Even the shortest guy back there couldn't stand upright without knocking his head on something.

"And noisy as hell, too. They had to sleep through the constant whining of that engine and the churning of the prop. None of them could hear a goddamn thing. They had shit and grime under their fingernails all the time, and their trousers were always dirty at the knees. But for as filthy as they always seemed to be, that engine room was the cleanest place aboard that boat.

"The chief back there was Danny Oppvaskkum—a great guy—who knew the physics and chemistry and engineering of that ship like he'd invented and built it himself. Couldn't tell which way the wind was blowing, but he could've taken that thing apart and put it back together with a screwdriver."

"How old was he?" Noah asked.

"Danny must've been about forty-five."

"Was it"—Noah paused, hoping a second's delay might make the question seem more delicate—"you know, was it his fault?"

"Oh, Christ no. No, no. Danny was innocent in that mess. He probably gave each of those boys an extra hour of life with his thinking."

"There's a picture of all of you in the maritime museum down in Duluth. Did you know that? You look like a football team in it."

"They might as well have been a football team, being as they were young and lean to a man."

"Did they have any idea, do you think?"

"Any idea of what?"

"Any idea they were about to die?"

Olaf closed his eyes, appeared to be thinking about it. "The storm was bad, no doubt about it, but we were killing it. It was snowing like hell, and it was cold as hell, and there's no doubt some of those boys *wished* they were dead, but none of us thought we were going to die. Not in our wildest, worst dreams." He'd rolled up the magazine and tapped his knee with it. After a second he concluded, "At least none of them were thinking about it then."

Outside, it was still snowing and the leafless trees were all tangled in a stiffening breeze. Inside, the air suffocated and the stove continued to ping.

Olaf, whose hands were crossed over his lap, was thumb-wrestling himself. He looked up. The few seconds of silence had clogged up his voice, and he had to clear his throat before he asked Noah how long it takes to brew a pot of coffee and make a couple turkey sandwiches.

"I don't know," Noah said.

"Think about it."

"Five minutes?"

"It took me twenty minutes from the time I stepped into the little galley in the crew's quarters to the time I had a fresh thermos of coffee and sandwiches for the boys on the bridge. The way that goddamn thing was yawing, I dropped a full jar of mayonnaise, beat the hell out of my knee on the corner of the icebox, nearly burned my left hand off making coffee. I was a goddamn fool for trying."

"Was the walk back up to the bridge as scary as the walk down?" Noah asked.

"It was no stroll on deck," Olaf said as he set his head back against the chair.

Noah tried to place the story his father was telling in the context of what he already knew himself, or had at least read. None of the books that dealt with the wreck differed much in terms of what happened. His father returned to the bridge to find a panicked captain. The three methods of communicating with the engine room from the bridge had all failed. Noah could picture the brass Chadburn standing like a giant keyhole with the black-handled lever that, when set to a certain position in the pilothouse, would signal the engine room to adjust some aspect of her speed or bearing. He knew that if the Chadburn failed there was an onboard telephone line that connected the two ends of the ship. If both of those failed, there was a system of bell messages that the bridge could send to the engine room. *Two whistles check*? he wondered. *Four whistles all right*?

In each of the histories written about the *Rag*, the authors told similar stories of the simultaneous failure of all three modes of communication. None of them knew, though, precisely why the engine room had taken so long to comply with the captain's orders. The reason they didn't know was that the only man who had witnessed or been privy to the finer points of the communications snafu and lived to tell about it had never bothered to do so.

"Why didn't you ever set the record straight on why they weren't answering Jan's command? It makes the whole thing seem sort of fishy, doesn't it?" Noah asked.

"Nothing fishy happened on that boat," Olaf said. "Not unless you consider twenty-seven men burning and drowning fishy.

"The reason I never gave those goddamn reporters the details is because what happened out there was nobody's business but ours. Selling newspapers on account of our bad luck seemed like horseshit to me. If people wanted to know what it was like to get out of something like that with your life, they should have signed up to ship out at Superior Steel and taken the chance on finding out for themselves. It was between us and the lake. The big-bellied newspapermen weren't interested in what happened, they were interested in making a circus out of us, in selling their goddamn advertisers an extra ad in a special section."

"Don't you think there were plenty of people who just cared enough to know?"

Olaf dismissed him with a wave of the hand.

"The Coast Guard and National Transportation Safety Board reports both said the same thing—that when you got back to the bridge Jan was upset because he couldn't contact the engine room and he wanted to check down because you were about to round Isle Royale."

"How in the world do you know what the Coast Guard and NTSB reports say?"

"It wasn't just the newspapermen who wanted to know," Noah said.

Olaf cast a glance at Noah, one he interpreted as apologetic, even sheepish. "Jan's agitation was as simple as that, yes," he said, steeling his voice as best he could. "When I got back up to the bridge, he was trying to get them to check down. We were about to pass the northern end of Isle Royale, and he wanted to be prepared to assess the seas."

"Were you in danger?" Noah asked.

"None that we knew of. Jan was taking things slow because of the whiteout, but we weren't in danger. At least not because of the weather, we weren't going to run aground or founder under those seas."

"But not being able to get in touch with the engine room . . ."

"*That* was cause for concern," Olaf said.

One of the things that had never added up for Noah was why— after only two minutes of trying to reach the engine room—Captain Vat had become so anxious. He remembered being on midsummer cruises with his father when the *Rag* was still running on coal. He recalled his impression of the engine room after watching it in action for an hour or two. If not chaotic, it had certainly seemed perpetually hectic. All the levers and gauges, the noise and motion, so many pipes steaming or dripping with condensation or whistling out of the blue, and so many guys, even on calm days, tending to the countless details, led him to believe it was a miracle they had time to listen to orders of any sort. He couldn't even begin to imagine what the commotion must have been like back there on the night she went down.

"So what did Jan do?"

"He nearly panicked, that's what he did. When I got back up to the bridge he was sounding the bells for the third time. Three whistles," Olaf said, "it meant they were to check down. When they didn't respond after the third try, he thought about sending a couple deckhands back to see what the hell was going on. In fact, he went so far as to summon them to the pilothouse.

"I'll tell you what," Olaf continued, "the look on the faces of those kids said as much as anything about the shape we were in. We'd been at it for years, right? Jan and myself and Joe? But these kids were just starting out, just finishing their first season. It was the first big blow any of them had seen. When Jan told them to put on their life vests and they took turns looking out the window into that wildness, Jesus, you'd've thought he was sending them right to hell."

"But he didn't send them, did he?"

"Goddamn," Olaf said. "I sure as hell didn't want him to. I thought it was a suicide mission."

"But *you* had to cross it."

"I did, later. But it was different when he asked me to go because I expected to. I was used to those responsibilities. These boys just wanted to go to bed. As it turned out, not sending them cost them any chance they might have had." Here his voice trailed off again. Noah could practically see the parade of crewmates passing through his father's memory.

"Anyway, Danny finally called, and Jan lit into him like I'd never seen. 'Goddamnit, Oppvaskkum, I almost sent two boys across that deck. Do you have any idea how dangerous that would have been? Do you realize ignoring calls from the captain—even in emergency situations, *especially* in emergency situations—is unacceptable if not outright insubordinate? We're fighting a monster up here and you don't have the time to heed my calls?' " Olaf was doing his best impression of a man with a much deeper voice than his own.

"But he was trying to contain the leak. It wasn't his fault," Noah said.

"You're right, it wasn't his fault that the line was leaking, but I can't imagine what kind of trouble they were in—or how fast that trouble must have found them—to justify not responding to the bridge. We're talking about one of the cardinal rules here."

"So even if a guy's up to his ankles in diesel in a place as combustible as that, it's more important that he pick up the phone right away than figure out how to stop the leak?"

"The point is that by not picking up the phone, he jeopardized the whole order of things. Because he didn't pick up the phone, two guys were about to be sent out into that storm. Because he didn't answer the phone, the guy in charge of the ship was paralyzed, see?"

The line of reasoning was so familiar to Noah that he almost laughed. How many times had his father used the same hierarchical theory to make Noah paint the garage or shovel the sidewalk at their old house on High Street? "Aren't there exceptions to the cardinal rules?" Noah asked.

"I've never seen one," Olaf said. "And I've seen a lot."

That was familiar, too, his father slapping down the trump card of experience.

"What did Danny finally say that made Jan send you across the deck?"

"Danny knew right away how serious the problem was. As far as I could tell—and I never knew for certain—the main fuel line had ruptured near the tank, which was in the forward half of the engine room where the coal bunker had been the season before. The leak was serious enough that the entire engine-room crew, including the porters and steward, were busy trying to clean it. It had to have happened so goddamn fast—gotten out of hand so goddamn fast—that there was no chance to even sound an alarm.

"When Danny finally got around to calling the wheelhouse, there was no question about what kind of shape we were in. I only heard one side of the conversation, but there wasn't much doubt about our dire straits. Jan decided in an instant that we'd have to seek shelter, and his last words to Danny sent a hot chill up my back: 'Double-lash anything that could cause a spark, and keep a couple of those boys at the ready with fire extinguishers, we're going to come about.'

"Now, how'd you like to hear something like that from the boss's mouth?"

"It'd scare the shit out of me."

"Well, it scared the shit out of me, too. Jan and Joe and me got together in the chart room. Old Jan, he briefed us. We got our position figured out, and we decided to bring her around and head straight west for Thunder Bay, where the *Lachete*, *Prudence*, and *Heldig* were already at anchor.

"We had a little shelter from the worst of it, being as close as we were to the north shore, but it wasn't like we could just tip our caps and wave good-bye to those seas. We were going to pay for it. The good news was that once we got around, the wind would have been behind us and getting to Thunder Bay would have come pretty easy. Anyway, it was the only option we had.

"Goddamn," Olaf almost whispered, "I remember like it was yesterday. He had the engine going slow astern while he waited for just the right lull—it seemed like days—and as soon as he felt it, he ordered engines full ahead and the rudder full left. Everyone in the wheelhouse swayed and lurched and grabbed for a railing or something to hold on to as she slid down one side of a trough and up another. She listed bad for a second or two while a big swell washed over the length of the deck.

"We took a couple more waves before we got on course, but we *did* manage to get turned around. We were looking at two and a half hours," Olaf mused. "Two and a half, maybe three. That's nothing. It's the amount of time it takes to play a baseball game or drive from Duluth to Misquah. It's *nothing*."

"But it was too long," Noah said.

"A half hour would have been too long," Olaf concluded, making to stand up. He planted his slippers two feet apart, rested his elbows on his knees, lifted his head from beneath his drooping shoulders, and straightened at the knees, still bent at the waist. As he labored, a spasm of pain must have shot through his stomach because he fell back into the chair clenching his guts.

Noah jumped from the sofa and found himself standing over the old man with his hands out. His father's face was frozen and gnarled in pain. "What can I do?" Noah asked. "Can I help?"

Olaf took a deep, tremulous breath and rolled his head back. "It's cold in here," he said. "I was going to put another log on the fire."

Without a word Noah opened the stove and put a heavy piece of wood in among the embers.

"I need a pillow for my back," Olaf said. "Could you get one?"

Noah went into the bedroom and grabbed one of the down pillows from his father's bed.

"Here," he said as he helped his father forward, pushing the lumpy, uncovered pillow down between the chair and his father's lower back. "Do you want some aspirin or ibuprofen?"

"Nah," Olaf wheezed.

"A glass of water?"

Olaf looked up at him. "I could use a glass of water."

Noah brought him the water. "Lift your head," he said.

When Olaf did, Noah took the afghan from behind him. The old man's head fell back and rested on the chair again, and the soft, white, wrinkleless flesh of his neck was exposed in the lamplight. Noah stopped and stared at it. He wanted to touch it, to feel it, to confirm that it was as delicate and velvety as it looked.

"What?" Olaf asked, rolling his eyes up to look at Noah.

"Here," Noah said, handing him the glass of water and putting the afghan over his father's lap. "How often is that sort of thing happening?"

"Not often," Olaf said. "Not often at all." Again he waved his hand. "Grab that book over there." He pointed at the bottom shelf of the chest-high bookcase next to the sofa.

"Which book?" Noah asked.

"I forget what it's called. The black one."

Noah pulled a book from the shelf. "This?"

"Let me see," Olaf said. He took the book and thumbed through to the back of it. "This is the one, it's got transcripts of the radio contact between Jan and the Coast Guard and the other boats in the vicinity."

"Dad, we don't need to talk about this anymore. I mean, maybe you should get some rest."

"I'm all right." He handed the book back to Noah, who opened it to the first transcript, a communiqué between the *Ragnarøk* and the U.S. Coast Guard station in Gunflint.

"Read that," Olaf said.

Noah did:

22:15

Captain Vat: *Pan-pan, pan-pan, pan-pan. All stations, this is SS Rag-narøk, SS Ragnarøk, SS Ragnarøk. Our position is* [pause] *48 degrees 10 minutes 7 seconds and 88 degrees 20 minutes 7 seconds. Repeat, 48°10' 7" and 88° 20' 7". We are in heavy seas, wind gusts up to 78 knots, sustained winds 45 to 65 knots. Wave size variable to 20 feet. Report a major diesel leak in main fuel line. Repeat, major fuel leak in main line. Bearing 268° for Thunder Bay. Wish to alert any vessels in the area and U.S. and Canadian Coast Guards of our situation. Have a crew of 30 men; cargo 12 tons of taco-nite. This is the SS* Ragnarøk, *over.*

U.S. Coast Guard: *SS* Ragnarøk, *this is U.S. Coast Guard station Gunflint, change to channel 68, over.*

Captain Vat: *Roger.*

Coast Guard: *SS* Ragnarøk, *do you copy?*

Captain Vat: *Roger, we copy.*

Coast Guard: *SS* Ragnarøk, *do you require assistance?*

Captain Vat: *Negative. I only wanted to make you aware of our situa-tion. The leak is bad, I've got a dozen men working on it, and the heavy seas aren't helping, but we should be okay. We're heading for Thunder Bay—speed of 7 knots. Should be sheltered by 0:30. Over.*

Coast Guard: *Roger, SS* Ragnarøk. *We'll keep an eye on you.*

Captain Vat: *Roger that.* [Pause] *Are there any other vessels in the area?*

Coast Guard: *Negative,* Ragnarøk, *you're alone.*

Captain Vat: *Roger. Out.*

Coast Guard: *Out.*

Noah saved his page in the book with his thumb. "How far were you from Thunder Bay?"

"The last position I charted we were twenty-four nautical miles from the entrance to Thunder Bay. That's what, about twenty-eight miles?"

Noah opened the book and scanned the page. "And how fast is seventy-eight knots?"

"Seventy-eight knots?" Olaf closed his eyes to think. "About ninety miles per hour."

"That's like a hurricane."

"It was blowing, no doubt about that."

Noah shook his head in disbelief. "So you make the pan-pan. Then what?"

"Then Captain Vat made the decision that saved my life. In the chart room behind the wheelhouse, he ordered me and a crew to the stern in order to assist Danny. He told me to take three guys, one of whom he wanted at the phone the minute we got to the engine room. The rest of us were to help out any way we could."

"Why'd he send you?" Noah asked.

"I was pretty good with mechanical things," Olaf said. "I guess he thought I could help."

Noah paused, sure the question he wanted to ask was the most delicate so far. He put himself in the position of being ordered across an icy deck with winds gusting to ninety miles per hour. He thought about Lake Superior exploding across the deck. He thought about getting to the engine room, where thousands of gallons of diesel fuel were smeared across so many combustible engine parts. He thought of the nearly eight hundred feet of water beneath the keel of the ship. And he knew he would have been terrified. "Were you scared?"

Olaf looked up at the ceiling. "I don't remember being scared, no. But I sure wasn't excited about what we had to do."

"Why didn't you use the tunnels?" Noah asked.

"The *Rag* didn't have a tunnel."

"But you could have just walked on top of the ballast tank."

Olaf smiled. "I forget how well you knew those boats. The *Rag*'s ballast tanks didn't have square tops. They were slanted to meet the bulkhead without any straight angles.

"The object of the design," Olaf said, "was twofold. First, it was made to make cleaning the cargo hold easier. Without a straight ledge to sweep, we would save a half hour's labor every time we changed cargos. That adds up over a season. It was also an engineering concept that allowed more of the ballast-tank water—when the ballast tanks were full—to sit lower in the bulkhead, creating a lower center of gravity with less water. This way it would take less time to pump the water out. The idea was a flash in the pan, and no other boats I ever knew were built the same way.

"It wouldn't have mattered anyway. We got across the deck fine. It's what we found when we got there that was the problem.

"I stopped in my berth and changed into some dry clothes before I gathered the men to come with me. I stripped out of my damp pants and socks and shirt and put on my union suit and dry pants, fresh socks and a turtleneck. I grabbed my pea jacket, my mittens, and hat, and when I was all bundled up I topped myself off with the raincoat and the orange life preserver that had sat for years in the wooden basket above my desk.

"For some stupid reason I checked the four porthole windows in my cabin," he said. There was surprise in his voice, like it was a memory that had only come back to him then, all those years later. "I wonder why I did that.

"Whatever the reason, it gave me the minute I needed to remember my watch. Your mother had given it to me the Christmas before. It was on a sterling chain in my desk. I kept it there for safety.

"When she gave it to me she told me it'd bring me luck. I decided I wanted to have it with me when I died. In fact," Olaf said as he dug into his pocket, "here it is." He handed it to Noah.

It was beautiful, a tarnished nickel-silver pocket watch with an analemma on its face. The movement was visible behind a rear crystal, and when Noah flipped it open he saw the name of the watch company engraved on the bezel. UTVIKLING URMAKER—KRISTIANIA 1920.

"I've never seen this before," Noah said.

Olaf was settling stiffly back into the chair. "It needs to be polished," he said.

"So you put the watch in your pocket?" Noah asked.

"I did."

"And then you went to get the other guys?" he said, handing it back.

Olaf began fingering the clasp with one hand as he tried to remove some of the patina. "It's a damn strange thing, isn't it?" he asked. "This flimsy little watch, this soft metal chain." He looked up at Noah. "And that big old boat. Steel made from the ore of her predecessors, steel they'd made army tanks from. Almost a million rivets, two football fields long, eight thousand tons. One of them made it and the other one didn't."

Olaf worked the patina on the watch with his fingers, his jaw quivering in a now familiar way. The look of concentration on his face had given way to drowsiness.

"How did you pick the guys to cross the deck with you?"

"I picked Red because he was the single strongest guy I ever knew," Olaf said. "Short bastard, built like a brick shithouse, with a red beard that hung to his chest and eyebrows the same color, bushy as a hedge. He had a cannonball of a gut, rock solid and sticking out there like a pregnant woman's. Huge shoulders"—he hunched his shoulders up for effect—"but the smallest goddamn feet you ever saw. Like a bird.

"And a goofball, too. Always laughing and joking and playing pranks, good guy to have on your boat any time of year but especially in the fall, when everyone's good and goddamn tired of each other. He wore the damnedest red boots.

"During a lifesaving drill earlier that year, he hauled one of the lifeboats twenty yards up a Lake Ontario beach. Might not sound like much, but I could have picked any team of three other guys on that boat and together we wouldn't have been able to do the same thing. Amazing. I'm sure I had that in mind when I told him to bundle up."

"Why Luke?"

"Luke was the guy I trusted most on that boat. He was the only guy—aside from Jan—who I believed would do anything to save another guy's life. You said something about heroes, well, Luke was as close as we got.

"He was in his cabin, and I poked my head in and said, 'Luke, we're going aft. We've got trouble,' and he was up and in his gear in thirty seconds. Keep in mind he was asleep in his drawers at the time. Always willing to help, always had the best interest of the crew in mind." Olaf yawned, twitched his nose, and tried to cross his legs but couldn't.

"And why Bjorn?"

"Bjorn was sitting closest to the door."

Again the photograph in the maritime museum of the three men huddled on the beach came to mind. The distance between Bjorn's place at the card table and that otherworldly beach suddenly seemed like an impossible span. Noah wondered how much the picking of that particular group of men mattered. He wondered if Red had been a weakling, or if Luke had been less willing, or if Bjorn had been asleep in his bunk, whether things would have turned out differently.

Olaf interrupted Noah's thought. "We were out on the deck within minutes. I instructed the boys to keep together and latched myself onto the lifeline. I went first, then Red, then Bjorn, and Luke was last. The lifeline was a taut, half-inch steel cable that ran from the bow decking to the stern decking right down the middle of the boat. We had lines attached to our waists that we clipped onto it.

"We each had a flashlight or headlamp. Red had a walkie-talkie. There were half-a-dozen lamps running down the edge of either side of the deck. On a clear night they lit the *Rag* up like a boulevard, but they barely cracked the darkness that night. And the spotlight Jan had shining down on us from the roof of the pilothouse was just a little glimmer in the dark. Might as well have been a star on a cloudy night for all the good it was doing.

"The darkness wasn't the terrible part, though. It was everything else. Even though we'd gotten the ship turned around, we were still taking some pretty heavy seas, and our big problem was the ice. The deck was covered with it, the lifeline was heavy with it, and in no time at all we were covered in it ourselves. And the wind—Jesus Christ, the wind—so strong at times it'd just whip up behind us and send one of us sprawling face-first onto the deck.

"And the snow," he said finally and whistled.

"And cold?"

"So goddamn cold I felt like I was on fire," Olaf said.

One of the few points of difference in the chronicles of that night was the moment at which the fire became the central fact of the catastrophe. Although Bjorn had told a reporter during an interview a few weeks after the wreck that they could smell the fire while they were crossing the deck—a detail that should have put the speculation to rest—some refused to believe this could have been true. They argued that it would have been impossible to smell the fire, seeing how the smoke would have been contained in the engine room, how by then the wind would have been coming from behind them. These same people argued that any fire would certainly have resulted in an immediate explosion that the men on the deck would have heard and felt despite the rough crossing. Noah doubted these speculations. Although it seemed fair enough to assume that they might have felt or heard the explosion, it didn't seem out of the realm of possibility that they might not have, either. As for smelling the fire, Noah had little doubt that the stench could have escaped from any of a hundred crannies in the decking.

"How soon did you know she was burning?" Noah said.

"Hard to say. We were probably better than halfway across the deck when it dawned on me that something smelled wrong. It was like burning hair is what it was, but there was so much other goddamn commotion that it must have been another minute or two before it hit me. We'd crossed under the hatch crane and were probably only thirty or forty feet from reaching the decking when the stink took over.

"All at once I knew what was happening, and no sooner had I put it all together than Red grabs me by the shoulder. I thought he was falling and using me for balance, so I didn't turn around right away. But when he shook me again I turned, and he was shining his flashlight on the walkie-talkie.

"'Boss,' he said, hollering at the top of his goddamn lungs, 'the captain's calling.'

"There was so much static and interference from the noise in the background that I could barely hear what Jan was saying, but the long and short of it was that we were pretty well sunk." He looked off into the corner for a few seconds.

"He told me we had no steerage, that the engine room was incommunicado again. That's what I gathered from the static anyway. But then his voice came clear: '*The* Rag *is burning,*' he said. It seemed absolutely impossible." He looked down and quit talking.

"Jan must have already made the mayday, huh?"

Olaf lifted his eyes slowly. In the dim light Noah might have mistaken their glassiness for tears.

"Hand me the book," Olaf said. "And grab my glasses off the counter."

Noah did.

"I don't know exactly what time it was when Jan radioed us on the deck, but it had to have been some time around quarter of eleven. Everything was happening so fast." He had the open book under his nose in the lamplight and was scanning the page with his long, thick finger. "He made the mayday at ten thirty-three. And I'm sure he made the mayday before he signaled us."

"You said something about all the answers being in the mayday transcript," Noah said.

"I said as much as we'll ever know is in here." Olaf looked back down at the page for a second. "In the mayday," he said, closing the book but keeping it marked with his finger, "he gives them our position—which had hardly changed from the time of the pan-pan—and tells them there's a fire in the engine room, that he's lost contact with the stern, that he's got four men en route to investigate, and that he's lost his rudder.

"We know the fuel line was leaking. We know that everyone on

the stern was busy trying to contain the leak. We know that sometime
between, say, ten twenty and ten thirty, the whole thing went up, and
that within minutes the steerage was shot and Jan made the mayday.
It's safe to assume that there was some sort of explosion because a fire
alone wouldn't have put the rudder out of commission so fast. It's also
safe to assume there was an explosion because we never saw any of
those boys alive.

"When we finally reached the stern, I sent Luke and Red down
below to see what was going on while Bjorn and I went up to the
boat deck to see about steering that son of a bitch."

"What do you mean steering it?"

"At the very stern of the ship, behind the stack, up on the boat
deck, there were two emergency wheels. Jan told us he'd lost the
rudder, so up we went. I'll tell you what, there couldn't have been
a more wide-open spot for heaven to piss on us than the ass end of
that ship."

Noah was trying to piece it all together. "But you didn't have a
compass, you didn't have a radar or the charts."

"We knew which way the wind was blowing, though. I figured if
we kept it behind us, we'd be okay."

Olaf pinched the bridge of his nose as he took off his glasses.
"We were fighting it, you know? We had no idea what in the hell was
going on but that we had to keep the boat pointed in the right direction." He was shaking his head and suddenly sounded as if he were
pleading to a jury. "After a while—right before we ran aground—
Red and Luke came up to the boat deck. Bear in mind, we're still
right in the middle of hell. It was cold and windy and we were
soaked and coated with ice and standing up on that deck with tar-
gets on our chests, just waiting to get dead. We've got no idea what
the hell is happening below us until Luke comes back up. In the

middle of all that screaming wind he tells me we're done, that the engine room and her crew are gone, that right below us all four decks are up in flames: The fantail deck, the windlass room, the cabins—everything—poof"—he exploded his hands—"roaring away. He tells me they didn't see anyone, that we've got no chance. Jesus Christ," he said under his breath.

"And I'm thinking to myself, those goddamn boats sitting tight in Thunder Bay better damn well be on their way, and the Coast Guard better have a cutter and a few helicopters coming to search or we're as good as dead.

"My mind was all tangled up. I was sitting on a time bomb with all the water in the world exploding around me. It's so goddamn dark and cold and my guys are telling me that right beneath our feet half the crew is cooked." He closed his eyes, looking, Noah thought, like he was trying to erase the picture from his mind. "I didn't know what the hell to do, so I grabbed Red by the arm and we went back down.

"I told him to stay right with me, that we were going to slog it back into the engine room and see if there was anything we could do."

"But they'd just been down there. They said it was impossible."

"I had to see it for myself, I guess. As much as I trusted Luke, I knew it would haunt me forever if I got off that boat without checking on those guys.

"Jesus, it was something. We entered by way of the galley, grabbed fire extinguishers, and worked our way to the dining room and then toward the gangway that led into the crew's quarters. I sounded the alarm, tried to make it into the cabins. But we had to stop. We couldn't have gotten ten steps into those rooms without going up in flames ourselves.

"The strange part was that nothing in particular seemed to be on fire. It was like the air was on fire, all of the air. We were getting tossed around, of course, and each time I got thrown against the wall I could feel how goddamn hot it was. If I hadn't been soaked through and halfway frozen, I probably would have come out of there with burns everywhere. Instead it was almost a relief if you can believe that."

"How long were you down there?"

"Impossible to say, five, maybe ten minutes I'd guess. Once our extinguishers went empty we had no choice but to get back up on deck with Luke and Bjorn."

"I can't imagine."

"Why would you want to?" Olaf asked. "Why in the world would anyone want to imagine that hell?"

Noah took the question as a cue and sat there silently trying to remember what he knew about the ships that had laid up in Thunder Bay—whether it was just two or all three of them that had responded—and whether it was a search plane or helicopters that the Gunflint coast guard had dispatched when the wind weakened.

After a few minutes Olaf broke the silence again. "It had to be Canoe Rocks," he said.

"What did?"

"Where we ran aground. The death blow."

Olaf labored to his feet again, this time staying bowed at the waist as he took a few steps across the living room toward a wall shelf that sat behind the dining table. It was cluttered with cast-iron cookware and decorative Norwegian dishes, unused cookbooks, and antique cans of mosquito repellent. From the top of the shelf he grabbed what looked to Noah like a poster that was rolled up and tied with blue-and-white string.

"This is an old chart of Superior," Olaf said, as he tried to catch some of the faint light in order to read a curled-up edge of it. "Right up your alley, come to think of it."

"Let's have a look at that." Noah pushed the mugs and magazines and books on the coffee table to one end.

Olaf fiddled with the knot for a couple of seconds before he gave up and handed it to Noah, who fidgeted with it himself for a moment before biting through the string and unrolling the map on the coffee table. Olaf had grabbed a couple of heavy books from the bookcase and set one at each end of the table to keep the chart from coiling back up.

It was an old Loran-C chart published by the National Oceanic and Atmospheric Administration that Noah recognized at a glance. It covered the north Superior shoreline from Grand Portage Bay, Minnesota, to Shesheeb Point, Ontario, and included the entire Isle Royale archipelago. People were always coming into his shop in Boston hoping that the folded and faded maps they had found in their attics were priceless relics. More often than not, they were just like this one, worth nothing more than what it would cost to mail them.

Olaf had turned a couple of lamps on and sat down knobby-kneed next to Noah on the sofa. "You see here?" he asked, dragging his nub pinky up the length of Isle Royale to its northeastern tip. "These are the Canoe Rocks. And this," he said, dragging his thumb another couple of inches straight north, "is where we came about, where Jan made the mayday. The wind was coming from there," he said, stretching his arm toward the dark corner of the great room and then signaling the direction with his thumb by pulling it back toward them, "so you see, the rocks were the first things in our path.

"We came about at ten fifteen, the fire starts at about ten thirty, you factor an hour of powerless drifting in, and we'd have hit the rocks about eleven thirty. From Canoe Rocks we drift a little farther southwest for a half hour or so and sink exactly here," he said, thumping a black X scrawled on the chart with his thumb.

Noah sat up, retraced the path his father suggested, and leaned in to have a closer look at the sounding marked on the chart. "It says here the water's only five hundred and eighty-two feet deep. I thought the *Rag* was deeper than that."

Olaf pointed at the fine print along the upper edge of the map. "This chart was published in 1964. After the *Rag* sank, during the investigation they spent a lot of time using sonar equipment and whatnot trying to determine the exact whereabouts of the wreckage. They discovered the original soundings were off a couple hundred feet."

"No small error," Noah said.

"Discrepancies on these lake charts only mattered if they were in shallow water, in the harbors and along the coasts. The difference between five hundred and eighty feet and eight hundred feet doesn't mean much to a boat drafting twenty-five."

They both sat back and sighed and turned to face each other. After an awkward second Olaf looked away and patted Noah's knee before trying to stand up. The edge of the couch was lower than the chair, though, and he couldn't get his legs to lift him. Rather than trying to get up again, he let himself slide back into the cushions.

Noah had stood impulsively and found himself hovering above his father for the second time in as many hours. Instead of lingering this time, he walked around the table and looked for something to distract them from the awkward moment. A couple of seconds seemed like a couple of minutes before he finally grabbed the afghan and spread it over his father's legs.

"Thanks," Olaf said, then gestured toward the stove. "Is there room in there for another log?"

Noah opened the stove door, knew another log wouldn't make any difference. He took one from the wood box and tossed it in. When it hit the smoldering pile already in the stove, the logs collapsed and spread across the bottom of the stove in a bright, pumpkin-orange flash. The new log caught fire immediately.

"Close the damper a bit, too, would you?" Olaf asked.

Noah did. As he stood there within a few feet of the open door, watching the bark on the split oak disappear into ash, he figured the temperature in the cabin must have been at least eighty-five degrees, maybe ninety.

He closed the stove door and went to the kitchen to pour himself a glass of water. "If there was an explosion, isn't it possible that *that* was the cause of a rupture in the hull?" Noah asked.

"Sure, sure," Olaf said. "In fact, I'd be surprised if serious damage hadn't been done by an explosion, the fire alone, even. But the fatal blow was the rocks."

"How do you know?"

"It wasn't more than a couple minutes after I got back on deck that we ran aground," Olaf said. "Imagine that big boat butting against a line of rocks, each as big as a house. The jolt knocked me right off my feet. We were lucky we'd had time to get ourselves reattached to our lifelines. If we hadn't, we would've been in the water—and probably dead.

"You see, when the boat's adrift in the open water, the waves are up against a moving target. When the boat's beached on the rocks, in the shoal water, they're free to pound whatever's there. I remember trying to get my feet back under me and the water crashing up over the deck. I didn't have a whole lot of hope right then, that's for damn sure."

"It must have been terrifying," Noah said, imagining himself in the same situation. "What do you think about at a moment like that?"

Olaf looked at him from the corner of his eye. "Have you ever been in a rumble?" he asked.

"What do you mean? Like a fistfight?"

"Yeah. You and another guy mixing it up."

"No."

"I've been in one fight," Olaf said. "In Westby, Wisconsin, of all places. I was sixteen years old. I remember because it was the year I won the ski jumping tournament down there—you won there once, too, didn't you?" he asked but didn't wait for an answer. "We were in one of the bars in town after the tournament, and some local guy got it into his head that I was trying to move on his girl—which I probably was." Olaf smiled. "He cussed me out, and before I knew it, he'd cracked my head with a beer bottle. It wasn't a clean hit, but it was enough to knock me down. Then he sets to work kicking, punching, crashing bar chairs over my shoulders every time I tried to get on my feet. I didn't know what in the hell had hit me, but I knew I had to get up. I thought that son of a bitch might've been crazy enough to kill me.

"The point is, I'd been getting the shit knocked out of me: the walk across the deck, the time on the open boat deck, running aground and taking that pounding, that all adds up. It would've been easy to just cling to that icy deck and hope."

"Why didn't you give up?"

"I guess there was some instinct to survive," Olaf said. "And I knew I probably wouldn't if I just sat there holding on for dear life."

"Did you think you were going to die?"

Olaf thought about it for a second. "I don't suppose I thought I was going to die, no. It was more a matter of thinking I wouldn't survive. There's a difference, or it seemed so at the time.

"We were only hung up on the rocks for a couple of minutes, but that was time enough for me to put some perspective on our situation. We had no engine, no engine *crew*, no steerage, no communication between ends of the ship, no communication at all, with anyone. We were thirty miles from safe harbor, stuck on a rock in the middle of Lake Superior, it was below zero, a near whiteout, with fifteen-foot waves. And we were already soaked to the bone.

"Now, I don't care if you have two minutes or two days to make decisions when you're in a mess like that, the fact is, there just aren't a whole lot of options. You asked me if I thought I was going to die. If I'd had the time, I might've. But I didn't. I had to decide whether to launch the lifeboats or get back with the rest of the crew on the bow."

"Why would you have done that?"

"They were my crewmates," Olaf said without hesitation. "I was an officer aboard a ship in peril."

The notion of the crew's importance touched an unidentifiable nerve in Noah. "I don't understand," he said. "Crossing back to the bow would have meant leaving the lifeboats. If you leave the lifeboats, you've got positively no chance."

"That's true *if* you know the boat is sinking. We didn't."

Noah shook his head. "You didn't know you were sinking? You're on the rocks, the lifeboats are ten feet from where you're standing, half the crew is already dead—probably dead, anyway—and you hesitate to get off the ship?"

"They were my goddamn crewmates, I wanted to save them more than I wanted to save myself. How could I have helped anyone by getting into a lifeboat and rowing into the goddamn night?"

"How did you intend to save them by leaving behind the only means of escape?"

Olaf was clearly riled. "Oh, hell, I don't know. Maybe I thought there would be safety in numbers, maybe I thought one of those lifeboats out on the open water would have been suicide—I mean, hell, it nearly was. Or maybe I just didn't know what to do. There's no manual for surviving the end of the world." He balled both hands into lopsided fists and pounded them against his legs.

"It doesn't matter anyway," he concluded. "No sooner had the four of us met back on the deck than we came off the rocks. As soon as we did, I knew exactly what we had to do."

Noah got up again, went to the kitchen, and wiped his face with a dish towel. Outside, it was dark, and Noah caught a glimpse of his reflection in the window. His hair was messy and on end, and he looked drunk. He hadn't shaved since he'd left Boston, and his stubble darkened his chin. His eyes were slack but bright. There was fog on the outside of the window, and he figured it would have been frost if not for the heat inside.

"Understand something," Olaf said, "until we got off the rocks, I still had the notion that everything was going to come together. I still thought—and it's easy to see how ludicrous this sounds in hindsight—that somehow we could come out of it, you know? That we could avoid the end. Stupid, but it's true.

"And another thing, contrary to conventional wisdom, when you're on the edge of life—like that—and falling off, you don't stop and reminisce. At least I didn't. What you do is look for something to hold on to."

Noah hoisted himself up onto the kitchen counter and crossed his legs. "I guess," he said but didn't understand. The notion that the old man's crew of nobodies should take precedence over his mother and sister and himself still didn't make sense.

"And maybe there was a chance up until we came free, you know? Maybe everything going through my head wasn't just fear or indecision."

Noah thought, *He's pleading. Maybe not to me, but he is.*

"It's all the same, though, like I said, because when we did come off the rocks, all I wanted to do was get off that goddamn boat. It was the only thing left to do."

Noah looked up at him. "So that's when you knew she was going down."

"There wasn't much doubt about it. I mean, despite the fact that we couldn't see a thing, you could tell she was wallowing." He paused. "Whenever I imagine what she must have looked like from God's view, all I can see is the dying light."

"How fast did it happen?"

"Can't say for sure, but between the four of us we couldn't have gotten the lifeboat launched in any less than fifteen or twenty minutes, and considering how far from the rocks she ended up, it was probably a little longer than that."

"Not enough time for any of the other ships to get there?"

"No way."

"Or the Coast Guard?"

"What were they going to do even if they'd been able to get there? Searching for us on a night like that would've been like looking for a cotton ball in a cloud. They never would have found us."

"And the rest of the crew?" Noah asked, almost in a whisper.

"Don't know what happened," Olaf said and put his head down.

They sat in silence for a while before Noah slid off the counter and went back to the armchair. "You look tired," he said.

"I'm always tired."

"I'm tired, too," he said, looking at his watch to find that it was only six o'clock. "Why don't you get some sleep?"

"I think I will," Olaf said. "Give me a hand, would you?"

Noah skirted around the coffee table and took his father by the elbow. His arm was thin and soft. Noah helped him around the table.

"Gotta hit the head," Olaf said.

"Me, too."

"You know, I never thought much about it, but the worst part of the whole goddamn night came after we got the lifeboat in the water."

They walked to the door and stood in the dusky light coming off the kitchen, pushing their feet into a pile of unlaced boots by the door.

"*That's* the real story," Olaf said.

"Why don't you save that part for another time, huh?"

"It was a hell of a thing, you know? A hell of a thing."

"I've no doubt about that," Noah said as he pushed the door open. The air was biting, and no sooner did Noah step outside than his body drew taut and a shiver rippled up his back and through his shoulders.

They walked to the edge of the glow from the house and stood next to each other beside a tree, their shoulders almost touching.

"Already stars in the west," Olaf said, pointing through the trees. "It's going to clear up."

"Hopefully warm up, too."

"What, it doesn't get cold in Boston?"

"Of course it does, it's just that we usually hold off on the snow until winter."

"Ah, hell, that wasn't snow."

"It looked like snow to me. It got me thinking about your dog." Noah could picture Vikar somewhere in the middle of the woods, wet and bloody-muzzled, devouring a freshly slain rabbit.

"Don't worry about him. He's been roaming these woods for a long time now," Olaf said as he climbed the three rickety wooden steps back into the house. Noah held him steady by the elbow.

When he opened the door, Noah could feel the warm air surge out of the house. The blustery evening had cleared Noah's head—had invigorated him—and when he stepped back into the house, he thought it smelled like boiling rutabaga. It was a smell that reminded him of his mother and the dreaded Friday-night fish boils of his childhood. He was instantly sapped again.

He kicked off the boots and sat back down on the couch while Olaf filled a glass jar with water from the pitcher. He drank it, then filled it again, took two chalky tablets from a canister on the counter, and dropped them into the jar. Finally he dug into his mouth and pulled his teeth out and dropped them in the jar.

"What?" Noah said. "Since when do you have dentures?"

"Six years ago. I hate the goddamn things," Olaf said, picking up the jar and holding it to the light. His lips seemed baggier without his teeth, and it made him look even older.

Noah ran his tongue across the front of his own teeth. "I didn't know you had them."

"I guess you wouldn't."

"I guess not."

Noah rolled the chart back up and returned it to the shelf. Standing at the window, he thought, *That's it then. That's the dead come back to life.* "I'll have some dreams tonight," he said.

Olaf set his teeth on the counter. "You're lucky enough to still dream, huh?"

S I X

What a sight the old man made. On one end of the couch his bushy-rimmed head rested on a pillow. A collage of quilts covered him, leaving only his clownish feet—snug in thick wool socks—dangling over the other end of the sofa. His arms were folded over his chest, the sleeves of his union suit coming apart at the cuffs. He might have looked like this in a coffin, Noah thought as he walked past, slid on a pair of boots, and stepped outside.

A ribbon of beguiling fog curled up the trail from the lake, and he followed it down. Pockets of complete darkness still haunted the woods on either side of the path, heavy, wet, and eerie in a polka-dotted dawn. He could see the lightness above the lake and the still-black water exhaling mist. He thought again of Natalie's arriving today.

When he came to the beach he walked to the edge of the water and kicked at a clump of limp grass. He wore only a sweatshirt and his boxers, and the cold air gripped his legs. He flexed his body to stave off the chill. All around the rim of the lake the woods hoarded a darkness that didn't seem to make sense—coming, as he had, down the faintly lit path—but when he turned around to look back at the house, it too was gone in the darkness.

Across the lake, above the rolling treetops, the sky was turning a muted red that faded upward, seamlessly, through a hundred shades of pink and back to black. He stepped onto the dock, the planks and pilings creaking under his weight. The boat sat in the water, tied to the dock by two expert knots that appeared ready to hold the old thing there forever. Noah tiptoed into the boat and sat on the splintered thwart, watching the ripples roll out on the otherwise placid lake. *Natalie will love this place,* he thought. He could picture her on a warm summer afternoon, sitting on the beach with a magazine and sun hat under the shade of an umbrella. She would squint at him and smile and lick her thumb before turning the page. At lunch she would tell him peaches were out, blueberries in, according to the latest health craze she'd just finished reading about. He'd make himself a summer-sausage sandwich and look at the kids, two of them—twins, he'd decided—three years old and sitting in the clearing in the yard, on a picnic blanket in the sun. Fair-skinned and straight-haired, they picked at a caterpillar. He'd touch Nat on her knee and bowl into the sunlight, arms wide, to scoop them up. The kids would jump up and scream happiness and stutter-step in circles until he captured them. Nat, clearing the paper plates, would watch them, shielding her eyes from the sun with her hand.

A fish rolled lazily out of the water beside the boat, a big fish, and Noah's reverie was lost. *She's sleeping,* he thought, looking at his wrist for the watch not there. *She'll be on her way soon.* In that instant he realized—almost as if he'd always been aware of this fact—that his father's story mattered only if Noah could someday tell it himself, to a son or daughter, to another Torr who could keep it alive—here, on a blustery November night—for a third generation. He stood up, thankful for Nat's fortitude, and started back toward the house.

Midway up the path, though, he froze. The trees swayed and murmured, and when they went silent he heard something else in the distance. It was faint, lilting, and it stopped almost as soon as it started. He took another step and froze again, turned back toward the lake, and heard it again, louder and more mournful this time. A howl, a wolf's howl. One wolf usually meant many.

He tried to move in a lull after the second cry but couldn't—he was spellbound. The light had come fully up but was still drab. A third cry went up, and he walked back to the beach. *God, it's beautiful*, he thought. And no sooner had he thought it than the howl was answered. The wolf song permeated the air, seemed even to warm it. He fixed his eyes on the shoreline, scanned it from the cliff face they'd fished off the other day to the impenetrable spruce stand on the north shore of the lake. He couldn't see them, but the howling had entered him. It filled him the way the foghorns had as a child.

They sang for a long time. He wondered if the hunt was over and they were celebrating their kill, or if they'd simply been lost in the night and were calling each other back to the den. Maybe there were pups, maybe it was a long call to danger.

When they stopped he started back for the house. He considered its black windows as though from a distance they might let onto something other than what was really there. He saw a light flicker on in one of the windows and his father's head appear. It looked like a scene from an Impressionist painting. But the image only lasted for a second before the old man turned and disappeared from the light.

"BRIGHT-EYED AND BUSHY-TAILED," Olaf said. "You hear the wolves?"

"I looked for them." Noah stopped in the kitchen.

"There's a pack in the neighborhood. Their turf comes right up to the shore across the lake. Far as I can tell anyway. If you're quiet and sit still long enough, sometimes you can see them watering themselves in the morning."

Noah filled the kettle and put it on the stove.

"I saw you down there listening. Awfully brisk morning to be out in your skivvies." His father's union suit hung on him, and he had the afghan slung over his shoulders like a shawl. "Twenty-eight degrees according to the thermometer." He pointed out the kitchen window.

"I'll bet it's five degrees colder once you get away from this house. You're killing me with these fires."

"I can't feel it," Olaf said, dropping back on the sofa. "I can't get warm enough."

"That why you slept on the couch last night?"

Olaf nodded, settling back under the quilts. "The bedroom gets so cold."

Noah sat in the chair. "I'll get back at that tree in the gulch today. We'll restock this place with firewood yet. And I'm going to get that chain. I'll leave as soon as I finish the coffee. You want to come with?"

"I'll stay put. But you can take my truck again if you want. Knutson's opens at seven. Better fill the gas can, too."

"I will."

Olaf laid his head down on the pillow and let out a long, quiet sigh. "I feel better today, out here on the sofa. Like I'm on vacation or something. A night at the Ritz."

"If only we could call for room service," Noah said, getting up. "I could use one of those breakfasts you were talking about last night."

"They've got good cinnamon rolls at the Landing. Bring a few back with you."

"I'll do that. Don't go anywhere."

A smile turned up half of Olaf's mouth.

AT THE HARDWARE store a half-dozen men, all as old as Olaf, milled about a deer stand that, according to a handwritten sign, had just arrived in stock. Each of the men had a Styrofoam cup of coffee in his hand and wore a plaid or blaze-orange hunting vest. Noah walked to the back of the store and rang the service bell on the counter. One of the men in the group excused himself and hustled back to help Noah.

" 'Morning. What can I do for you?"

"I need a length of chain."

"Any particulars?"

"Is there such a thing as three-quarter-inch . . . something? Polyurethane coated? I need twenty feet of it."

"Let me show you what we've got," he said, motioning with his long arm for Noah to follow.

A couple of aisles over several spools lined the shelf. "This what you have in mind?" the old man said. "It's your standard high-test, shot peened, poly coated. What do you need it for anyway?" He put his nose up in the air and looked at Noah through the lenses of his reading glasses.

"I don't know exactly. It's not for me, but it looks like it'll do."

"If it doesn't work, bring it right back and we'll get you what does." He hollered toward the back of the store, and a tall teenager with a baggy Gunflint football jersey hanging on him stepped from behind a door. "Cut me twenty feet of the three-quarter-inch poly, all right?"

"Sure thing, boss." The kid hurried behind the counter for a chain cutter.

"He's a good worker," the old man said. "Hard to find up here."

"Good help's hard to find anywhere," Noah said, meaning to sound conspiratorial.

"Of course, you're a Torr. I've been trying to figure it out since you walked in. All you Torr fellas are twelve feet tall. But I must've known you when you were knee high to a grasshopper." He cleared his throat. "Your grandpa bought everything he needed to build that place from my pop, one of our first big customers. He used to play poker with him right back there." He gestured to an office behind the counter. "How's your dad doing anyway? Haven't seen him in a while."

"He's okay."

"Tell the old codger Knut says hello. Tell him to come down and have coffee some morning."

"I'll do that."

The kid brought the chain and set it on the counter. Knut put it in a paper bag and took eight dollars from Noah. "Remember," he said, "if that doesn't work for you, bring it back."

"I appreciate it," Noah said. "And I'll tell the old man you say hello." The bag seemed to weigh a hundred pounds.

At the Landing he filled the gas can and the truck before he went inside. The empty gravel parking lot and old-fashioned gas pumps finally made the place seem as remote as it was, and he imagined everything buried in snow. He pictured himself clamping his feet into a pair of cross-country skis and getting back to the cabin by way of fresh tracks in the spring corn. He imagined the labor, sweat, and reward. He could hear the fresh klister wax singing under the skis.

When the tank was full he went inside to pay and pick up the box of cinnamon rolls his father had requested. A bell chimed as he opened the door and walked into the deserted store. No cashier greeted him, only the smell of baking bread thick in the air. In the bakery case pastries as big as his feet lined the shelves. They looked better than anything he'd ever seen.

OLAF STOOD IN the middle of the yard wearing his ancient pea-coat, mukluks, wool cargo pants with pockets ballooning on either leg, and a pair of worn choppers. He held a thermos in one hand and an unlit cigar in the other. Noah parked the truck, took the bag with the chain from the seat beside him, and met Olaf in the yard.

"What are you going to wear when it starts getting cold?" he asked.

Olaf smiled. "Any luck with the chain?"

Noah held the bag up. "Knut says hello. Nice guy. There's not much you couldn't find in that store of his, either. It's doubling as the local coffeehouse. Told me to tell you to come down some morning and join him for a cup."

Olaf lifted the thermos. "I make my own coffee. But he runs a good business, been around since the Voyageurs." He looked in the bag.

"That going to work?"

"This is fine," Olaf said.

"Where are you headed anyway? Looks like you're ready for a polar expedition."

Olaf suddenly seemed bashful. He slapped his hand against his thigh, turned to look toward the shed, made a tentative step in its direction but stopped and faced Noah. "Come here," he said.

The padlock on the shed wasn't locked. Olaf took it from the hasp, hung it on a nail pounded into the siding, and tugged the warped door open. He stepped into the shed and pulled aside the curtain, barely illuminating the heaps of junk everywhere. Car parts and oil cans occupied a whole wall of shelves. There were mildew-stained cardboard boxes, splintered canoe paddles, busted lawn chairs, a step-ladder missing every other rung, a mattress and box spring leaning against the back wall, two pairs of Noah's childhood skis propped in the corner, vintage life preservers hanging from hooks on the wall to his right, and on the left a table that must have been his father's work-shop, as evidenced by the hacksaw, the stainless-steel tubing, and the mayonnaise jar full of nails and screws atop an oak door that spanned two sawhorses. The place stank like ripe, wet wood.

Where, Noah thought, disgusted, could her ashes possibly be in this mess? "This place is a sty," he said, stepping over a stack of mag-azines.

Olaf was clearing his toolbox from an old wooden barrel that sat on the floor beside the makeshift table. He shrugged. "You and your sister used to sleep out here. There's a nice breeze in the sum-mer." He pointed the hacksaw at the cracked window. "Comes up off the lake."

"It could use a breeze now. It smells awful in here." Noah was trying to figure out how to ask about his mother's ashes.

Olaf poured a cup of coffee from the thermos. "You recognize this?" He pointed at the barrel.

"This? Yeah, I sure do."

Olaf pried the lid off, exposing thousands of taconite pellets.

"Your mother hated these things. Thought they were messy. She hated a mess."

Noah picked a handful from the barrel and rolled them around in the palm of his hand. "They were," he said. "They still are." He showed his father the black smudges on his fingertips.

"I used to bring a pocketful of these home for you each run. Like they were goddamned lemon drops."

"I remember that," Noah said.

"You loved it. You thought it was the neatest damn thing."

Noah wanted to smile at the memory but couldn't. "Where are her ashes?" he said.

Olaf had turned his attention to the chain and didn't look up when he said, "Somewhere. It's been a long time since I had them out." He slung the chain over his shoulders. "I used to keep them in the house but got scared I might use them instead of flour to bread the trout."

"You're joking."

Olaf set the chain on the workbench and said nothing, only smiled.

"And now they're lost."

Olaf sat down, took a piece of the stainless-steel tubing, and threaded the chain through it. "They aren't lost. They're somewhere here. You can spit from one wall to the other, wouldn't take long to find them.

"Anyway, forget about the ashes for a minute. I need help getting this down to the lake." He kicked the barrel at Noah's feet, finally looked him in the eye. "And there's something else. All this stuff"— he gestured toward the workbench—"it's for an anchor. The chain, it's for an anchor."

"What anchor?"

"For my burial in the lake."

Noah looked at him for a hard moment. "Have you gone completely nuts? Your burial?" He raked his hair back and shook his head in disbelief.

"Settle down, would you? I know what's going on here"—he put his hands to his stomach—"I know what's happening to me. I'm not a fool."

"You're wrong about that. You're exactly a fool." Noah stepped toward his father. "First of all, we can take you to the doctor. We can get help for whatever's happening to you. They cure this stuff nowadays. I mean, you don't even know what's wrong. And don't tell me we covered it already," Noah insisted, anticipating Olaf's retort. "Let's be reasonable instead." Now he took the chain from his father's shoulders and let it slink to the floor.

In a firm voice Olaf said, "I've lived a long time and deserve this much." He bent to pick up the chain. "I know you think it's ignorant or selfish or *nuts*, I guess, but the simple fact of the matter is that after you've lived as long as I have, after you've come to terms with everything you've wrecked in this world, everything you've loved, once it's all tucked away and measured out, six more months or a year don't matter anymore."

"Maybe it doesn't matter to *you* anymore." Now Noah sat down. "Do I understand you? Do you really believe the things you're telling yourself?" He shook his head in disgust and in sadness. "Listen, there's no way I'm going to chain you up and drop you out with the fish. You can't ask for something like that. I'm glad I'm here and can help. But this is out of the question. You can just forget it." Noah stepped to the door. "Don't ask me again."

Inside the house Noah tore through his bag, put on a flannel shirt, took his dirty jeans from the bedpost and a pair of leather gloves from a shelf by the door, and headed back outside, only stopping long enough to fetch the chainsaw and the full gas can from the back of the truck.

He hurried to the fallen oak. When he reached the tree he paused and looked down into the creek bed. He swung into the gulch, tugged on the cord, set the chain against the trunk of the tree, and pulled the trigger.

He worked first with the saw above his head. Balancing against the steep incline of the gulch's wall, he let the saw rip through the oak as it rained sawdust on him. When the saw slipped through the top side of the trunk he flinched, expecting the tree to shift or fall when the first bole fell. It didn't.

On the bank of the gulch ropy stalks of bramble grew from the clumps of rusty soil, and he used them to pull himself up. There had to be an easier way of doing this. He stepped onto the trunk. He started the saw again and tiptoed backward out onto the tree. It couldn't have been much more than eight or ten feet above the ground, but it seemed much higher, especially when he looked toward the lake.

Measuring off a foot and a half, he set the saw onto the tree and hit the trigger. From this angle the saw worked much more easily. In less than half the time it had taken him to make the first pass from the underside, it cleaved the first stump. He made eight or ten more stumps from the trunk, and when he choked the saw off and looked behind him, he saw that he was a solid quarter of the way across and suspended above the nettle as if he were on the bowsprit of a ship.

His body thrummed with the lingering vibrations from the saw. He caught his breath, tightened the gloves on his hands, and brushed the sawdust from his sleeves. *Now the hard part*, he thought. He dropped back into the gulch, set the saw on the bank, and stacked the stumps into a pile at the base of the incline. Then he began hoisting them out of the creek bed. The first, narrower half of the bunch were light enough that he could toss them up. The second half required a plan. He managed to get the first big stump onto his shoulder. The thick bark bit his face as he crawled up the embankment. His feet churned in the loose soil. Laboring, the stump sliding around his neck—it must have weighed seventy-five pounds—the bark burning his neck, he imagined it crushing his ankle. He strained against the stump, finally rolled it up over the edge.

He collapsed onto the bank, half standing and half sitting, and felt his pulse throbbing in his wrists. Breathing heavily and sweating profusely again, he eyed the remaining half-dozen pieces of oak. *If not right now*, he thought, *I'll never finish*. Besides, the wind funneling up the gulch felt fine. He took off a glove, felt the back of his neck, and saw blood on his fingertips. He stanched it with the collar of his shirt. After he caught his breath he hefted the other stumps from the gulch. When he rolled the last one over the lip, he crawled out himself.

The wheelbarrow was parked where they'd left it. In its rusty, dented bottom, shallow pools of water had formed. Noah carted it to the edge of the gully and muscled the two biggest pieces of sawn oak into it. The trail, with its tree roots, potholes, and rocks, made steering the barrow difficult. But he managed eight trips. On the last he stopped midway back and looked up at the ski jump. Several times since he'd been back he'd thought of climbing the rickety old thing, but each time the thought crossed his mind he'd been distracted. Now he set down the empty wheelbarrow and kicked his way through the overgrowth to the lopsided steps that led up to the base of the scaffold. There were four telephone poles supporting the top of it and two more midway up the inrun. On the left side of the ramp thirty steps made of two-by-fours were pounded into the plywood floor under the handrail. He took them two at a time.

When he got to the top he stood for a minute looking down the inrun. The wind—a headwind he fondly recalled—blowing almost violently now, caused the scaffold to sway. Beyond the takeoff, on the left, the coaching deck his father and grandfather used to huddle on had completely sunk in the overgrowth. It was easy to imagine them standing there, their hushed voices carrying up to him as he latched his boots into the cable bindings and lowered his goggles over the rim of his white leather helmet. It was the flattery he overheard on those mornings that gave him his first sense of vanity, though neither could tolerate his lack of concentration.

He had no trouble concentrating now. *It looks so damn big*, he thought. Though the jump was awfully small in contrast to the Olympic-sized jumps he'd competed on as a teenager, the years of forgetting almost entirely about the sport had skewed his perspective. The landing hill was overgrown with new trees and thistle, and the takeoff was buried in the scrub, but he could easily imagine the whole scene packed with snow. Even though the lake frothed in the wind, he could see ski tracks narrowing in the distance.

The brightness of the sun glinting off the snow, the cold toes and windburned cheeks, none of it was lost after all. His skis squeaking against the hard snow at the top of the jump before he pulled himself onto the inrun, the speed gained as he hurtled down the ramp, the serenity and silence of the flight, the camber of both his skis and his body in flight, the exultation of flight. The perfect instinct to land and the explosion of consciousness in landing . . . *none* of it had been forgotten.

He looked back toward the house. Why had he been so quick to condemn the old man's project in the shed? Why had he been so quick to deny him this favor? Didn't the million mornings standing on that coach's platform in the wicked wind and chill of the Minnesota winter add up to something?

For all his horror at the thought of dropping his old man in the lake, the idea was not altogether unbeautiful. Again he thought about the story his father had told him the night before, this time pausing to reflect on the type of eternity his father had so narrowly avoided. Maybe the will to be buried in the lake was born of the notion that it was his honest fate, not merely some screwball's version of an interminable penance. None of which meant, Noah thought, that he'd be able to carry out the old man's wishes.

He wheeled the last load of wood back to the yard, noticed the door of the shed still open. He saw his father working, could see, through the papery curtain and dirty glass, that the old man had somehow managed to lift the barrel of taconite onto his workbench.

The sight of it made his entire morning's labor seem feigned.

SPANNING SIX OF the barrel staves, the words SUPERIOR STEEL & STEAMSHIP COMPANY were branded black. *The barrel must be a hundred years old*, Noah thought as he rubbed his thumb through the tarnished grooves of the lettering. He imagined piles of these barrels in the hull of an old turn-of-the-century bark, loaded with iron ore. He remembered this particular barrel hidden behind the furnace in the house on High Street.

One of the pieces of stainless-steel tubing was already attached to the barrel with a dozen finely placed bolts. In a pile on the table another dozen bolts appeared ready for the same purpose, and the second piece of tubing was apparently being shortened by something less than an inch. At least the hacksaw blade halfway through it suggested as much. Noah wrapped his arms around the barrel and lifted it off the workbench. It took all his strength. Though he could not imagine how the contraption might work, he admired the old man's vision. No doubt he had a plan, and no doubt that plan would work. Had he not been a sailor, Olaf might have made a fine life as a builder. Noah had often wished for his father's advice while in agony over how to install a new toilet or hang a chandelier from the dining room ceiling. Any of a hundred household tasks at which he inevitably failed. Long weekend afternoons with hammer-bruised thumbs. He smiled now, well removed from them.

The old man was at his afternoon nap. Later today than the day before.

Noah walked outside and crossed the yard. He began stacking the wood around the splitting stump in the yard. He thought of Nat, on her way now. He thought back through the travails of their childlessness. He remembered how the first couple years of trying had been almost magical in their ability to bring the two of them closer together. There had been such solidarity of purpose, such a marveling at prospects. It wasn't until after the first pregnancy and miscarriage that things had actually started to seem both urgent and unlikely.

He could remember that morning vividly. He had startled himself awake from a deep sleep and found her side of the bed cold and empty. He could hear the sound of the bathroom faucet and in the grainy light could see Nat's bare legs beneath the sink. Under the stream and splashing of water, he heard her unappeasable, almost silent, sobbing. When he stumbled into the hallway and stood in the bathroom door, she didn't even look up. "No, no, no, no," she muttered above her sobbing. He tried to console her, tried to hug away her quivering, but for the first time in their lives together she rejected him.

The other miscarriages had been worse in their ways—one had been twins, miscarried two days apart—but it was the first that had taken the deepest stab at their hope. The late-night talks about rearing the wonder child disappeared, her explanations of the tests and procedures her doctor was performing to isolate the cause of her infertility also ceased. So did talk of next steps. Over the next two years their inability to have a child had come to seem like an illness. It was mired in an unremitting despondency that might pop up at any time. They'd see a duckling in the pond at the park, and Nat would fall miserable for three days. If they saw a pregnant woman in the grocery store Nat would forget what they were there for. It was her sadness that had come to matter most to him, he realized. *She's somewhere near*, he thought as he headed for the lake. *She'll be here before dark.*

Down at the lake steely clouds mixed in the sky. The wind-whipped water curled up in waves that washed on the beach. He stepped onto the dock and bent to untie his boots. He took off his jeans and shirt, his socks and drawers, and stood naked at the end of the dock. Instantly the sweat that only a few minutes earlier had been dripping from him dried—seemed almost to encase him—as the wind curled around him. He stood there, distracted by the cold air, and had only a single moment of clarity, of apprehensive panic, before he jumped feet-first into the lake.

From the instant he went under he could feel the water seizing him. Although he'd been anticipating something like it, he could never have expected the grip of the water. If he hadn't kicked and pulled for the surface the instant he was submerged he might have ended up sunk.

Crazy though the idea of the bath had been, both his father and grandfather had been inclined to take late-autumn and even early-winter baths. It was a point of pride between the two men. Noah could remember watching them—their long arms and lean, muscular legs, their hairy chests and long beards—as they dove into the water while the early-winter snow whitened the sky. It was a rite of passage Noah had not grown up fast enough for. As he climbed onto the dock he took a cracked bar of Ivory soap from its wooden nook on the dock, wetted it, and began lathering himself. The air felt warm in contrast with the water, and he washed away the day's hard work and grime. He scrubbed his underarms, legs, and feet. He wetted the soap again and lathered his hair and face, his neck and arms. He washed his back. And before he could fear it, he dove back into the lake. He experienced the same convulsions, the tightening in his lungs, the stardust behind his closed eyes, but he needed a second to rinse himself, so he messed his hair with his hands and kicked wildly while he watched the soap disperse in the dark water.

Back on the dock he stood in the bracing wind as water puddled at his feet. He dried himself in the gale. Nat would not have known him there. He could not have known himself. He was—if only for a few long minutes—more his father than he had ever been. More than ever he was his son. A sense that ought to have brought with it a feeling of benevolence brought instead a pale choler. Nat would be here soon—was perhaps already up at the cabin—willing herself and Noah into parenthood with her resoluteness alone, stopping literally at nothing to add a branch to the Torr family tree. And here Noah stood, half an orphan for most of his life. He'd learned to live without his father, almost without the memory of him. He'd reinvented himself in a fashion with Nat's help, had evolved as a man even as his father had receded ghostlike into the Minnesota wilderness. Thoughts that should have been spent on memories of the old man, on anticipating times to come, had been spent on what instead? He toed the soap back into its nook.

Aside from Nat—from their life together—and these few other things, what did he even think about? Of their childlessness, sure, but less and less even of that. Was he not entitled to recompense for the void? Would it have been better if his father had died on that night all those years ago? Whether this last was said or only thought he did not know, but soberer for it having crossed his mind, he forgave the old man all at once. Forgave him everything. He wondered whether his father would forgive him.

In the spirit of being his father's son, he walked back up to the cabin in his boots alone.

SEVEN

I leave you alone for a few days and this is what I come to find?"
Nat stood at the kitchen basin, scrubbing a bunch of radishes, staring at her naked husband. She was trying to make light of things, Noah knew, but the effort felt stilted. She seemed unsure of her own presence. "Hurry and dress. Soup's on."

In the middle of the great room, before the now tempered woodstove, the card table was prodigiously set. Noah took a piece of cheese, sniffed it, tasted it. "Brown cheese," he said, then stepped into the bedroom.

When he emerged again Nat was helping Olaf to a seat at the table.

Noah said, "When did you get here?"

"About a half hour ago."

Olaf ladled creamy gruel from a plastic container.

"What's that?" Noah said.

"This is black pot," Olaf said. "What your grandmothers would have called *sort gryte*."

"I'm dying to hear about this," Noah said, heading for the refrigerator. He added the smoked salmon to the feast.

"There's not much to hear. I found this place online." She searched for a paper bag under the cluttered countertop. "It's called Kafe Forny. 'Kafe' with a K. I'm afraid it's all cold." She handed Noah the bag and an open bottle of beer. She offered Olaf a bottle, but he declined with a turned-down chin.

The label on the bag had a Duluth address under a Norwegian-flag logo. The beer bottle read, HANSA-BORG'S BORG BOKKØL. Noah tasted the beer. He looked at his father spooning the soupy black pot into his slack mouth, the look on his face giving away a deep satisfaction. "So you left Boston this morning, stopped at a Norwegian deli in Duluth, drove up here, and now you're serving me a beer and something called black pot."

"And *lutefisk, lefse*, that cheese, *krumkake* for dessert."

"And radishes."

"And radishes," Nat confirmed. She set a plate of them on the table.

"Chrissakes, this is good eating," Olaf said.

Natalie sat next to Noah. "Dig in," she said.

A taste for these flavors had long been lost to Noah, but when he saw Natalie sprinkling sugar onto a buttered sheet of *lefse*, when he saw her slicing another piece of *Gjetost* cheese onto her plate, even when he saw her daring a quivering spoonful of lutefisk taken from a pan atop the stove, his appetite became tremendous. He ate everything. Olaf ate everything. Noah drank one and then another bottle of beer. Olaf suggested they turn on the radio, which they did, but when they found no station in the twilight hours they settled on old stories told around the table. Food stories all. Natalie recalled the always overcooked pork and dumplings stewed in cans of storebought soup from her childhood. Neither Noah nor Olaf could imagine it. Noah's memories settled on Christmas cookies so fine they defied his power of description. And for Olaf it was Thanksgiving turkeys cooked in the cavernous roasting pans of steamship ovens; his own mother's *lefse*, made of nearly rotting potatoes for their sweetness; her own antique *krumkake* irons; and finally her homemade butter on the *lutefisk* she made every Friday night.

Natalie, despite her labor in setting the table and the still too-warm room, wore her favorite sweater of Norwegian wool. She looked wholly native to this spot in the woods, so far from Boston and their life and her cautionary and conservative upbringing. She looked, Noah thought as he sat back for the last sip of his beer, more like his wife in that instant than in any other moment of their life together. It wouldn't have been possible for him to say that he loved her any better, but neither could he remember a moment in their history to match the intensity of his conviction that here was the woman whose wisdom in all things made *him* a finer man, finer for the life with her and finer for the child she would—he was suddenly convinced again—bear to this world and to their lives. With this thought came another: that whenever that child did come, Noah would no longer reign in the boundlessness of her love, that that domain was forfeit to the child.

When Nat unpacked the *krumkake* and offered to make coffee, both men declined. Instead they nibbled at the cookies with waning enthusiasm, Olaf admitting that his mother's old recipe had nothing on the cookies from Kafe Forny. Enough food still lay on the table for another such feast, the black pot congealing in its cream, the gelatinous lutefisk in the pan, the *lefse* stacked like tortillas in a plastic bag.

They talked for an hour as if such gatherings were a weekly occurrence. Natalie was the most garrulous, telling Olaf about her work with her usual seriousness on the subject. Her intelligence was on fine display, and Noah could see that Olaf was impressed. When the subject of Noah's business came up—and when Olaf circled back to his original skepticism about the very idea of an antique map— Natalie offered her opinion, reiterating Noah's point about them being artistic more than utilitarian but also explaining how purchasing the business fitted into their retirement years down the road and how, most importantly, it made Noah a happier man. Noah could tell her explanation was far more satisfying than his own had been those few days before.

It was well past dark when the conversation wound down.

"Well," Olaf said, laboring up from the table after a lull in the conversation, "if I were younger, now's the time I would have gone outside for a smoke. Might have finished the night with a finger of hooch. But I'll be goddamned lucky to make it to bed. Natalie, I don't have thanks enough. I'm off to bed if you two will clean this mess up." He took a couple of steps toward his bedroom door, turned. "Noah could tell you how early I rise, but I sleep like I'm dead until then. Good night."

Noah and Nat said good-night together.

"Where does a girl go to the bathroom around here?"

"The outhouse is in the woods, up a path behind the shed. I'll get the flashlight and go with you."

"You don't need to go with me, just point me in the right direction."

WHILE NOAH CLEARED the table and put the food away, Natalie sat on the sofa with her feet tucked beneath her, a glass of water in her hand and the sweater folded beside her. She commented quietly on the inventory of the cabin. "What does he do up here?"

"So far he fishes and tells stories."

"Can you imagine living here?"

"There's a radio show he listens to in the morning sometimes. I guess he reads a lot."

"Wouldn't you get lonely?"

"Of course I would, but I'm not him."

Nat looked at him. "You two aren't so different."

"Really?"

She looked at him again, a look to quell further comment if he read her right. "He was so sweet, Noah. While you were down at the lake we just sat here and talked like long-lost friends. We talked about everything. He's got me scared of the bears and wolves. Did you know he makes himself pasties every Sunday night? I don't even know what a pasty is."

Noah finished cleaning. He leaned on the counter, listening.

"He's glad you're here. That's plain to see." She took a small wooden box from the shelf behind the sofa. She opened it. Within were photographs, a pipe, a skeleton key. An old fountain pen.

Noah sat down next to her. "My grandpa carved that box, I'm sure of it. I think it was a gift for my mom. Maybe it was for Solveig."

Nat handed him the pictures. They were all of Noah's mother. So beautiful. One of his parents on their wedding day. One with Solveig on her mother's lap, little more than an infant. "Jesus, the things I'm finding around here," Noah said. He put the pipe in his mouth.

Natalie took the pictures from him. She took the pipe. She re-packed the box and set it back on the shelf. She sipped her water. "So you're not mad, are you?"

Noah put his arm around her. "I'm sorry."

"Don't apologize. Now that I'm here, I understand. If anyone should apologize, it's me."

Noah leaned in and kissed her neck.

"This is so weird," she said. "That's the other bedroom right there? There's not much room for privacy."

"We can be quiet."

But how to be quiet on that bed, in that house so used to its own silence? How to be quiet when the only other sound was the stove fire and a dying gale outside in the woods? Noah had lit a candle, its amber glow left the last corner of the bedroom in darkness. He set it on the nightstand. At the foot of the bed they undressed, hanging their clothes on the bedposts for want of anyplace else to lay them. When they kissed—there at the foot of the bed—the touching of their lips seemed as loud as a drumbeat.

Natalie said again, "This is so weird."

But Noah put his finger to her lips and led her to the side of the bed. He pulled back the covers. When Nat lay down the ancient bedsprings tolled. When she put her arms around him she also put her mouth to his ear, "Your skin is cold," she said. "You smell good. Like the air up here."

"WHAT TIME IS it?"

Noah angled his watch toward the candlelight. "It's only nine o'clock."

"God, it feels like three o'clock in the morning."

"It's always earlier than it seems up here."

She took his hand under the quilt. "So, you think there's anything going on down there?" She moved his hand to the bottom of her stomach. "The doctor said there were at least six follicles ready to release. We could have sextuplets."

"I'd take anything, but better to start with one."

"What," she said, shifting her weight up onto an elbow and looking at Noah, the candle aglow in her eyes, "don't you think I'd make a capable mother of six? I thought my performance tonight with the Norwegian food was pretty impressive."

"Some of that food was awfully good."

"I could eat *lefse* every day."

Noah kissed her. "I don't know where we'd find *lefse* in Boston."

She lay back down. The bedsprings creaked again.

"It was terrific, all the food. My dad loved it. So did I."

Outside, the gale was weakening. Noah listened to the trees still swaying gently. "Every night the wind dies down," he said.

"Speaking of wind, you should have felt that plane land in Duluth this afternoon. It was terrible. But the view from the window was amazing. We circled out over Lake Superior. I could see the city below. There was a ship outside the harbor. We flew right over it. And there were these veins of reddish-brown water curlicuing from the shore out into the lake."

"Those are the creeks and rivers. Wherever they run into the lake they bring with them the color of the rocks and soil."

"It was so pretty. And I love Duluth. But cold."

"That's how everyone feels. The 'but cold' part."

She snuggled next to him. "Not here, though."

"Definitely not here."

They lay silently for a while. Noah thought she had fallen asleep. He was about to get up and blow out the candle when she said, "I'm sure this isn't even going to work, but it's like I have to try. Why else are we on this earth?"

Noah leaned up on his elbow now. "I've spent all day thinking about it. All this time trying, I guess it's just taken it out of me. You, too, I know. Of course you more than me." He lay down. "I don't know, I think all the failing, watching you be so sad all the time."

"You were sad, too."

"Of course I was, but it's different."

Again they lay silently, Noah stroking her hair, and again he thought she'd fallen asleep.

"Anyway, even if it doesn't work I'm glad I came."

Noah squeezed her hand. "I had a realization today. If we do have a baby, when we have a baby, I realize that I won't be the most important person in your life anymore. I'm okay with that."

"What in the world are you talking about?"

"I mean when we become parents things will be different. Children, they demand a lot of love. Especially if you're a good parent, which you will be. That's all."

"Only a man would say something like that. Only a man would be capable of thinking something like that."

"I didn't mean for it to sound bad."

"It just doesn't make any sense. Anyway, don't worry about it. I wouldn't love you any less if I had a million kids."

And now she did fall asleep. Noah rolled out of bed and blew out the candle.

SOMETIME BEFORE DAWN Noah lay in bed, the stillness all around incomprehensible. Even the stove fire's hiss was absent. Even the sound of her breath. He ought to sleep, he knew, was tired enough to do so, but his thoughts kept him awake.

After a time he heard his father's door open and his feet padding across the great-room floor. By his reckoning of the previous mornings, he made the time four or five. The first daylight was still two or three hours away. He stepped out of bed, pulled the quilt up over Nat's shoulder. She pushed her hair from her face but did not wake. He moved into the great room as the door outside closed with a quiet clap. From the window Noah watched his father cross the yard to the shed. Rather, he watched an apparition of his father, one blurred by the flashlight's bouncing. The windows in the shed were soon bright. When Noah stepped outside he could feel the frost melting under his bare feet. There were stars enough to see a mile.

Inside, he put a kettle of water on the stove and two of the left-over *krumkake* on a plate. He wished he had a newspaper to read. When the water boiled he made coffee. He poured a cup and pulled the peacoat over his bare shoulders. He took the coffee and cookies to his father in the shed.

"I thought I heard you milling around," Olaf said over his shoulder. He was separating two small piles of nuts and bolts on his workbench.

"I brought you some coffee." Noah set the plate of cookies and the coffee on the bench. "This is it, huh?" he asked, gesturing toward the anchor.

Olaf nodded. "Thanks for the coffee. Didn't want to wake you two."

"I figured as much."

Olaf took a long drink of the coffee. He removed a cigar from a drawer at his knees and unwrapped it. He bit off the end but did not light it, though he held a match between his fingers. "You sleep okay?"

"Yeah."

"Natalie staying a while?"

"I'm afraid she has to leave this morning."

Olaf smiled. A devilish look.

"I know," Noah said.

"She's about a hundred times the woman I remember from your wedding. What I remember from your wedding anyway."

"She's the best."

Olaf took another drink of coffee. "Well."

"Well, I guess I'm going back to bed."

"I'll be out here for a while. We'll have some oatmeal when you all wake up."

"Good."

As Noah left the shed he could smell the first licks of cigar smoke.

He undressed and climbed back into bed. In a voice groggy and pleased, Natalie asked him what time it was.

"A little after five o'clock. Go back to sleep."

"What were you doing?"

"Nothing, go back to sleep."

He had almost fallen asleep himself when he heard her whisper, "Look at all those stars still out."

Noah put his arm around her.

"Is your father still sleeping?"

"No, he's out working in his shed."

"I have terrible breath," she said.

"That's okay," he said, and again they made love.

When they'd finished Nat took her pillow from behind her head and put it under her bottom. There was a light beyond the stars in the window now, and they looked upon it. They lay so for a long time, both of them awake and silent. Her hair still smelled of its shampoo. Her skin so soft under his hands. He was exhausted but oddly restored next to her there in bed. He felt gluttonous. It was, perhaps, the most luxuriant hour of his year.

Finally Noah said, "What time do you have to leave?"

"My flight's at one. I guess I should leave by nine."

Noah didn't say anything, only held her.

"Unless you need me to stay for anything." She rolled over to look at his face, put her pillow back under her head.

"Like what?"

"I don't know. I could help you take care of him. We could try to bring him to the hospital. Whatever."

"He'll never go to the hospital, and I don't blame him anymore. It's his life. We'll be okay. I can take care of him."

"What about your sister?"

"She's going to come when she can. She can't just leave at a moment's notice. Tom is busy. The kids are busy."

"I feel so weird leaving like this. Your father must think it so strange."

"He knows what's going on."

"I guess this all worked out."

"It did. I hope it did."

"How long are you going to stay? What's your plan?"

"I have no idea."

AFTER BREAKFAST NAT was ready to leave. She stood at the open door of her rental car and bade Olaf thanks. Noah tossed her bag into the backseat of the car. She kissed Olaf on the cheek. She kissed Noah on the lips. She squeezed his hand.

"Stay over on the right side of the road here," Olaf said, pointing to the side of the trail up from the cabin with the most traction. "That track's damn near washed out. And be careful driving back to Duluth on 61. The deer will be out for breakfast themselves. They sit in the ditch next to the road." Olaf moved toward the house. "I'm going inside. It was good to see you. Thanks again for supper last night. It beat hell out of instant mashed potatoes."

"We'll do it again sometime," Nat said.

Olaf nodded. "Good-bye."

Nat smiled. "Well, I better get going. It's two lefts and a right, right?"

"A right at Lake Superior." He handed her the package holding the agate. "Open this on the plane. It's no big deal."

She put her arms around his shoulders and hugged him. He hugged her back very hard. Her car trundled up the road, slipping into the ruts, the wheels spinning, but she was gone in a moment.

EIGHT

A ll day Olaf slept while Noah split and stacked wood. Vikar had emerged from the woods to watch, and at noon Noah fed him a bucket of food. His own lunch he took to the top of the ski jump again, leftover black pot and unbuttered *lefse*, the remains of the smoked salmon. Vikar followed him but would not climb the scaffold. After lunch he went back to the gulch to inspect the oak. He tried to devise a plan but realized he needed a much bigger saw, it was as simple as that. He would ask his father about it.

He checked on his father at one o'clock. The old man still slept, deeply but with great agitation. Noah went down to the lake to fish. He rowed across the lake to the spot off the cliff. He cast his line, waited, and jerked the jig across the bottom of the first step. For two hours he cast his line up the step. And for the second time in as many efforts he didn't catch a thing.

THE SUV PARKED in the yard had North Dakota plates.

Inside, Solveig sat on the sofa beside their father, her arm around him. Olaf, his eyes glassy, his hair messed from the long day of sleep, looked both thrilled and desperate. "I wish you wouldn't have asked her to come," Olaf said before either of his children could speak.

"I didn't ask her to come."

"Of course I'd come, Dad." She put her hand through his hair.

"Well, there's no need to sulk," Olaf said.

"Come on, Dad," Noah said.

"I'm okay," Solveig almost sang. "I'm glad I'm here."

"When did you get here?"

"Just now. I can only stay for a couple days. The kids are with Tom's folks." She took a deep breath, trying, Noah saw, to stave off tears.

"You just missed Nat—it's a long story. But this is great," he said. "Here we all are."

As pleasant as the previous night had been, this night was dour. Solveig, for her part, seemed immobilized by her grief at the sight of the old man. No question he had worsened from the day before, but even Noah thought his sister's worry exaggerated. Olaf could hardly stand it. The thought occurred to Noah that Solveig—with her fretting melodrama—was handling her father's illness much as his mother had handled the morning of the wreck so many years ago. Though in many ways she was as sweet and incorruptible as his mother, Solveig was also the child of a different generation, and what had been forgivable in his mother was less so in his sister.

Instead of eating dinner the three of them snacked intermittently on leftovers from the night before. They seemed incapable of coherent conversation. Finally Olaf asked Noah to bring the piano in from the porch.

The old Acrosonic sat in a corner, buried beneath mounds of junk—a fishing net, empty boot boxes, a telescope with a cracked lens, empty bags of dog food, a spare truck tire—against the lake wall.

Noah cleared a path, unlocked the wheels on the legs of the piano, and rolled it into the living room. A long time ago, Noah remembered, the piano had been refinished with a deep, wine-colored varnish. Now the glassy finish was obscured and gauzelike.

"It's a ghost piano," Noah said. "Doesn't it look like a ghost?"

"Been on that porch for the better part of ten years," Olaf said. "I should have taken better care of it."

"It's not as if you play, Dad," Solveig said. "And besides, this house isn't exactly built for a piano. They take up a lot of room."

"Even so," Olaf said, "it's a shame."

Noah had wheeled it across the floor and was positioning it against the wall. "Toss me a dishrag," he said to Solveig, who stood at the kitchen counter now with her hands on her hips. She flipped him the rag.

Noah had hoped that dusting it off and getting it in the soft lamplight might restore some of its luster. But it looked perhaps even worse. When he lifted the cover off the keys and stood over them playing "Chopsticks," its wail startled him. Every third or fourth key failed to strike any note at all, and the keys that did hit the strings sounded more like shrieks than music.

He looked over his shoulder at Solveig, who covered her ears with her hands. "We'll get a piano tuner up here. You can't play on this now." He stood, closed the keyboard cover, and wiped his hands on his pants.

"Good luck getting a piano tuner up here," Olaf said. "You're in Misquah, not Boston or Fargo."

"Don't be ridiculous," Noah said as he headed back onto the porch to retrieve the bench. "We'll find a piano tuner."

As he rummaged through the mounds of rubbish he could hear Solveig giving the piano another try, some wail approximating a classical number. By the time he'd found the bench under an old kerosene stove, Solveig had mercifully quit playing. He lugged the bench into the living room, set it before the piano, and wiped his hands. "We've got to clean that porch up," Noah said.

Olaf said nothing, a look of despondency conveying all. He stood, kissed Solveig atop the head, and adjourned to his bedroom.

Noah and Solveig sat opposite each other on the sofa. Noah was flushed again from the heat of the fire. He felt exhausted beyond sleep. "I'm not wrong about this, am I?" he said. "He's as bad as I thought, right?"

"I think so," Solveig said. Her voice quavered, but she kept from crying.

"He's building some goddamn contraption out in the shed."

"I know. He told me that he wants you to bury him in the lake." She paused. "We can't bury him in the lake, Noah."

Noah nodded half yes, half no.

"I told him we would bury him properly in a cemetery. I told him he didn't need to do an eternal penance for something that happened so long ago and was entirely out of his control."

"I bet he loved hearing that."

"He didn't say anything."

"Of course he didn't."

She folded the afghan and draped it over the back of the sofa. "I talked to Tom about having him come stay with us. He was wonderful. He said he'd do whatever I wanted, that we could hire a nurse to live with us."

"That's awfully generous."

"I'm sure there's no way Dad'll do it, though," she said. "He's got other plans in mind now. I can see that clearly."

Olaf came out of his bedroom. He stepped outside and returned in a moment. He prepared the water and effervescing tablets for his teeth. He said good-night again.

"Where were we?" Solveig said.

"We were getting nowhere," Noah replied.

They talked for a couple of hours about what to do before they went to bed. Solveig was inconsolable. Noah finally realized how necessary sleep was. His body ached. Somewhere in the intersection of his fatigue and forlornness he caught a glimpse of the old man's reason, saw how it might all play out.

THE PATTER OF rainwater on the roof woke him the next morning. As he strained to hear his father or sister stirring in their bedrooms he could make out only the thumping in his own head. The rain streaming over the gutters and cascading down the windows blurred the morning. He thought of going back to sleep, even rolled over to do so, but decided he'd already slept too long and too hard. He rose from the sofa, felt the entirety of his fatigue, remembered his labor the day before. He remembered his dreams, too, and he replayed them with a child's intuitiveness, but their meaning never arrived.

Both of the bedrooms were empty, both beds made. The fire was as temperate as it had been since he'd arrived. He looked out the window and saw that his sister's truck was gone. He wondered where they were for a moment but gave up on the thought of them and felt an enormous relief in their absence. Given the weather, he could justify a day on the couch.

The morning had risen with more showers. All of the pine trees sagged under the deluge. Even the hardwoods—the poplar and aspen and birch—were limp of limb in the near and distant woods. The wind, though, was gone; he imagined the rain had quelled it, had drowned it.

Since he'd been here he'd felt a nearly constant sense of responsibility. Any moment not spent doing something was one spent wondering what he ought to be doing. Now, though, as his shoulders loosened, he felt no obligation whatever.

He looked through the refrigerator for breakfast but found nothing. He went to the piano and tried to finger the first few bars of an old piano-lesson standard, but between the lamentable tune and his own sorry playing, he gave up after his first try. He washed what few dishes lay in the sink. He put a kettle of water on for bathwater. He stood at the window for a long while watching the rain. Finally he took a magazine from the table and settled back onto the sofa.

It was the *Wisconsin Lawyer* his father had been reading a few days earlier. He checked the table of contents, turned to the shipwreck article. He read it twice, bored first by the tedious and arcane legal language and then by the clichéd images of Spanish frigates sunk with kings' ransoms off the coast of America. Though the article was pedantic and forgettable, it did trick him into a question that he spent much of the morning pondering: What was left of his father, his mother, his sister, even himself, on the bottom of Lake Superior?

He pictured his father's berth on the *Ragnarøk*, a place he knew well from the summer cruises to Toledo and Cleveland and Ashtabula that he'd taken as a child. He could envision the porthole windows and the steel bulkheads; the riveted floor and the braided rug his father kept at the foot of the diminutive bed—too short by two feet for his father; the officer's desk opposite the bed—mahogany, indestructible, stately, with an inlaid glass top—bolted to the bulkhead; the pictures of the four of them beneath the desktop, the sense of awe it gave him to think that a picture of him should be included in a place so sacred; the narrow locker in the corner of the berth, the black steel-toed boots polished to a dead flat shine that sat on the floor beneath the sweaters and coats hanging from pegs. Pictures hung on the inside of the locker door, too, one of them of Noah himself, mid-flight on the bunny-ears jump in Chester Bowl at the age of five. As far as Noah understood, the article suggested that all of these things no longer belonged to his father but to the state of Michigan or Minnesota, depending on which state's territorial water the wreckage rested in. It seemed unfair that some state historical society owned that part of his past, that the calamity of November 6, 1967, hadn't been damaging enough, hadn't taken the perfection of his childhood and crushed it, but that any proof of that perfection, even were it salvageable, wouldn't belong to him.

The kettle whistle blew. Noah mixed it with cold water from the ten-gallon drum under the sink. He washed and shaved, stood naked at the kitchen basin. He felt a firmness in his shoulders he'd not noticed for many years. He dressed in clean clothes, the last such pair of drawers, the last such T-shirt and pants. A pair of cotton socks. He took the key to his father's truck from a nail pounded into the windowsill and went out. The torrent had weakened, luckily for Noah. The windshield wipers only worked on one slow intermittent speed.

FROM THE PAY phone at the Landing he called Natalie. Now the rain had ceased altogether and reddish water lay in pools all over the gravel parking lot, none of them reflecting sky. She answered on the second ring. "I was hoping you'd call," she said.

"How are you? How was the trip home?"

"I'm fine. The necklace is beautiful. Thank you. Whatever possessed you?"

"Sheepishness, I guess."

"I mean it. It's beautiful. I'm wearing it now." She paused, he could picture her caressing the glassy stone around her neck. "How's your father?"

"We're a stopover for damsels in distress now. Solveig came yesterday, the two of them are off somewhere."

"How is she?"

"A complete wreck. So is my dad. It's like he's worse for her company."

"I'm sure it's hard for both of them."

"Anyway, I don't get it."

Natalie took an audible breath. "I missed you this morning. It's not the same around here without you." She filled him in on several details. Her travel plans for the week. A conversation she'd had with Ed about the shop. He was fine. She was going to go to her parents' house to watch the Patriots on *Monday Night Football* after work. "But no beer for this one," she said. "I really feel like I'm pregnant."

"It was just yesterday, Nat."

"I don't mean physically feel, I mean I have a *feeling*."

"I hope you're right."

"When are you coming home?"

"I didn't tell you this, but the day you got here, my father asked me to bury him in the lake when he dies."

"What do you mean, bury him in the lake?"

He replayed the conversation in the shed. He described as well as he could the anchor his father was fashioning from the barrel. "And he told me about the wreck, most of it anyway."

"About his ship? What did he say?"

"It would take me all day to tell you everything."

"Tell me *something*."

"Let's just say I'm wiser now. Still, I have no idea what to do with him, no idea at all. No idea when I'll be home, that's what I was getting at."

"Well, I talked to Ed this morning, and he's fine. Completely fine. He might not want you to come home, the way he tells it." She paused. "Take as long as you need, Noah. I'm fine here, and I know you need to be with your father now. Just keep me posted. And say hello to Solveig."

"I will," Noah said. He felt light. "I'll call you when I know anything."

HE HADN'T NOTICED, standing outside the Landing talking to Nat, but by the time he got back to the cabin the day had become frigid. Ice had formed along the edges of the shallow pools atop the splitting stumps. Solveig's car was still gone. Vikar lay curled atop the steps, the stink of his wet coat noticeable as Noah stepped over him. Only the dog's eyes moved to check Noah.

He ate the rest of the smoked salmon and stale crackers for an early dinner and lay sprawled on the sofa afterward, the walls and all they held becoming familiar now. He thought of grabbing a book from one of the shelves but fell asleep instead. He woke much later to darkness and the sound of Olaf and Solveig returning.

When they came inside—his father first, held at the elbow by Solveig, the old man swaddled in full winter wear again—Noah sat up to meet them. Olaf looked at Noah with blank eyes. Solveig appeared drained, her eyes swollen, her face splotchy.

"Where have you been?" Noah asked. "I've been worried."

Solveig helped Olaf out of his coat, she led him to the chair. "I left you a note," she said.

"Where?" Noah looked under the magazines and mess on the table.

"I didn't want to wake you this morning."

Olaf sat down heavily.

"Are you all right?" Noah said.

Olaf looked at Solveig.

"We went to the hospital in Duluth. That's where we've been, that's why we've been gone so long."

"You went to the hospital?" Noah asked his father.

Solveig spoke for Olaf. "We talked about it yesterday, Noah. While you were outside, I guess." Solveig had found the note under the table. She handed it to Noah. "Don't be mad."

Noah read, *Took Dad to St. Mary's. Be gone all day. Wanted to tell you but he wouldn't let me. Sorry. Love, Sol.*

He read the note again, folded it, put it in his shirt pocket. "Well?" he said, at a loss for words but suddenly filled with a kind of hope. "What did you find out?"

"Let's get Dad to bed. We can talk later."

"Good idea," Olaf said, his first words since arriving. "I can get to bed myself."

While Olaf tended to his dentures, Solveig took several small plastic bottles from a white paper bag. She sorted a half-dozen prescriptions. After Olaf stashed his teeth and poured himself a glass of water, he kissed Solveig good-night.

Solveig caught Olaf by the arm. "Take these, Dad," she said.

Olaf looked at the pills in the palm of her hand. He took them from her and went into his bedroom.

"How did you . . . all those pills . . . he looked so . . ."

"Come sit over here," she said, patting the couch. She straightened up, wiped her eyes dry with the heels of her hands.

"I'll stand," Noah said.

"Don't be upset, Noah."

"I'm not upset," he assured her. "I just don't understand how you got him to the hospital. What did they say?"

"They did tests. They took a lot of blood. They did a proctology exam and took tissue samples. X-rays. They wanted him to stay, naturally."

"Of course he wouldn't."

"No." She trembled visibly. "I'm so sorry we went without you. I wanted you to come, but Dad wouldn't hear of it."

"Don't worry. Just tell me what they said."

"The prescriptions, they're mainly to help with pain. The doctor said he must have a lot of discomfort. The proctology exam showed advanced signs. She said the first test results would be ready on Wednesday. You're to call her at noon." She handed Noah the doctor's business card. "She said she'd be surprised—very surprised, she said— if they don't confirm what she suspects, that the cancer is beyond treatment, that it has probably spread to his liver and lungs, that it's probably only a matter of time. She said he was a big, strong man. That doesn't mean anything, but it doesn't hurt."

"How was Dad?" Noah motioned to the bedroom door.

"He hasn't heard any of this. He told the doctor to tell me, said he didn't want to know. I wish we hadn't gone. I just thought maybe there was something they could do." She began to tear up.

Noah sat down. "Hey, they gave you prescriptions for the pain, that's something at least. It's good you took him. He should have gone sooner. Listen, we knew, like you said. You seem surprised."

"I'm not surprised, Noah. I'm sad. My father—our father—he's dying. We should be sad. I should be allowed to cry."

Noah put his arm around her shoulders.

Soon she gathered herself. She asked for a glass of water, which Noah poured and brought her. She drank it all at once. She wiped her eyes with the sleeves of her shirt. "I only got him to go because he wanted to see the old house."

"In Duluth? The house on High Street?"

She nodded. "We went first thing, before the hospital. We were sitting there idling in front of it. The man who lived there, who must have lived there, was cleaning his gutters. He was up on a ladder. Dad just stared out the window. God, it was weird. It looked the same, just exactly the same. I felt ten years old again." She handed Noah the glass as if to ask for more water. Again he filled it and brought it to her.

"After five minutes Dad said, 'Okay.' Halfway to the hospital he said, just out of the blue he said, 'A lot of times I couldn't remember what our house looked like. Not lately, I mean when I was gone, out on the Lakes. I'd try to picture it but couldn't. I should have taken that for a bad sign.'

"God, it was sad, Noah. I told him how I used to wait for him to get home. I'd sit in the window in the living room and watch the harbor entrance."

"I'd do the same thing. Before the wreck." Noah paused. "Maybe we were waiting for two different people."

Solveig looked at him. "He loved us the same before and after. He just didn't know how to feel about himself."

"It's not so simple," Noah said.

"What's not simple?"

"There's a long list of things that aren't simple about it."

"Maybe. Anyway, I could use a drink."

"There's nothing here. Amazing but true."

"It's not amazing, Noah."

"He told me about quitting. He should have had his epiphany about twenty years earlier. Things might have been different." Even as he spoke he realized that the rancor was all but gone. "But better late than never, I guess."

"That's just what I was going to say."

They talked long into the night and were exhausted in the end. At midnight they turned in, Noah to a sleep absent of rest.

"YOU BAKING A pie?" Noah said, one eye closed, the other squinting at the dull shimmer of the kitchen light.

"You could say that," Olaf said.

There were eight or ten Mason jars sitting on the kitchen counter, each fuzzy with freezer burn. Olaf had two more under his arm. He was already dressed.

"Seriously, what is all that?"

Olaf set the last jars on the counter. "This is for you and your sister."

Noah had rubbed the sleep from his eyes. He stood and stretched. He yawned. He walked to the counter, picked up one of the jars, and held it to the light.

Olaf took it from him and put it back on the counter. "Wait until your sister gets up."

Noah's jeans hung on the chair. He hiked them on and sat back down. "Want to tell me about the trip to Duluth yesterday?"

Olaf rearranged the jars into neat rows on the counter. "Your sister didn't tell you about it?"

"She told me some."

"I went for her."

"Those prescriptions they gave you, are they making any difference?"

"Will you grab that box and put it on the coffee table?" Olaf said, pointing at a wooden whiskey crate.

Noah picked it up and moved it to the table. "The prescriptions?"

"I didn't take them."

"Of course not."

Olaf finally sat down on the sofa. "Solveig drove me by the old house," he said.

"She told me."

"It's a nice house. Someone's taking care of it."

"I give up, Dad."

"You give up?"

"The doctor, the prescriptions, everything."

Olaf smiled. "You promise?"

Together they reminisced about the old house. Memories like photographs. Olaf told Noah about the night of his birth, Noah in turn about his forays into the old man's office and how he'd pretend to be his father while the elder sailed the Great Lakes. After the sun rose Solveig emerged from her bedroom.

"What's all this?" Solveig asked.

"Noah," Olaf said, "there's a box on the dresser in my room. Would you grab it for me?"

Noah did. He placed it before his father.

"This," Olaf said, making a wide gesture that encompassed the room, the jars on the counter, the two boxes on the table, the house in general, "this stuff all belongs to you two. We have some business to take care of." He unscrewed a Mason jar. "This is your inheritance," he said, pulling a block of frozen hundred-dollar bills from the jar. "Round about two hundred thousand dollars. You split it. On top of that, there's another fifty grand, plus or minus, in the bank. This is all in a file marked 'Lake Superior Savings and Loan.' The bank is in Gunflint. You're both on the account."

"Jesus, Dad," Noah said, looking at Solveig, whose face was frozen in shock. "That's an awful lot of cash to have in the freezer."

Olaf nodded as if in agreement. "A lifetime of savings," he said. "I don't know how it works in terms of claiming the inheritance—tax-wise, I mean—but you two can figure it out. You're both beneficiaries on a small life insurance policy, too. By small I mean small, probably not worth a bag of bread crumbs." He furnished another file marked "Life Insurance Policy."

"Aside from the cash, all I have is the house and the land. People say property values up here are booming, but I have no idea what it's worth. Anyway, don't sell it. Your grandpa built this house and it belongs in the family."

"Slow down a minute," Noah said. He stood up, looked at the Mason jars lining the counter. He counted them. There were ten. "Hold on."

"Dad," Solveig said, her voice uncertain, "this is all very surprising."

Olaf looked back and forth between them. "What? I'm executing my will. This is something we have to do. Bear up, will you?"

Solveig buried her face in her hands. Noah stood in the middle of the room, equidistant from the two of them. He felt his pulse quickening.

"Sit down, would you, Noah? And stop moping, Solveig. You've moped enough, there's no need for it."

Solveig persisted. Noah could not move.

"Please," Olaf said without kindness, "sit down."

Noah stepped to the chair and sat down beside Solveig.

Olaf cleared his throat. "Listen, you two, there are things you need to know about. Business, all right?" Without waiting for a reply he continued, "This is the deed for the house. Taxes are paid through next year. They were twenty-eight hundred dollars this year. I'm putting all this information in a file labeled 'Estate.'" He held up a brown accordion file, then tied it shut.

"The rest of this stuff is all yours." He removed from the box something wrapped in newspaper. He tore it away. It was a ski jumping trophy. "CLASS FIVE, FIRST PLACE, 1966," he read from the engraved brass plate. "CLOQUET SKI CLUB JUNIOR INVITATIONAL."

It was, Noah remembered, the first trophy he'd ever won. A brass-plated ski jumper in flight sat on a white marble base. He took it from his father. "I remember this. I remember the day. Before I got the trophy you told me I had to shake the man's hand."

"There's a box of these things out in the shed. I pulled this one. I remembered it, too." He searched the box for a red folder. "This is yours," he said to Solveig, handing her the folder. Inside was a Chopin score with a pink ribbon stapled to it.

She clearly recognized it.

"You were a freshman in high school," Olaf said. "Nineteen seventy-nine, third prize at the city competition. I loved to listen to you play."

He presented each of them with relics of their youth. Old report cards and school projects, acceptance letters to colleges, pictures of prom dates, newspaper articles from the *Herald* about ski jumping tournaments, piano recitals, commendations for planting trees on Arbor Day. The right person might have fashioned a biography for either of them from the miscellany that now sat spread out on the coffee table. By the time he'd finished unpacking the folders and boxes, his energy was flagging. He had one box left.

"These are your mother's figurines," he said, unwrapping a miniature ceramic ballerina. "For the goddamn life of me, I never understood why she liked these things." He unwrapped another figure, a two-inch-tall man in a tuxedo and top hat. He held it up as if to prove his point. "You get the picture," he said, wrapping them back in newspaper. "There's other stuff, too. Just be careful going through it. Who knows what's hidden in this house?"

Noah said, "Dad, who keeps their life savings in Mason jars? Why isn't the money in the bank? Why isn't it invested?"

"Never my thing," Olaf said, as if the matter had but one simple answer. "You got your paycheck, you cashed it, put a little in savings, a little in checking, otherwise you managed with what you had."

"We're talking about two hundred thousand dollars."

Solveig asked, "What are we supposed to do with all of it?"

"Whatever you want. Solveig, sweetheart, it's yours now."

Olaf's voice, Noah thought, was deteriorating with each word he spoke. No amount of coughing or throat-clearing helped. This lent his words an almost religious timbre that was as hypnotic as it was sad.

"We are not dropping you in the middle of this lake," Solveig said suddenly, in a voice now controlled. "It's a ridiculous idea. Absolutely ridiculous."

"Please listen to me," Olaf said.

Solveig started again but stopped. Noah could not speak.

"Are you done? If you're done I'd like to say what I have to say," Olaf said. He looked at each of them in turn. "When you get to be as old as me, and when you look back on your life, it's impossible not to regret every other step you took. I do anyway. But you also get to see the wonderful things. The most wonderful of the wonderful things for me were days spent here, with the two of you, when you were little kids, before so much went to shit. The happiest days of my life were our Christmas mornings here. I remember the looks on your faces as you pulled toys and candy from your stockings. And your Christmas oranges. I remember feeling like, *My God, these are my children!* Sometimes the only good things I can remember are those mornings and the huge feeling that came with them." He paused, set his chin on his chest in that gesture now familiar to Noah. "If that sounds sad or like I'm feeling sorry for myself, it's not meant to.

"Anyway, I'm not a religious man. I reckon the nearest we come to an afterlife is how we're remembered by our children. I figure the more often you think of me when I'm gone, the happier my ghost will be. If I'm here, where I belong, as opposed to some cemetery in Duluth or Fargo where you'd come once every ten years, you'll remember me a little more often.

"So," he said, putting his hands together as if to pray, "I'm sorry if it makes you uncomfortable, but a dead man's a dead man no matter where he rests. I want you to bury me here. The lake is more than a hundred and fifty feet deep over by the falls. Do it there. Nobody will ever know."

Noah looked at his father. He looked at Solveig. "Since when are you so eloquent?" he asked his father.

"I've been practicing that speech for a long time."

LATER THAT MORNING Solveig put her suitcase in the backseat of her truck. She turned to Noah. "Could you do it?"

Noah closed the truck door. He looked first at the house, then at the shed. "I don't know. It's hard to imagine, that's for sure."

"Who would come up with a plan like that?" She was thinking out loud more than asking a question. Or so Noah thought.

"How would I explain it to the authorities? It would look suspicious," he said.

"To say the least. But you'd have to tell someone. The sheriff?"

"Tell them what?"

Solveig shook her head as if to erase the thought from her head. "What are we talking about, anyway? This is nuts."

Again Noah looked at the shed. "It is and it isn't."

She gave him a look half imploring.

"He's never asked anyone for anything. Not ever. Does he deserve it? Do we owe it to him?" he asked.

She leaned against her truck. "When he first mentioned it I thought he was completely bonkers," she said. "Hearing him talk about it, I'm not so sure."

"That makes two of us," Noah said.

They looked at each other.

"What would Mom do?" Solveig said.

"Whatever Dad wanted. Without a second thought."

"You're right about that."

There they stood. Noah hoped his sister would make a declaration on the matter, but she did not. His gaze kept falling on the shed, drawn by the hideous and marvelous trove of its contents. Each moment deepened his mystification.

"I'll hurry back," she said.

Noah looked at her, understood her complete lack of confidence in the utterance. "You have to tell me what to do if you don't make it back in time."

She closed her eyes tightly. "I couldn't do it, Noah." She opened her eyes. "I picture myself alone up here, with Dad, that terrible contraption he's making . . ."

"That's no answer."

"It's the best I can do."

HER BID TO take Olaf with her had been rebuffed as swiftly as it had been offered. Noah and Olaf stood shoulder to shoulder in the yard and watched as her SUV bounced up the road. When it disappeared beyond the last curve Noah turned to his father. "If you're up to it, why don't you show me how that contraption works?"

Without a word Olaf led him to the shed. There he explained how the tubing was attached to the barrel. He demonstrated how the barrel should rest on his chest while the tubing extended down the length of his legs. He showed him how the chain should cross his back, under his arms—which were to be bound behind his back—and through the tubing. Noah stood with his hand on his chin trying to comprehend the instructions.

"Do you think it will work?" Olaf asked.

"What happens after you've been down there for a while? What about decomposition, things like that?"

"The water is cold enough at that depth I won't decompose. Cold and dark both."

"How will I know where to do it?"

"Anywhere under the falls is fine. It's plenty deep over there."

"I just toss you into the boat and row over there? Pitch you over the side? Between you and the barrel, that's a lot of weight."

Olaf pulled something like a section of dock from between the table and the wall. "This will fit across the boat, gunwale to gunwale.

Lay me across it. When you get to the other side of the lake slide it right over. Keep your weight opposite the side you drop me. The boat should be okay."

Noah stood dumb for a moment, trying to imagine actually doing it. "What about everything that goes along with it? I mean, what about a death certificate? What about notifying Social Security and Superior Steel? How can I drop you over there and still take care of that?"

The elegance of his father's earlier plea was getting lost in the crude details. Olaf didn't know about death certificates and pensions, nor did he seem to care. "You're smart, you'll figure it out," he said. "I still have to get the chain threaded in there. I'll do that tomorrow. Right now I need to rest."

Noah led him out of the shed and helped him across the yard. Inside, sitting opposite each other in the sofa and chair, Noah said, "What if I can't do it?"

Quietly, Olaf said, "You will."

III.

The Darkest Place in the Night

NINE

Five years after the wreck of the *Ragnarøk*, a poet from the Ontario town of Point au Baril on Georgian Bay and a woodcut artist from Duluth collaborated on a short book to commemorate the anniversary of the disaster. It was Noah's favorite of the many books written about the wreck.

Five hundred copies were printed and bound in the woodcutter's garage. It was a poem—billed as an "epic"—called *The Darkest Place in the Night*, and except for friends of either artist or aficionados of the Superior shippery, not many people knew about it. That changed five years later, when the *Herald* ran a feature on the ten-year anniversary of the wreck. Rather than leading with the customary, now famous photograph of the washed-up survivors—the same photograph that hung in the maritime museum in Duluth—it printed one of the woodcuts from the book and the last two lines of the poem. The woodcut showed three abstract figures clutching the icy gunwales of a lifeboat in portentous, black, fine-lined seas. A striking image. The lifeboat rode the crest of a wave, and each of the three faces diminished into abstraction so that only the first was clearly a face at all, one meant to exude the nightmare. The clear-faced figure raised a giant

Thorlike hammer above his shoulders, poised to strike the ice from the boat. For Noah, the image captured his own sentiment about what had happened, or how he imagined it had happened.

The poem itself became something like a belated anthem for the wreck, its final lines the standard epigraph for anything written about it. Strange, Noah thought, watching his father sleep with difficulty on the sofa in the wake of Solveig's leaving, how one verse of an obscure poem could become so automatically associated with the fact of the disaster, but it had. Enough so, in fact, that even for Noah the famous quotation and the wreck had become irrevocably linked. In the five minutes he'd been looking at the book he'd managed to memorize again the last couplet. He sang it to himself: *The slaves of the lake beseeching the light, / Adrift in the darkest place in the night.*

After they'd finished in the shed, Olaf had lain down to sleep on the sofa without a word of any sort. Noah, at a loss again, tidied the house, refilled the wood box, and took the thawing cash from the Mason jars. His plan was to deposit it first thing in the morning. He should have been awed both by the sum of his inheritance and the manner in which Olaf had presented it, but the fact of the matter was that nothing surprised him anymore. The week had cured him of his wonder. Now he sat with the book open on his lap, staring at the page.

"That guy came to visit me once," Olaf said, startling Noah, who had almost dozed off himself, the heat in the house stunning again.

"The poet or the artist?"

"The poet. Said he wanted to make sure he got it right."

"What did you say?"

"I told him I didn't understand his poem, that I was more of a plainspoken sort."

Noah tried to imagine the conversation, tried to imagine the poet's horror in confronting his father. "You didn't toss him out, I hope."

"Why should I? He was a nice guy."

"I prefer the woodcuts to the poem," Noah said. "I like this one." He showed him the opened page.

Olaf looked at it over the rim of his glasses and nodded his head as if to agree. "Whatever I thought about the poem, I liked the title. It's a good title."

"The other night you were telling me about the wreck. You never told me what happened once you were in the lifeboat."

"I ran out of gas, didn't I?"

"I think we both did."

Olaf struggled with the afghan. Noah helped it across his shoulders.

"Why did you think it was a good title?"

"What?"

"*The Darkest Place in the Night.*"

"You know, it's been a long time now. A long, long time. But I still remember the darkness. Maybe it's just easy to imagine the dark, especially up here. I don't know."

"You must remember other things, too. I suppose it's hard to forget."

"Not so hard when you're as old as me." He smiled. "But I remember things, sure. We were at the mercy of many things back there. We had the inferno blazing beneath us, the snow squall suffocating us, seas still washing the deck. And wind. Holy shit, that wind. The thought of launching one of those lifeboats, because of all that, seemed like the greater of two evils. I mean, those things were made for Sunday picnics on a lake like this here"—he gestured toward Lake Forsone—"not all-nighters on a stormy Superior. They had no real keel to speak of, no cover, they were just big rowboats with a few supplies stowed under the thwarts. I'll tell you what, it was awful damn hard to imagine rowing that thing across the lake.

"Where did you put that chart?"

Noah stood. "Here." He fetched it from the shelf and unrolled it on the coffee table again.

"We were here, remember? I more or less knew our position, knew what neighborhood we were in, leastways. What I figured we'd do was simply make our way west, thought we'd end up in Thunder Bay or some spot south of there. In all the commotion I didn't spend much time factoring in the hell working against us. No thought of wind, no thought of drifting, of the seiches. This was an oversight, I guess, but even after I decided to launch the boat I didn't think about the ordeal we'd have ahead of us until we were actually lowering.

"There was some light back there. Floods on either side of the stack, the creepy glow from the fire beneath us, my headlamp and the flashlight Luke carried, but it was still hell to see anything. The lifeboat was set to two davits, the davits to two cables, the cables to winches that you lowered manually. There was a canvas tarp covering the boat lashed with Manila rope who knows how old? On a sunny day in July, lowering that boat might have taken three minutes. Clip the rope, pull the tarp off, unlock the winches, swing it out over the deck, and crank it down. The ladder that went over the side was just sort of piled atop the deck. Made of chain and steel rungs. Toss that over the deck, too. You could have had the crew in boats in five minutes. That night the whole goddamn operation was covered in ice six inches thick. Might as well've been set in concrete."

"What did you do?"

"Red cut the rope off the tarp. Got two hammers from the tool-box in the lifeboat. He and Luke went at hacking the ice. I crossed the deck to the stack. You might not believe this, but I ripped a rung from the ladder that climbed the stack. I worked on the davits with the rung. Bjorn was in charge of the ladder. I don't know what he used, but by the time we got the boat over the deck, ready to lower it, Bjorn tossed the ladder. too."

"It's amazing what people are capable of in times of desperation," Noah said.

"Listen, the four of us might have been able to portage that whole goddamn ship up the Soo, we were so desperate. Far cry from now," he said, rubbing his biceps.

"I suspect you're stronger than you think," Noah said, remembering the barrel in the shed, how the old man must have lifted it onto the workbench.

"Anyway, we were ready to lower it. I ordered Luke and Bjorn into the boat. By then the ship had come about in the storm so the port side of her was taking all the seas. That created a lee for us on starboard. This was both good and bad. Good because it gave us a calmer spot to load the lifeboat, bad because that foundering son of a bitch was going to be right on top of us when we got in the water."

"Wasn't it dangerous to lower the lifeboats with guys in it?"

"No more dangerous than anything else that was happening. Normally there wouldn't be anyone in the boat while it was lowered, no. But I figured there was an awful lot that could go wrong once the boat was in the water, and a couple guys down there to handle things wouldn't be a bad thing. It was a gamble, sure, but we were so short on odds that it didn't matter anyway."

"What did you and Red do once the boat was in the water?"

"We scuttled our asses over the side of that boat, that's what we did. Now, if you want to talk about spooky, let's talk about getting down that ladder. You take the wind, the water, the ice, the fire. You take the darkness. You put it all together and try to imagine hanging over the side of that ship, climbing down to that boat bobbing all over the water." Here Olaf stopped, a look of intense concentration on his face. Noah read it as the look of a man trying desperately to remember something he'd worked his whole life at forgetting.

"Did you see Red?"

"Did I see Red, what, go into the water?" He looked away with a surprising suddenness.

"Yeah, did you see anything?"

It was well documented in the annals of the wreck that after Olaf and Red had gone over the side of the ship, first Red, then Olaf, and after they'd passed the fantail deck and the flames without, Red had dropped from the ladder, not to be seen again until his body washed ashore on the rocks at Hat Point. The only scenario ever suggested was that he'd simply lost his footing in the chaos, managed to get hold of a rope once he was in the lake, and then managed to attach himself to the rope and so been towed behind it through the night.

"I did not see him fall." Olaf faltered. "I did not hear a splash. Or a scream. There was nothing, I didn't even know he was gone." He let out a soft moan.

"I sent Red over first, thinking the sooner he was in the lifeboat the safer he'd be. I thought it must be written into my rank. Hell if I knew."

Again he paused. Longer this time. He looked like a man in a confessional mood.

"I remember getting down that ladder. Rung by rung. Remember passing the decking, feeling the warmth of the fire. I remember the smell. I thought of all those guys in there. Cooked. I felt greedy for being on that ladder, greedy for being so close to the lifeboat. I didn't even have much faith in surviving the night, but I was glad of the chance. I still wonder why that chance fell on me. It seemed to me all these years that something more than luck had its hand in it. But for all the many thousand times I've replayed it, that's all I come up with. Dumb luck. I was lucky Jan sent me across the deck. I was lucky to get across the deck, lucky not to have been washed off the deck once we were aft, lucky I didn't fall from the ladder like Red. Chrissakes, that's all it was. Luck. Rotten luck."

"What's wrong with a little luck in a situation like that?" Noah asked, interpreting his father's words as an act of contrition.

"Oh, hell, there's nothing wrong with it. I was damn glad for it. But when it comes time to add it all up, saying you were lucky isn't a very good explanation."

"Maybe there's no need for an explanation. Maybe there *isn't* one."

"Maybe not."

"Did you see him again, I mean before morning?"

"Did I see him again? Jesus Christ, did I ever," Olaf said, turning his eyes to the ceiling.

"When I got into the boat Luke and Bjorn were already bailing. The lifeboat was twenty feet long, and they were together in the bow. Red was just gone. I turned my headlamp out onto the lake. I was shouting his name. We were already in a mess. The water, it was churning." He spit his words, made great gestures with his arms, whorling gestures that sufficed as testament to the nature of that lake. "That dark. Couldn't see a damn thing, not at first. But then he was there. In the water. Behind the lifeboat. I saw him, Noah."

This fact, to Noah's knowledge, had never been revealed. Not to the investigators at the NTSB, not to the brass at Superior Steel, not to anyone. "You saw him?"

"I did."

"Was he dead?"

Olaf closed his eyes slowly. "No," he said. "I had the headlamp pointing into the lake. Just there, between the lifeboat and the ship, bobbing in the water like a goddamn buoy, old Red. I hollered to him. I saw his hand go up for help. I saw his eyes blinking, for Chrissakes." He stopped, opened his eyes.

"Did Luke and Bjorn see him?"

"I don't think so. We'd all looked, but by the time I saw him they were both consumed with what they were doing, they were already working overtime just to keep that boat from capsizing. Goddamn, it was like being lowered into a lion's cage getting into that boat." He closed his eyes again. "And there's Red out on the water." Olaf lifted his head slowly, opened his eyes, and turned them to the ceiling. He shook his head. "I got the heaving line and made a couple tosses, but it was no good. He had no chance. That's what I figured anyway. We were taking such heavy seas. That goddamn gale was eating us alive. I needed to help Luke and Bjorn. I took the tiller, hoping to keep us in line with the wind." He brought his eyes back to Noah. "I didn't know what to do. I didn't know how to save him."

"Why didn't you ever tell anyone?"

"That I saw Red alive? It's my fault he died. I should have saved him. I should have jumped in after him. Maybe he had broken bones, he was probably hypothermic already. We all were. What do I do? I toss him a line. All he saw was the light from the headlamp and a goddamn *heaving line* coming toward him. I should have done more. I could have done more."

"Red couldn't have survived."

Olaf shot him a cold stare. "We did."

"You hadn't fallen from the ladder. You hadn't fallen into the lake."

"That's horseshit. His soul is on me."

"Jumping in for him, that would have been suicide. There was nothing you could have done."

Olaf got up. He walked to the door and looked outside. *My god*, Noah thought. *What do you do with a lifetime of that on your mind?*

When Olaf came back Noah steered him to the chair.

"And I bet you were sure you couldn't think less of me," Olaf said.

"What are you talking about?"

"Letting Red go like that."

"It's not your fault. You must know that."

"You're wrong. I took a few tugs on that rope once it was in the water. I might have thought about him for a minute. Then it was time to go. Who knows what Luke and Bjorn ever thought."

"Why is Red more important than the other guys? Why are you lugging his ghost around?"

"None of the others had a chance. Red had a chance. I was his chance."

They sat silently in the flotsam of his father's avowal for a half hour. Perhaps longer. The evolution of Olaf's face in those minutes was like that of a man relieved. Did Noah feel different now? Had history lied?

"Anyway," Olaf said finally, breaking a silence that had become palpable.

"It doesn't change anything," Noah said. He had decided this was true.

"It's not supposed to."

They fell silent for another minute. "I always wondered about the others. Why didn't they ever make a run for the lifeboats?"

Olaf looked out of words, like he couldn't say another thing. But he did. "Do you know the story of the *Mataafa*?"

"It rings a bell."

"I think it was 1905. Maybe the worst weather Superior's ever seen. The *Mataafa* was from the Pittsburgh line. It's morning, the boat steams out of Duluth. Right away they know they've made the wrong choice. So she comes about. Other ships had done the same thing, started only to reenter the harbor. The *Mataafa*, unlike the other boats, towed a barge behind her. She couldn't get back into safe water, was hung up on the rocks just outside the harbor. There were nine men on the aft end of the ship, the rest of the crew was in the bow decking. They're all taking a beating. Incredible waves. Wind. The day goes on and half the population of Duluth is on shore watching her wallow. They see a handful of men attempt to cross the deck. Three made it. One of the guys washed over but got back on board. He stayed astern. The water was so rough the Coast Guard couldn't even get out of the harbor. This ship is sitting literally a couple hundred yards off the shore and nobody can help.

"All night it storms. The temperature drops. Snow piles up. Now hordes of people are lining the shore to see what happens to this ship and her crew. At dawn the seas have settled some, and a rescue boat is dispatched. They make one pass and get the men off the bow. Fifteen of them. When they go back for the guys on the stern, they're all frozen. Literally encased in ice. Nine of them dead. Frozen to death, you see? They probably could have smelled the bonfires ashore, burning all night long. That's Superior.

"You asked why nobody else made a run for the lifeboats, and the answer is simple—I don't know. I don't know why or even if they thought it would be best to stay put. Maybe Jan had a plan. Maybe he thought there would be a rescue attempt and the odds were better up there. Hell, maybe they *did* try to get back to the lifeboats and simply didn't make it. It's impossible to say.

"All I know for sure is we were off that boat. Bjorn and Luke. And Red, somewhere in the water. We were in a mess all over again. Hopeless, I thought. Some light still came from the *Rag*, but mostly it was just us and the darkness. I was on the tiller. and with the wind behind us it didn't take long before we were a fair distance from the ship." He stared down at the chart spread across the coffee table. "It seems impossible to me now to think that the whole night he was riding behind us like a goddamn anchor. How he got himself hooked onto that line I'll never know. Why didn't it snap? How in the hell did he come crashing up onto that rocky beach in the morning?"

"How did you guys manage?"

"Believe me, we managed nothing. Right away we were bailing water and still we were up to our ankles in it. Not just water, Superior water, water so cold it would've hurt to drink. Luke was rowing, trying to keep it between troughs so we'd take less. But it did little good. Too many waves from too many directions. Bjorn was working on the gunwale ice while he bailed." Again he went silent. Noah didn't dare to ask any more questions.

"I remember all of it. The cold. The wet. The dark. It should have been impossible for me to notice the glow behind us with all that commotion, but I did. It was like a ghost already. In the snow and sea spray, I could see a hazy light where the ship was. Maybe four hundred yards behind us. The flames, I guess, and whatever onboard lights were still working. That spot just flickered, coming in and out of view as we rode the waves. The farther we got the fainter it got, of course, until it was gone. We rode up a wave and I looked and there was nothing but the night."

Noah had scooted to the edge of his chair in order to hear better. Olaf's voice had weakened with each word, or seemed to. By the time he said "night" there was almost no sound at all, just a little parting of his lips and an indiscriminate wave of his hands. Despite the ebbing and softening of his voice—or maybe because of it—the image of the receding light from the sinking ship resounded in Noah, seemed especially important in light of all the darkness to come.

"The wind was coming from every direction. So was the water," Olaf continued, his voice now barely more than a whisper. "We were soaked. Every thirty seconds another wave would wash over the gunwales and swamp us. Sometimes they were waves so big I thought we'd sink right under them. Sometimes they were easier. So we kept her afloat. It was like the water wanted us, but the darkness wanted us more. Sounds ridiculous, I know, but it's the truth. There were times I couldn't even see the other guys in the boat. I'd yell as loud as I could and they wouldn't hear me six feet away."

The utter silence of the house, broken only by the pinging stove and Olaf's labored breathing, compounded the image of the riotous night in the boat. The old man elbowed himself up on the couch. He rearranged the afghan over his shoulders. He cleared his throat.

"We kept the gunwales clear as we could. Kept from freezing by working so goddamn hard. Somehow we stayed in the boat. I mentioned luck before. No amount of luck earlier in the night measured up to staying alive all night in that mess. By the time morning broke I ought to have learned to believe in God."

"It truly was a miracle," Noah said, more to himself than to his father.

But Olaf heard him. "Here's the thing." He coughed to clear something in his throat not there. "It's a whole lot more remarkable-sounding now than it seemed at the time. Maybe that's obvious, maybe not, but the fact is, for those eight hours it was like we weren't really there. It was downright impossible that we could be so cold, so wet. That it could be so dark. And even though we were working hard to stay alive, I suspect that each of us was waiting to die, too. I know I was.

"I'd spend some minutes woolgathering over you kids and your mother all tucked under your quilts at home without realizing that my hands were so cold I could hardly grip the tiller. I wanted to say good-night so badly, wanted to touch each of your foreheads the way I always did. When I'd snap out of it, it was like I'd been shot. All the pain would surge up, all the panic. But just as quick I'd be back in some other trance, thinking about getting ready for church when I was a tyke back in Norway, thinking about my mother pulling the curlers from her hair. And the whole time we were just frantically working, rowing and hammering and bailing. I suppose I kept at it with thoughts of all of you because I knew that any minute the boat would heave me out into the lake and that would be it. That would be the end." He closed his eyes. Rested.

Noah looked at his father there on the sofa, bereft of the vitality he had once possessed so abundantly. For the old man's son there was as much sadness in the moment as relief. He suspected his father felt little of either, was likely unmoved and unchanged. Perhaps emptiness filled the place where once a secret had resided.

"I don't know," Olaf said. "It's amazing, the memories you carry around with you. Never once had I thought of my mother getting ready for church until that night. But there she was. Those memories are in you all the time. On a night like that they're just hurrying up for one last trip across your mind. I suppose a wise man might have learned something. But what did I do? I ended up wrapped around a tree growing out of the rocks on a frozen beach not sixty miles as the gull flies from where we sit now. You start wondering, why me?" He pointed feebly at his own chest.

Noah wanted to console him but didn't know how.

"You end up as the line in a poem, as the face in a picture in a museum. Meanwhile, your crewmates are dead and you haven't talked to your wife—honestly talked to her—in years. And your kids grow to fear you. And instead of making it right you let it ride. You drink in the raunchiest bars in eight states. Jesus, do you drink." He cleared his voice now and said more loudly than he had said anything in an hour, "And you lose all shame." In his faintest voice yet he concluded, "Chrissakes, that is some ancient grief."

Noah stood. He walked over to the sofa and sat down next to his father as if his proximity might ease the pain of the memory, as if the gesture could speak. He put his hand on his father's shoulder, moved the afghan to make the moment less awkward.

"So there's your story, Noah. Sorry as it is, that's it. We washed onto the beach at Hat Point and all I had in me was jetsam and you suffered for it. So did your mother and sister."

Noah thought, *I wonder if he's dying right now. In this instant. I imagine this is what it might look like.*

Instead Olaf said, "The morning broke and we could see the shoreline. We rowed like hell to get there. Did you know it was below zero that morning? We were sitting there like we'd just been for a swim, for Chrissakes. We thought about trying to build a fire but the only thing we might have burned on that barren shore was the lifeboat, and it was covered with ice. Bjorn, he was trying to light his coat on fire with his lighter." He mimicked Bjorn trying to start his sleeve ablaze. "But his thumb was just a lump of ice. Could have used it for a hammer.

"It's strange, but had we been out on the lake on a clear day, passing Hat Point, I could have given you our coordinates to within a minute each way. But pressed up against those rocks, that cliff looming behind us, snowy as the morning was, I wouldn't have guessed it with ten tries. Delirious, that's what we were, all of us. Hallucinating. We had one blanket among us, from one of the stows in the lifeboat. That was it. We were just waiting to die again." He paused and scratched his bald head. "And of course Red washed up."

"Red," Noah said.

They sat in silence for a moment before Noah continued, "How long before they found you?"

"Seemed like days but it wasn't long. We didn't have time to freeze to death, so that tells you something. First a plane circled above us, then we saw a cutter offshore. I tried to get up and wave, but I couldn't. I think we were all in shock. Everything was blurry. My eyes were coated with ice. None of us could talk. Soon enough an army of highway patrolmen and paramedics were there, coming up the shore like so many dreams."

"And you were saved."

Olaf looked at Noah, put his hand on his son's shoulder now. "That's one way of saying it. They got us out of our clothes, bundled us up in blankets and parkas and whatever else they had around. First they took us to a lodge, a place in Grand Portage. They worked on us there until the helicopters came to bring us down to Duluth. I asked for a cup of coffee, I remember, like we were getting up for breakfast." He actually smiled, halfway and to himself, to be sure. "Just like that, the whole thing was over."

Noah started to say he was sorry but Olaf interrupted him. "Actually, it wasn't over." He leaned over the coffee table, traced a line from the black X off Isle Royale to Hat Point. He traced it back. After a few minutes Olaf looked at Noah again. "For most of your life I've used that night as an excuse. Not because I wanted or needed one but because I had no control over what it did to me. I should have. Hard as it would've been, I should have beaten it.

"I never told anyone any of this before, son. Never told your mother, even though she deserved to know. Never told your sister. Never told any of the guys down at the Freighter, not even on my worst night. I never told it on the bridge of a single ship I later sailed. Hell, I never even told the NTSB or the bosses at Superior Steel the whole story. Everything I just told you, it's been rotting in me all this time."

"Why," Noah said, his own voice now faint, "did you tell me?"

Olaf looked at him. He leaned forward and took off his glasses. "You asked me, Noah. That's why. And you deserved to know. Aside from your mother, you deserved it more than anyone."

TEN

Cold the next morning, as cold as it could be in early November. He drove a half hour up the rutted highway to Gunflint with the sunrise, the road unwinding to lake vistas magnificent in the metallic onset of the morning and winter. There seemed equal resolve among both the day and the season.

On the south end of town a pickup truck waited outside the ranger station at the head of the Brule Trail, a solitary man leaning against the bumper smoking a cigarette. Otherwise the town hunkered ghostlike, a few streets along the lake that gave way behind them to an incalculable wilderness. No Wednesday-morning rush hour here. The semblance of a village nestled around the harbor. Cars were filling up at the Holiday gas station. Noah stopped at a traffic signal on Wisconsin Street. Next to him a white-haired woman in a Chevy sedan almost as old as his father's truck smiled as if expecting the codger. When she saw Noah she waved anyway. He had decided he loved driving that old Suburban and thought he'd never be able to drive his half-electric car again.

The bank was on the north end of town, and except for two raccoons, its parking lot was empty. He looked at his watch. The bank opened at eight. All morning he'd been feeling mixed up about hastening off with the inheritance. Though it was exhilarating in its way to think about the sudden boon of all that money—how could it not be?—he also thought anyone glancing at the situation would think it peculiar. A father so sick left alone, if only for a morning. An estranged son reaping a financial reward so significant. The simple fact was, he had assured himself repeatedly during the drive, that he'd never once imagined the possibility of an inheritance from the moment his father had called him until the first wad of frozen cash had been pulled from the first jar. Noah knew he could not have rested—much less taken care of the jobs around the house—until the money was safely deposited. His nature would not allow it. The sign before the bank flashed the temperature. Thirteen degrees.

Inside, two tellers stood behind the counter. A receptionist sat at a desk on the right. He walked toward the tellers, passing a table piled with jumper cables. A sign hanging above it enticed people with a free gift for opening a home-equity line of credit. It struck Noah as he hefted the duffel off his shoulder and onto the counter that it must be tough for a bank like this to stick it out, how with people like his father living in the hills above town, business must be difficult. Signs hung everywhere on the walls advertising auto loans, low-interest credit cards, and free ATM withdrawals.

"Good morning," one of the young women behind the counter fairly sang. Her name, according to the placard before her, was Ellsie. Her cheery disposition seemed misplaced in that sullen town.

Noah explained his situation. "My father's a customer," he said. "So am I if he tells the truth. He hasn't been here in a while. I've never been here. I'm not sure if you can help or not."

She interrupted, "If you're a customer here, I can help."

Noah smiled. He nodded as if skeptical. "Here's the thing, I have a huge deposit to make."

"Have you filled out a deposit slip?"

"I mean huge. It's cash."

"We accept cash deposits," she said. It took Noah a moment to realize she was joking.

"I have to count it," he said, unzipping the bag to show her. "I'm sure this looks a little strange, but I promise there's nothing fishy."

Without a word Ellsie set a THIS TELLER CLOSED sign before her workspace and asked Noah to follow with a wave of her hand. She led him to an office with an empty desk. She asked him for the account number and his driver's license. She copied this information on a Post-It note. "Okay," she said. "You start counting it here, I'll get the forms we need and fill them out. Put the money in stacks of fifty. Here"—she opened a desk drawer, took from it a box of rubber bands. "Remember, stacks of fifty, I'll double-check it when I get back."

For the next hour Noah counted the still cold hundred-dollar bills. Ellsie joined him a few minutes after she'd left. She verified his tally by running the stacks of money through a counting machine. Together they counted two thousand sixty-two hundred-dollar bills. When he explained how the money had ended up on the table, Ellsie assured Noah that stranger things had come to pass during her tenure at the bank. She moved the stacks of money from the table to heavy canvas bags. When they were finished she moved the bags into the vault. He signed the paperwork, inquired about wiring the money to banks in Boston and Fargo, and confirmed with her that his sister had equal access to the funds.

"Great," Noah said. The transaction felt somehow incomplete, but he thanked her, took his empty duffel from the table, and turned to leave.

A couple blocks back toward the harbor was a place called the Blue Sky Café. He stopped for something to eat, ravenous.

A stack of the Duluth *Herald* leaned against the cash register. He bought one. In a booth that overlooked the village, he ordered coffee from a waitress whose gray hair rose in three layers of buns to a peak atop her head. Her apron was starched sheet-iron stiff. She brought the coffee on a saucer with sugar cubes and a miniature pitcher of cream. He ordered the Lumberjack: two eggs, pancakes, bacon, steak, juice, coffee. When the waitress asked if there was anything else, he ordered one of the pecan rolls from the bakery case in front of the store.

Seated around a horseshoe-shaped counter, ten or twelve men dressed in hunting gear ate breakfast and drank coffee. Outside, the placid harbor water shone black under the gray sky. He could see the street of boutiques and galleries ringing the harbor, but commerce in late morning was no more enthusiastic than it had been at eight. A woman walked her dog. Three men and a child stood before a pizzeria talking. The trees on the hills above town appeared bronzed, the sky above them offered little illumination.

While he waited for the food to arrive, an uneasy feeling came over him. He attributed it to his being in the café at all while his father rested sick at home. Though there was business to tend to—he had to call the hospital and his sister, and he'd had to deposit the money—it seemed extravagant to him to be back in civilization. He thought about this as his food arrived and he ate voraciously. He drank four or five glasses of water, his juice, and was finally brought a coffeepot for himself when the waitress admitted she couldn't keep up with him. He buttered the pecan roll, salted the steak, and soaked the pancakes in maple syrup. As he ate he realized that his unease was easily enough explained. The anger and resentment and sadness that had colored the years of their estrangement were absent now. Not just absent but erroneous. What he'd mistaken for feelings of guilt at being in town were actually feelings of longing. He *wanted* to be back in the cabin, even felt a pull for the too-hot stove and the bland food, for the fishing lines in the water. He knew now that he could venture freely in the full range of his memories. No more caveats next to good times, or whole years' forbidden recollection.

When he finished breakfast he pushed the plate across the table and spread the paper before him. It was eleven o'clock and he still had an hour before he could call the doctor at St. Mary's. He skimmed the election coverage and read a feature on the economic doldrums gripping the shipping and steel industries. Everything suffered: taconite production, ship traffic, grain shipments, coal shipments. There were problems with the stevedore union, with the railways, with the mines. The economic implications were far-reaching, of course, to say nothing of grim. The forecast was even grimmer. The mayors of Duluth and Superior—in reelection mode, no doubt—were calling for tariffs on imported steel. Though it was interesting, Noah thought the article little more than a refrain. Some version of this story had been told since the first iron ore was ever mined in Minnesota, since the first ship full of taconite ever left Duluth harbor. Though it would have been impossible for Noah to dismiss the political and economic realities expressed in the article, it was not impossible for him to see that some things never changed.

But some things do, some things had. Something enduring had been built during the past week between him and his father. He could not name it, he only knew that it gave him permission to live the rest of his life. That was it. That huge, teetering part of him that for years had been resting on his resentment had been replaced by the whole story, bitterroot and all.

The bill at the restaurant was ten dollars and twenty-nine cents. He put a twenty on the table, rolled the paper under his arm, and walked back out into the cold hour before noon. He stopped at the Gunflint Trading Post and bought new socks and long underwear, a T-shirt with the words A LOON A TICK screen-printed across the chest, a pair of Carhartt jeans a size too big, and a pair of flannel boxers. He had the tags cut from everything.

He took a room at a harborside motel and unpacked his new clothes on the bed. He began to undress. He clicked the television on and watched the weather report. The forecast called for continued cold and snow, possibly heavy, later in the week. The thought of it appealed to Noah.

The hotel soap smelled of almonds, the shampoo like a fourth-rate barbershop. He took a long, scalding shower, washing and rinsing and washing again. He would have liked to shave but he had no razor. He toweled off.

In the nightstand drawer was a Cook County phone book. He looked in the yellow pages for a piano tuner. There were two listings, both in Gunflint. He called the first and made arrangements for him to come the next day at lunchtime and have a look. Noah gave careful directions. Then he turned the TV off. He fished from his pocket the doctor's business card. He looked at his watch. It was noon.

A one-sided and dispiriting conversation passed between Noah and the doctor, whose authority and competence seemed as unquestionable as the news was bad. She informed Noah that though not all the tests had been completed, she nevertheless had no doubt about the severity of his father's illness. She spoke brusquely but with compassion of biopsies and polyps, of tumors and blood, and of stages of sickness, particularly of a stage designated Duke's D. A terminal stage, she assured him. She told him the cancer was spreading rapidly and out of control. She said surely his father was in extraordinary pain. She did not mention treatment. "Under normal circumstances," she concluded, "I'd suggest your father visit us again immediately. That you make hospice arrangements. Though I understand that's not likely."

Noah agreed.

"The truth is, it doesn't matter much. If he were admitted he wouldn't leave again. His sickness is that advanced. The drugs we prescribed won't do for the pain what we would do here, but I suspect your father might not want them regardless. He may as well be at peace where he is."

She asked Noah whether he was able to stay with Olaf. She reminded Noah to give him the drugs, said he might not be able to watch his father if he didn't. She warned him of the possibility of hallucinations and of the suddenness with which things could turn. In the end she apologized for bringing such news. Noah might have said ten words during the entire conversation.

His conversation with Solveig required more speech, and he left no detail unsaid. She assured Noah she'd be back soon, as early as Friday if everything went as planned with Tom's folks and the kids. Maybe even Thursday if Tom could clear a court date. She told Noah to go back and take care of their father. When Noah asked her if she'd had any epiphany about the anchor in the shed, she admitted to none.

WHEN HE'D FINISHED on the phone with Solveig he dressed quickly in his new clothes. He paid the hotel receptionist for the phone calls. He nearly flooded the truck while starting it and drove out of town with white plumes of smoke huffing from the tailpipe.

The truck didn't handle the sharp curves of Highway 61 very well. It would lurch and slide and grumble when Noah braked hard midcurve, then sputter when he'd step on the accelerator coming out of one. Rounding one of the steep, uphill curves, he came upon an awesome panorama of the lake and skies. A battlement of cinder-colored clouds broke and the sun reflected off the water in a million different directions. The lake was well below him, down a granite cliff, and the distance eclipsed the reflection. He could stare right at the sun's image off the lake.

He stopped at the Landing before heading back up to Lake Forsone. He bought kitchen matches and lantern mantles. He bought coffee and hot dogs, oatmeal, roasted peanuts, and bread. He asked for ibuprofen, antacid, ChapStick, and Gold Bond from behind the counter. He asked for two Hudson Bay blankets. He stocked up on batteries and candles and toothpaste. When it was all loaded in the back of the truck, he drove back to the cabin.

A pall draped the house. Noah could sense it more than see it. The midday light settled more like dusk. He rushed to park the truck and hurried into the house.

Olaf knelt on one knee before the stove, adding wood to the fire. The only light in the room came through the windows. He looked over his shoulder when Noah walked in. It was as though he had aged five years since Noah had left that morning.

Olaf said, "The fire's out."

"The fire is not out, Dad. It's a hundred degrees in here."

Olaf tried to raise himself off the floor but stumbled onto his elbow in the effort.

Noah helped his father to his feet, ushered him to the sofa, and helped him to sit. After he spread the afghan over his father's legs, Noah went back and closed the stove door.

"Look at the ice on the goddamn windows," Olaf said.

Noah looked at the frost that had formed in the corners of the window panes. "It's going to snow."

"Sure it will."

"I mean it's in the forecast. We might get socked."

"Socked," Olaf said.

"What do we do about the road?"

"Laksonenn," Olaf said. "Laksonenn plows." Each word seemed a triumph from the old man.

"Someone named Laksonenn plows the road?"

"He does."

During the next few minutes Noah watched the old man's lips puckering and his face twitching, an expression between pain and exhaustion. Olaf fell back to sleep, to what terrible dreams Noah could not guess.

IN WHAT REMAINED of that day Noah trimmed the house. He refilled the ten-gallon buckets at the well. He restocked the wood box. Olaf slept motionless on the chair. Before dusk Noah went to the shed. He stood in the doorway and tried to imagine the spot his mother's ashes occupied. He may even have hoped that some ghost or ghost's messenger would present itself, would guide him in the looking. Instead he began where he stood, on the threshold of that welter of junk. He kicked over stacks of magazines, he moved un-marked boxes filled with old tools, truck parts, fishing tackle old enough that the barbs had rusted. He picked a lure from among many, held it to the dying light, and when he flicked the hook with his finger it disintegrated into dust.

He cleared a path to the back wall, and here he went through the contents of an old dresser. Clothes from his childhood. A kitchen mixer. A ledger marked 1972. Here Olaf's blocked scrawl tallied the year's receipts coming and going, a column for each. Noah studied the expenditures: groceries, oil to heat the house on High Street, electricity, clothes. There were two columns marked "Allowance," one for his mother, one for himself. *This,* Noah thought, *is how you end up with two hundred thousand dollars in your freezer.*

Noah saw a metal box beneath the dresser. He lifted it from the floor, set it on the dresser, and studied it. The moment felt religious. The box appeared to be waterproof, it was clasped shut tightly, un-rusted. Clearly something made to last. He unlatched the clasp. Within a Ziploc bag her ashes were interred. They appeared almost to spar-kle. Why he could not imagine, but he sniffed them. Only the other smells of the shack. He closed the box and brought it with him into the house.

His father still slept. Noah set the ashes on the coffee table. At six o'clock he ate a few crackers and half a jar of pickled herring. He thought of waking Olaf but didn't. The old man's sleep was fitful. He'd hiccup and sigh and his face would twist and fold in a hundred unnatural ways, all the while his hands fidgeted in the afghan and his feet kept time to some dream song. Twice during Noah's light supper Olaf's eyes plunged open and he stared at Noah, but as quickly they'd close again and whatever afflicted his sleep would begin again.

Noah himself fell asleep soon. When he woke at midnight he put another blanket over his father and went into his bedroom. He awoke at five-thirty to check on his father again. During the night Olaf had moved from the chair back onto the couch. He slept peacefully now, his chest rising under the mound of blankets, a silent snore from his hang-jawed mouth.

It was another sunless, sooty morning. Noah went to the shed. He wanted to study the anchor. He wanted to be prepared for whatever he might do.

Noah inspected the bolts that fastened the first piece of tubing to the barrel. He saw that holes had already been drilled for the second. He finished sawing through the tubing and began to fasten it to the barrel. He worked for an hour, breaking midway to look in on his father. When he'd attached the last piece, he puzzled the chain through the contraption. It looked, as he stopped on the way out to inspect it one more time, like a torture device from some earlier century.

Finally his father was awake. He stood at the sink basin rinsing his empty mouth with a glass of water. He had dressed himself in wool pants and a sweater thin at the elbows. The clothes fairly hung on him.

"Some sleep," Olaf said.

"I'd say." Noah looked at his watch. It was almost eight o'clock. "How are you feeling?"

"I've had better mornings."

"You want something to eat?"

"I don't think I could eat."

"How about more water? Could you drink? You should take these pills."

Olaf consented. Rather than expecting his father to swallow the pills—some were the size of almonds—Noah ground them on the counter with a spoon and stirred them into the water. Even drinking looked difficult. When he'd finished Olaf let out a soft burp. He handed the glass to Noah and went to the chair, his walk across the room a feat unto itself.

Olaf pointed at the box on the coffee table. "I'll be goddamned," he said.

"I found those out in the shed. I hope it's okay I brought them in."

His father replied with a look of deep regret, or what Noah took for one. "At least it explains my sleep last night." He sighed. "I always meant to bring them in. I knew it was a crime to leave them out in the shed."

"They're here now."

Olaf agreed. "She was beautiful," he whispered, his voice cottony with the memory.

"Always," Noah said.

"She was the love of my life."

These words startled Noah. Not because he was surprised at their meaning but because he'd never expected to hear his father say them. He'd always known it, he guessed. "She was mine, too, for a long time."

Now Olaf smiled. He pressed the heels of his hands into his eyes. When he laid his hands across his lap the smile disappeared. "What I did to her." He shook his head. "She broke my heart, Noah." The words were like something spoken years before.

"There were a lot of broken hearts back then."

"There still are," Olaf said, looking Noah square in the eyes. "But I guess it's a small price to pay. Everyone pays it one way or another."

"What do you mean?"

"A small price for the memories. Broken hearts or none, we all have them."

Noah thought about that. "You know what scares me more than anything? That I'm going to end up an old man without Natalie. That I won't have all the memories I want. Sometimes I don't care about anything but making it to old age with her. I see folks in restaurants or walking down the street and I get terrified we'll end up apart. It's a terrible feeling."

Olaf listened with a look of intense concentration. "You feel that way because you figure once you've made it to old age, the hard times will be behind you. You'll have made it." He paused. "I think I used to believe that, too, when your mother and I were young. But our lives changed. Those thoughts of mine changed. Hers, too, if she ever had them."

"I know she did."

This put another smile on the old man's face. "The problem with your mother was she was too smart for her own good. She was so much smarter than me. It was impossible sometimes."

"What do you mean?"

"I met that wife of yours. I suspect you know what I mean."

Noah said, "I guess you're right."

"She got stuck with me, your mother."

"I don't think I believe that," Noah said. He didn't believe it at all, in fact. "She loved you."

Olaf wedged himself up so his feet were flat on the floor. It was not an easy task. He took the afghan from behind the chair and spread it across his lap. "She may have learned to, but she was stuck with me to begin with. Your mother was pregnant when we got married. In the middle of her third month."

"She was what?" Noah did the math in his head. It didn't add up.

"She miscarried two weeks later. Gave him a name. Per Olaf. She wanted to bury what came out."

"Per Olaf?"

"That's what I wanted to name you." Olaf scratched his neck beneath his beard. "I wanted to tell you when you were talking about Natalie. Figured it wasn't the best time."

"She named a miscarriage?" Noah had gotten lost in the memories of his and Nat's own ill-fated pregnancies. That there was something like a history in the family was surprising to him.

"I was passing through the Soo when I found out about it. July 1958. I was never so confused in my life."

"Why confused?"

"I thought maybe the end of the pregnancy meant the end of our marriage. Your mother was so damn pretty, so damn good, and I thought the only reason she'd settled down with me in the first place was because she got herself pregnant."

"You got her pregnant."

Olaf seemed almost to blush. "We met at a dance hall, of all the goddamn places. This was back when people still danced. She told me right off she didn't want a sailor. I told her she should dance with someone else, then. But she didn't. There was something underneath all that primness."

"We're talking about Mom."

"Sure we are. We danced and danced. She smelled like rosewater, I remember. She always did. She had on a pink dress and a white sweater and with that blond hair it was like she had claim on half the purity in the world." He shook his head. "But she knew what she was doing. It was unfair is all."

"You were defenseless, huh?"

"Anyone would have been, that's the truth. I would have bought anything she had to sell. But she wasn't selling anything. That's the thing. At the end of the night I walked her home. She still lived with her parents over on the west end, by Wade Stadium. Warm March evening. At the door she told me she didn't want to get old before her time. Said that's what sailors did to you."

Olaf paused, clearly reveling in the memory of it all.

"Well, I know it didn't end there. Something must have happened between then and, what, May? April?"

"We were already shipping that year. I had two days."

"So?"

"So the next morning I'm walking back to my apartment from the diner on the corner and I get home and your mother is sitting on the stoop outside my building. I said, 'I thought sailors were off limits.'"

"What did she say?"

"Said she changed her mind. Said she'd make an exception."

"And she did."

"The thing is I fell in love with her like a kid. Immediately. I was stupid in love with her. Your mother? I was practically an old man when we met and your mother was no spring chicken, not by the standards of those days. She fell in love with me, ended up with me anyway, because twenty-eight-year-old women weren't single in Duluth back then."

"I saw enough reason to the contrary to believe that. Mom loved you. Very much."

"Not how I loved her." He paused. "That day, that Sunday in March, right after I met her, she invited me out for a lemonade. Right then. We walked down to Wahl's, sat at the counter, and sipped our lemonade from paper straws. She told me everything I'd ever need to know about her. Then she put me through the wringer. Where did I grow up? Did I miss Norway? Did I wish I still lived there? Why did I work the boats? Why wasn't I married? What about girlfriends? Did I like my job? What about my parents? Did I love them? Did I want to have my own kids someday? A goddamn deposition.

"At the end of the afternoon I walked her home. I told her I had to leave the next day. I told her I wanted to see her again. We were standing there on the porch of her parents' house and you know what she said? She said come in, she said her parents were in Minneapolis." He shook his old head slowly no. "I told her I had to go, that I had too much to do before the next day. That was hard."

"You were smitten, just like that," Noah said.

Olaf nodded.

"You've never struck me as the smitten type. You've always been pretty tough to crack."

"Your mother never had any trouble cracking me."

"Just the rest of us."

"Solveig never had any trouble, either."

"I guess not."

"She was waiting for me when I got back. Like a bird, sitting on the stoop again when the cab dropped me off. She came up. We listened to the radio on the couch. Rosewater all over the place. I had no chance. None."

"And from this you decided she was only in it for the husband?"

"Ah, what the hell do I know?"

"A lot more than I thought," Noah said.

There was enough freight in the words that passed between them to require one of his father's old ships, but Noah let it pass by way of fond memories. He recalled mornings from his early childhood when the three of them—father, mother, son—had luxuriated in their happiness. The feeling of security in the booming laughter of his father. The way he would wrestle Noah on the living room floor, the Duluth winter outside the big bay window little more than a backdrop for the times of his life.

"Of course a lot changed," Olaf said, as if to check the mood. The tone of his father's voice confirmed for Noah something he'd only ever suspected: that Olaf knew about his wife's affair with Mr. Hember, the insurance salesman who lived across the street. Noah had always accepted her indiscretion as the solace in her long, lonely days. Whatever pain it had caused his father, if he knew about it at all, well, Noah had chalked that up as his due. But now the perverse pleasure he had for so long taken in his mother's infidelity was replaced with the shameful recognition that there was another side of the story. The fact that this knowledge was shared passed between them as though an unspoken accord had long ago been reached. They continued talking now as though they had discussed Phil Hember many times.

Noah looked at his father. "What did you expect her to do?" he said. "You set her up for a very lonely life."

"It's not all your mother's fault, what happened. Phil Hember."

Noah got up and poured his father another glass of water. He brought it to him. "Phil came along ten years after your boat sank. What happened in between?"

"What happened," Olaf said, pausing to take a long drink of the water, "was life. She was pregnant with you pretty damn quick. We bought the house on High Street. You were born. Solveig was born. My boat sank. I sank. Your mother and I sank. Hember took over for me while I kept the Freighter and the Tallahassee in business. That's the story. Here I am today."

"A little simplistic, isn't it?"

"No," Olaf said.

"No cause and effect? No regrets?"

"There's nothing but regret."

For twenty-five years Noah had been scratching his head over it, trying to see all the angles, to measure his disdain in proportion to the events that formed it. "Mom was screwing the dope across the street. You were sopping up gin drops in those rat holes. And your kids were at home trying to figure it all out. That's as complicated as it gets?"

The old man looked at him as if in slow motion. "Are you looking for answers? For explanations?"

"I don't know what I'm looking for," Noah said.

"Listen, Noah. I hated myself. It's true I hated your mother, too, and I hated what our problems were doing to you kids. But your mother did take up with Phil."

"Mom didn't want Phil Hember. He was your fill-in, like you said. He was the cat in the yard while you disappeared."

"I used to think he was queer. Living alone in that nice house with the lilac bushes. Sitting on his porch sipping tea." He shook his head. "I used to lend that son of a bitch my toolbox." He paused and shook his head again. "Anyway, what do you know about Phil? You were a kid."

"I grew up pretty fast."

"And you were an expert on marital relations?"

"I didn't need to be. I saw her sitting in the living room window watching the harbor. I watched her in the hospital, holding on for one last look at you."

Olaf put his chin on his chest. "She still shouldn't have done what she did. I may have checked out, your mother may have wanted more, but she shouldn't have done it the way she did."

Olaf leaned forward. He picked the box of ashes from the table and held them on his lap. For ten minutes, maybe longer, he stared at the box while Noah stared at his father. The silence in the room was a tribute to sadness if nothing else. Finally Olaf set the box back on the table. He looked at Noah. When he spoke his voice cracked. "I'm very glad you love your mother so much. I'm glad you loved her through it all. I loved her myself."

Noah looked at his father. He saw the age in the lines of his face. He saw the whiteness of his long beard. He saw him as a younger man, as the father of a young child. Of two young children. "I love you, too."

At this Olaf smiled. "Take care of those for me, okay?" He gestured toward the ashes.

"I will. Solveig and I will."

"Good." Olaf stood with much evident pain. Noah helped him. "I'm going to try and sleep in my bed for a little while."

"Sure." Noah helped him across the room. He helped him into bed and spread the quilt. "You want me to close the blinds?"

"No. Leave the blinds open. Maybe I won't sleep so long."

ELEVEN

Now passed an hour of sadness beyond words. Noah stood
at the kitchen window staring into the yard. The wood
was split and stacked. The ground had frozen during the
last two days. It sat hard as bedrock under the brown grass. It would
not thaw until April. There had never been a moment better made
for reckoning, still Noah could not think past his heartache.

He watched as the clouds broke. He saw noon come. The draft
from the kitchen window tempered the warm room. He ate the second half of the jar of herring. He knew he should call Solveig. Had a
strong inclination to call his wife. He thought the sound of her voice
might quell his grief, thought, in any case, it would help him through
the afternoon. But he had made a promise to his father and he would
not leave him again, come what might.

It was soon after lunch that he saw the truck driving down the
hill. A red piano painted on the driver's-side door. In the heaviness of
the morning's conversation Noah had forgotten about the piano
tuner. The man stepped from his truck, an ox and a slob. His shirttails
hung from behind his barn coat, his haunches filled it out. His boots
were untied and what hair he had appeared greasy. His black pants

were flecked with something, paint perhaps. He took from the back of his truck a toolbox the size of a suitcase and carried it to the door. Noah met him, let him into the house, said hello.

"I almost forgot you were coming," Noah said. "Any trouble finding the place?"

"None at all." He held his hand before him. "Gordy Nelsen."

"I'm Noah." They shook hands.

"Nice spot here. Quiet, peaceful."

Noah raised an eyebrow, one of his father's gestures. "That's one way of looking at it."

"Here's our culprit?" Gordy pointed at the piano sitting against the wall.

"It is."

Gordy tapped a key. He tapped another. He opened the top of the piano, took a flashlight from his toolbox, shined it into the piano. "I've seen worse," he said. "Though not much."

"Can it be fixed?"

He sat at the bench, put a foot on one of the pedals. He ran his fingers across the keyboard. "I can fix it, but God's truth is, it ain't worth it. For what it'd cost you could nearly have a new one."

"All I want is to be able to get a sound out of it. One that won't hurt the ears."

Gordy was up and in the piano again. He had already pulled two strings from the guts of it. "It'll take all day. I'll have to replace a few strings. Realistically, the whole action needs to be replaced. I think I see a crack in the soundboard." His head disappeared into the piano. It came back out. "There's a crack. Not the end of the world but not good, either." He got on one knee, looked at the pedals. "Is it an heirloom?"

"Something like that."

"I can fix it. Check the action. Repair the pedal. I do all that and you'll be able to play it. I can't promise it'll hold a tune for more than a minute or two. But I can do it. Heirlooms are heirlooms."

"Do whatever you can, okay?"

"Right." He smiled.

"Sorry about the heat. My father's sick, he needs it warm. He's sleeping in there." Noah gestured toward Olaf's bedroom.

A look of genuine concern spread across Gordy's face. "I can come back another time," he offered.

"Oh, no. No. Thanks, but it's not necessary. He probably won't even know you're here."

Gordy took off his sweater. Already his undershirt was wet with sweat. "This his place?"

"Yeah."

"Well, maybe a little music will make him feel better."

"That's the idea," Noah said.

"You have any more light?"

"Not much," Noah said, stepping from lamp to lamp and turning them both on. "How's that?"

"That'll help."

Gordy unscrewed the top of the piano and removed it. His big arms reached into the instrument. "This is going to be some job."

For two hours Gordy worked, pulling busted hammers and rusty strings from the piano, looking over his shoulder with a wrinkled brow and puckered lips as if he were a customer at a restaurant pulling a long black hair from his plate of spaghetti. He hummed while he worked and talked of all manner of things. He kept returning to the topic of the weather, specifically the snow that was on the way.

He assured Noah it would start that night. At one point he warned Noah to get the truck and car up on the county road. "If you don't, you'll be buried down here for the next five months."

Noah thanked him, and then asked, "Isn't it early for so much snow?"

Gordy took a break from his work. "We've had less snow the last few years, but we can still get walloped. They're talking about one of those El Niño winters again. Warmer but wetter. I'll make that trade every year."

"It's been a long time since I've been here in the wintertime," Noah said.

At this Gordy plied him with questions about Boston and Boston winters. He told Noah about the vacation he and his wife were finally taking to Florida, a place he'd seen only in brochures. He set back to work, still humming.

Noah got up to check on Olaf. He sat up in bed, his arms folded across his chest, his eyes open.

"How are you?" Noah whispered.

"I could use some water."

"I'll get a glass." Noah stepped back into the kitchen and got one. He ground another round of pills and stirred them into the glass. He brought it back to his father. "The guy's here fixing the piano," he said.

Olaf nodded as he drank the water. He wiped his bottom lip with the sleeve of his turtleneck. He was out of breath from drinking. He closed his eyes.

"Are you sure you're okay?"

"Chrissakes, I feel like hell."

Noah sat on the edge of the bed. "And there's nothing I can do?"

"I think I'll sleep again. Let me know when he's done with the piano. Maybe I can come out to the great room."

"I'll do that." Noah tucked his father in again. Took the empty glass back to the kitchen, rinsed it, filled it, and returned it to his father's bedside table.

When he came back out Gordy was refilling his own water glass. "I hope you don't mind."

"Of course not," Noah said.

Gordy went to the window, looked up at the sky as if to gauge its intentions. "Sixty-one is a hell of a road in a blizzard, that I can tell you. Especially spots where the highway's exposed to the lake. You can get some pretty deep drifts." He ambled back to the piano.

Noah watched him work. He had by now examined the action and soundboard and decided to leave well enough alone, to simply replace the hammers and strings and hope for the best. This plan he passed by Noah. Noah agreed. He told Noah he could have it done in the next couple hours.

For all of his ambling around and small talk, Gordy worked quickly and with apparent precision. He never had to correct something he'd already fixed. Except for the sweat now soaking his shirt, he appeared completely at ease.

Noah sat on the couch watching him restring the piano.

"What did your father do that he could get away living up here?"

"He worked on the ore boats," Noah said. "This was his father's place before him. My grandpa built it."

"Ore boats, huh? What did he do on them?"

"He retired captain," Noah said. "More than fifteen years ago now. He worked for Superior Steel."

"How about that? What about you, what line of work are you in?"

"I have a small business. I sell antique maps."

Gordy worked with both hands in the piano now. "Couple of interesting guys, you two. There aren't too many antique-map sellers, I don't suspect. Nor too many ore-boat captains."

"I guess not," Noah said. "Nor many piano tuners for that matter."

"Fewer and fewer all the time," Gordy said. He worked with great efficiency, seemed to be accelerating as the daylight faded. "My own grandpa worked on the docks in Two Harbors. He was a stevedore. Died on the job when I was only in kindergarten. Fell into a cargo hold, was crushed by a basketful of iron ore."

"Are you kidding?"

"No, sir. Happened a long time ago."

"My father survived the wreck of the *Ragnarøk*."

"Your father was on the *Rag*?" Gordy said. He stopped what he was doing and looked seriously at Noah. "My grandpa used to load the *Rag*. Can you believe that? Small world."

"It is a small world."

Gordy set back to work. "So he was one of the three." It wasn't a question so much as a statement of awe. "I was in high school back then. Remember it like yesterday."

"So do I," Noah said.

"And he kept sailing after that?"

"For almost twenty years."

"No way you'd have gotten me back out on that lake."

"He could hardly be seen on land," Noah said.

"He's damn near famous, I guess."

"Don't tell him that."

Gordy rested his arms atop the piano. "So you know the real story, I bet."

Noah smiled. "As a matter of fact I do."

"I'll have to tell my son about this. He loves the shippery."

Gordy finished an hour earlier than he'd thought he would. After he reattached the lid he pulled the bench up, cracked his knuckles, and launched into a beautiful rendition of *Rondo capriccioso*. He played like a virtuoso, the mass of his body ecstatic as he moved from one end of the keyboard to the other, an exultant look on his face. When he finished the air literally vibrated with the last notes. Noah applauded as if he were cheering the soloist from the Boston Pops. "That was my mother's favorite piece," Noah said. "She played it all the time."

"My favorite, too. I play it after every piano I tune."

"I hope my father was awake to listen. Maybe you could play another?"

He cracked his knuckles again, let his fingers hover over the keyboard for a moment. "Grieg?" he said and without waiting for a reply began.

Again it was beautiful. Noah listened, transported.

Gordy slid off the bench finishing the last few notes. "That's the opening to his concerto in A minor. I love it."

"I'm no expert, but I know a pianist when I hear one. That was just terrific."

He was packing his toolbox. "Thank you. It's what I do." His modesty was as genuine as his look of concern for Olaf had been when he first arrived. "Not much use for it, but it's what I enjoy."

"The world would be a better place if more people could play like that."

"The world's not such a bad place," Gordy said.

He wrote a receipt for Noah. Noah paid. He walked him to the door. It was cold.

"Tell your father I hope he feels better. I hope the music cheered him up."

"I'm sure it did. I really appreciate your coming. On such short notice, too."

Gordy turned up the collar of his barn coat. "My pleasure." He looked skyward. "It is on the way. Get your vehicles up this hill."

"I will."

And with that he left.

BACK INSIDE HE heard moaning coming from his father's room. Noah opened the door. The light from the living room filtered in and he could see his father stabbing the air with his fingertips. What he'd mistaken for a moan was actually humming that sounded vaguely like music. The smile on his father's sleeping face belied his voice, which was clotted and out of tune. Noah stood in the doorway and watched for a minute. His father soon set his arms down, quit humming, and settled back into sleep.

Noah moved the truck and his rental car up the hill as Gordy had suggested. Darkness was coming, and the cold was fierce. It even smelled of snow.

For a couple of hours Noah worked on one of his piano-lesson standards. It must have cut quite a contrast to the effortlessness of Gordy's playing. When, between notes, Noah heard his father coughing, he went in to check on him. Olaf sat up in bed, his eyes sunken in the darkness. Noah opened the bedroom door fully for the light.

"Hey, you okay?"

Olaf looked at him, appeared stunned. "Noah? Is your mother here?"

Noah went to his father's bedside. He sat. "No, Dad, Mom's not here."

His voice was so soft. "That's funny. I heard her playing the piano. She was playing my favorite piece."

"That was the piano tuner. He's gone now."

"Tell her I'd like to see her," Olaf said, looking up into Noah's face. A look both empty and full of something.

"You'll see her soon," Noah said, though he had no faith in heaven, nor any in hell.

"I want to talk to her."

"Tell me, and I'll tell her for you."

Olaf began to hum *Rondo capriccioso*, the sound a whir, barely a sound at all. Midsong, he stopped. "Tell her I'll be home soon. Tell the kids, too."

"You are home, Dad. I'm here with you. I see you."

Again Olaf looked at him. "Good," he said, then shut his eyes and eased back into his slumber, silent now.

Noah stayed at his bedside for some time. The wind had returned, it assailed the house. When he rose to turn in himself, he looked from his father's bedroom window. He could see the first of the snow slanting through the darkness, offering its whiteness. He imagined Vikar wincing under the bite of the driving flakes, bounding through the forest to beat the storm home.

TRY AS HE might Noah could not sleep. He lay in the bed and watched the snow radiating such paleness in the dark frame of the window. It fell furiously. He thought only of his wife now. He longed for her in a way he hadn't in years, with a kind of abandon he attributed to his father's love story. He'd come to realize, without any effort of thought, that he and Natalie had probably endured their bouts with failure. Those many failed pregnancies had been their trial, and now closer to fifty than to thirty years old, and with the education of the last ten days, he figured they had a pretty good chance. This thought appeased him deeply but also kept him awake when he wanted to sleep. There was a kind of euphoria attached to it.

Outside, he could see the spooky glow of the falling snow. He strained to listen, thought he could actually hear it. After a while he got up. He went to the kitchen and poured himself a glass of water. The temperature in the great room must have been twenty degrees warmer than it was in the bedroom. He pulled his T-shirt over his head and stood bare-chested at the window.

The snow, the snow.

At nine o'clock he heard groaning from his father's room. It stopped. It started again. When he cracked the door to peek in, he could see Olaf struggling to rise from the bed. He turned on the lamp near his father's bedroom door and stepped into his room.

Olaf's eyes cringed shut. His big hand went up to shield his face from the light. The moan went baritone, as if the light had changed the severity of his pain. "Chrissakes," Olaf said, his voice slurring the profanity. "Goddamnit, goddamnit."

Noah hurried to the bedside. "What is it, Dad?" he said, helping his father remove the blankets and quilt from his legs. "Are you too hot?"

"Ah, shit."

"It's okay. Tell me what to do."

"Shit," Olaf repeated. His legs were free of the bed covers. He swore again.

Noah took him first by the elbow, then sat next to him and put his arm around his shoulders. "Tell me what's wrong."

Olaf's shoulders crumpled, his chin fell, his eyes fluttered, and his arms went limp. His feet were on the floor now, his lips crusty and shuddering. In a voice barely more than a whisper he spoke into Noah's chest, "I have to go, Noah. To the outhouse."

Without a word Noah helped his father stand. He helped him into his wool trousers. He helped him walk into the great room. In the light the old man's pain became evident. He leaned lightly against Noah, would not have been able to stand without him.

Noah hurried him into his coat. He had Olaf hold on to the doorjamb while he put the old man's boots on. He tied them tightly. He took from the shelf the blaze-orange hunting hat and a pair of leather mittens. He helped his father into these. Then he put on his own coat and boots and took the flashlight. He put his arms around his father again and opened the door.

Already snow had drifted six inches deep. Noah kicked it away as they stepped into the mean wind. The going was slow. Olaf relied entirely on Noah for balance. He felt light in his son's arms, and after a few more difficult steps Noah simply handed the old man the flashlight and picked him up. He carried him up the path to the outhouse.

For fifteen minutes, maybe more, Noah held him steady, the two men alone in the utter dark now that Noah had turned off the flashlight. He'd hoped it would lend a hint of privacy to the ordeal. It was so cold.

On the way back Olaf clutched helplessly at Noah, his arms around Noah's neck, a grip so feeble. Finally Noah lifted his father in his arms and carried him back to the house, snow now creeping over the tops of his boots.

Back inside, Noah undressed Olaf to his union suit. He offered him something to drink. Olaf declined. When Noah began to help him back into his bedroom, Olaf stopped.

"I'll sleep in here," he whispered, pointing at the couch. "Warmer."

"Okay. Good," Noah said, somehow buoyed by the suggestion. "You'll be more comfortable in here."

Noah helped his father into the chair while he fixed a bed for him on the sofa. He then carried him over to it. The old man's head disappeared into the pillow. Noah covered him with the quilt and afghan. He tucked both under his feet and turned out the lamp. A dull slant of light from the window shone into the room. He could see only his father's outline on the couch.

"You all set? You comfortable?" he asked.

Olaf reached for Noah's arm.

Noah touched his father's hand. He held it there. "I'll be right in there if you need anything. Just call."

Olaf was already fighting sleep.

THE NEXT MORNING blazed bright, sunny and white and windless. A profound silence had beset the house, beset the wilderness around it. Noah stood at the window inspecting the weight of snow hanging on the pine trees, the whiteness everywhere a testimony to the vagaries of that place. The whiteness was disturbed only by the bark on the south side of the trees, on the limbs of hardwoods too thin to hold snow. He tried to gauge the snow's depth, but the drifts confused him. Snow sloped gently on the north side of the shed to the eaves but had been blown nearly clear on the south side of the roof.

He turned to look at his father, still asleep on the couch. His rest appeared easy now, the rising and falling of his chest steady if not slowing.

He stepped into his boots. Snow knee-deep had drifted onto the top step. He kicked it away and surveyed the yard. He thought he'd never felt air so cold or seen any so clear. He contemplated the fate of the wolves in the deep snow, contemplated the fate of Vikar, wondering why the dog hadn't come home for the storm. He lingered there, bracing himself against the cold, a new abundance of faith in the days ahead.

Back inside, Olaf lay awake. Except for his right eye, which was bruised, the old man appeared better, as if the long sleep had done something to whittle away at his dying. Noah asked him how he felt.

In a voice practically inaudible he asked, "You seen the dog?"

"I haven't. I was just wondering about him."

Olaf coughed. He cleared his throat and sat up to spit in the water glass on the coffee table. "Put a bucket of food out for him. He usually comes around after a snow. Builds a den under the steps."

Noah opened all the curtains. "I'll put the food out in a minute. Will he be all right, with the snow and cold and everything?"

"He usually is. Maybe he finally ran off with the wolves."

"The call of the wild."

"Your favorite story when you were a boy."

"Get out in the woods and stay," Noah said.

Olaf propped himself up on an elbow. "I need a hat. Something to keep me warm."

"I'll find one."

Noah fetched the orange hat from its peg on the porch. He gave it to his father, who struggled for a moment before handing it back to Noah and lifting his head slightly. Noah put his hands inside the cap, stretched it out, and pulled it down over the old man's ears. Olaf leaned back on his pillow.

Noah went to the kitchen counter. He ground more pills and mixed them with another glass of water. He helped his father drink the potion.

"What day is it?" Olaf said.

"It's Thursday."

"In the morning?"

Noah looked at his watch. "It's ten o'clock, a little after."

Olaf closed his eyes. "How much did it snow?"

"More than a foot, I think. There's a drift to the eaves on the shed. And it's cold. Below zero."

"The high after the low," Olaf said.

Knowledge like that I'll never possess, Noah thought.

Now Olaf opened his eyes. He looked at Noah. "It hurts. Bad." He coughed. "It has for a long time."

Noah sat on the coffee table facing his father. "What can I do?"

"There's nothing to do."

"I wanted to call Solveig, but I'm not leaving."

"I'm glad she's not here. I've got to be a sight."

He was. "You look good. Better than last night."

Olaf looked at the piano. "I dreamt of music."

"You're dreaming again? That's good. You slept pretty peacefully last night."

"I feel better when I sleep."

"You want to sleep now?"

"Wish I could." He took a deep, unsteady breath. "I feel hollow."

"Is there anything else you want?" Noah asked.

"Pull the quilt over my feet," Olaf said. "And just sit here with me."

Noah tucked the quilt around the old man.

Olaf began humming, more tunefully this time than the night before. Midway through the song he looked at Noah. He almost smiled through his baggy lips. Noah smiled back. He put his hand on his father's.

After a moment Olaf said, "Your child, name him well."

"Or her," Noah said.

"Or her," he echoed. "And love them."

"Of course."

"Tell you what. Take all the love I never gave you and heap it on your child. Maybe you'll remember me a little more kindly that way." He picked up the tune right where he'd left off.

"You don't need to worry about me remembering you kindly, Dad."

He hummed the rest of the song. "My watch is on the nightstand. I want you to have it. Get it fixed."

"I will. I'll treasure it."

"I wish we could call Solveig. I should have had a phone line put in here years ago."

Noah got up to look at his cell phone. There was still no service. "I can go into town and call her. Do you want that?"

"There's no time for that. Just tell her that I love her, too. And the kids."

"I will."

"Is it November yet?" Olaf said.

"It is," Noah said, again checking his own watch. "November seventh."

"It's always November," Olaf said. Now he looked out the window. "Sit down for another minute, would you?"

Noah did. Olaf reached up to touch his face. He held his son's look. He pulled the boy to him exactly as he had thirty-five years ago.

He kissed his forehead. Noah stayed there, close enough that he could feel his father's breath. He wanted to tell him that he understood now. That he understood how his love had become cruel. He wanted to tell him he loved him. He couldn't say anything.

Soon his father said, "Go put the food out for Vikar. I'm going to get some rest. I'm glad you're here. I'm glad you came back."

Noah sat up. He'd closed his eyes in his father's embrace but opened them now. When he did the old man was already sleeping again. He slept through the morning and the afternoon. He slept through the evening. He was still asleep when Noah himself dozed off on the chair sometime late at night.

TWELVE

The next morning Noah dressed warmly and shoveled a path down to the lake. Two hours' labor that proved he'd underestimated the snowfall by half if not more. Again the sun shone and again the whiteness nearly blinded. He looked upon the lake bisected with skim ice, an arc of placid black water disrupted beyond the ice by thin ripples that flared under the cold, stiffening breeze. He felt a moment's reprieve before he stepped onto the dock. But the ice cracked under the sway of the posts and he realized it was paper-thin, that the rowboat could easily break through it. As for the boat, it was buried like everything else under the snow. He shoveled it out, shoveled the dock, too.

The room had been very cold when he'd awoken. He had not stoked the fire during the night. In that lightness and chill he'd seen his father, seen the quilt not rising. He'd watched, hoping to convince himself that what he knew was wrong, that the light was insufficient or that the old man's breathing had become that short. When he finally stepped to Olaf and touched his cheek, his knowledge became irrefutable. His father's face was the same temperature as the air. Noah simply pulled the quilt up over the old man and knelt beside the sofa. Anyone passing by would have thought he was praying.

Back up in the yard he cleared a path to the shed. The sun did little to warm him, and his fingers and toes grew numb despite his exertion. He first took the wheelbarrow from the shed. Looking down the hill to the lake, at the snow everywhere, he pushed it aside and retrieved instead the old Radio Flyer ski sled from the rafters. He tied a rope to the back end of it. Now he stood before the anchor, the consequences of its purpose beyond any intelligence he possessed. Solveig was not there. Nor Natalie. He put his arms around the old barrel. With great effort he carried it to the sled sitting in the snow. He set it upon the seat, took one of the pieces of tubing in one hand and the rope in the other, and guided it down the hill. At the lakeshore he set it on the dock. He towed the sled back up the hill and retrieved the platform his father had fashioned to sit on the gunwales. By now the sting of the cold on his face drew his skin tightly to his cheekbones. The lobes of his ears had gone numb. He brought the platform to the dock and set it across the boat with some difficulty. The ice around the boat cracked as it had when he'd first stepped on the dock, its sound full in the otherwise silent day.

Finally he returned to the house. He scratched the frost from the kitchen window and read the temperature on the thermometer. It was below zero. He turned to regard his father. For a long time he looked at the shape beneath the quilt. He counted back the time. It had been only some hundred and sixty hours, a simple week ago, that he and his father and Natalie had eaten so festively the Norwegian feast she'd brought. Only three days before that he'd arrived here at the lake. And just two days before arriving he'd received his father's call. The measuring of those days and hours confounded him in contrast to what lay ahead for the old man now. To what lay ahead for himself.

He stood before the stove blowing into his hands and tapping his toes. The question of whether or not to dress his father now came to him. He walked to the couch. He lifted the quilt. That ratty union suit appalled him. So did the messed hair, the toothless mouth, that pinky half gone. Noah covered him again and went into his father's bedroom. In the small closet he saw the old man's wardrobe. A corduroy jacket. Three pairs of woolen trousers sewn by Noah's mother and distinguishable only by the wear at the cuff, at the knee. A white cotton shirt with a button-down collar. An assortment of plaid flannel shirts. On the shelf above these meager hangings a short stack of sweaters. Noah found the thickest one. He held it up. It had a roll-neck collar and patches on the elbows. He slid a pair of the wool trousers from a hanger. From the top drawer of the small chest in the room, Noah took a pair of red wool socks and went back into the great room.

He pulled the covers back again. With as much difficulty as trepidation he began dressing his father. He lifted the old man's head and pulled the sweater over it. His rim of hair lay flattened. The lids of his eyes seemed almost translucent. Noah paused to look on them. The skin was the same gray color as his eyebrows and lashes, the same gray color as the sweater.

The sleeves of the sweater presented a problem he'd not expected. His father's arms were stiff, seemed flexed at his side. It took a modest feat of strength for Noah to bend them at the elbow. He fixed the collar at the old man's neck. He straightened the sleeves. Next he pulled the wool socks onto the feet. The feet too were stiff. The pants he slid on easily. He thought of putting on boots but was dissuaded by the rigid ankles. Instead he put a hat over his father's head. He put mittens on his hands. Finally he wrestled the peacoat onto the man. Noah stood back. He stepped again toward Olaf, put his thumbs between his father's lips, and pried his mouth open. He retrieved the dentures from their jar on the counter and pushed them into the old man's mouth. With one hand on top of his father's head and one beneath his chin, Noah muscled the lips together again.

He thought of hiking up the hill to the truck, of driving into Misquah to call his sister, but decided against it. Instead he removed his mother's ashes from the shelf on which he'd placed them. He set them on the kitchen counter and stared at them as if she might materialize and give him counsel. His capacity for thought had diminished with his tasks, and when his mother offered no advice he decided to row his father across the lake.

He guided the sled down the hill a last time. On the dock he untied the rope from the sled. He put his father's hands behind him and tied them together with a length of braided nylon rope he'd found in the shed. The arms resisted as if in protest. He thought how his father might have chastised him for the knot. It satisfied Noah in any case, and he proceeded with the barrel. It weighed more than his father, or so Noah reckoned. He laid the contraption on his father's chest. He aligned the pieces of tubing with the old man's legs and crisscrossed the chain behind his back, around his ankles, his father's instructions returning to Noah unexpectedly. Noah could hardly believe how it all went together. He felt a small sense of pride at his part in its execution.

He managed to load his father onto the boat. He centered the old man and his anchor and stepped cautiously into the boat himself. The oars broke the ice easily. Between pulls he could hear the bow cutting through the ice. Midway across the lake the ice cleared and he was in open water. With his back facing his destination, he used the dock in front of him as his fix, knowing that if he kept in a straight line at about a forty-five-degree angle from the dock he'd end up abutting the cliff in the deep water.

He rowed. The wind bit at his neck and wrists and poured through his coat. He worked with absolute purpose, steadily and smoothly, his father balanced between the gunwales. The labor warmed him. He began to breathe hard. He kept his gaze on the dock, now so small a point of reference in the distance. He figured he was halfway, and when he paused to check saw that he was right. Again he turned, looked toward the dock. He saw upon it his father's dog—or the ghost of a dog—his nose raised to the wind. Noah wiped his eyes to clear his vision. Then the dog was gone. He put his head down and dug the oars into the lake again.

And then he was at the spot where they'd fished so recently, so long ago. The sun at its apex reflected off the small waves that came with the winter wind. Except for the sound of them against the boat's wooden hull there was no sound at all. He looked around. He didn't know what he was looking for, but neither could he find it. He heard Solveig's voice, her reticence, her declaration that she could not do it. He thought again of his mother's ashes. He thought of Natalie's innate confidence in him. Maybe he deserved it, for once. Some version of his father's plea to bury him here replayed in his mind. There had been such elegance in it. And in the story of the *Rag* as his father had told it. There was his father now: dressed for winter, the afghan trailing in the water like a seining net.

Noah edged his father to starboard. He edged himself to port. The boat rocked. He tilted the platform. His father, rigid, splayed to the anchor, slid almost without a sound into the water. Instantly Noah put a hand into the water. He watched his father cartwheel toward the depths and out of view. It seemed to take forever.

Noah sat. He took the oars again, steered the boat around. He sculled back across the lake, thankful for the blinding whiteness.

Epilogue

Natalie still slept as he crested the last rise heading east into Duluth. The sun had just broken and cast its light onto the hills east and north of the city. A sight beyond his capacity to describe, but not to relish, which he did. It was the opposite season of his last arriving here, and the contrast in every way was lovely.

He followed the interstate down into the city. At this hour on a Saturday the roads were nearly vacant. He passed the first neighborhoods, the first industry. His ears popped. The harbor bloomed in the distance, all grays and inky blacks, the water coursing brilliantly and white beneath the sun. At the top of his view he saw the aerial bridge.

He nudged Nat. "Hey, sleepyhead. Look at this."

She pulled her head from the pillow on which it lay next to the window. Her eyes adjusting to the light, she stretched. "Where are we?"

"Duluth. Breakfast in five minutes."

She sat up. She scanned the view. "It looks a lot different."

"It's April, not November."

He drove on. They'd planned on having breakfast at Canal Park, so he exited at Fifth Avenue. He turned over the tracks and stopped at Commerce and Railroad Streets. To his right the elevator silos and docks beckoned. "You mind if we make a detour? It won't take long."

"What for?"

"I want to show you something."

He turned right. He passed two vacant slips not fifty feet from the road. The pier that jutted between them was wholly derelict. A little farther six pyramids of taconite five stories tall and black as obsidian rose against the harbor. Natalie asked about them.

"That's what this town survives on. Or used to survive on. It's taconite."

"What your father spent all those years lugging around in his boat."

Noah looked at her. "The same stuff."

He turned onto Garfield and drove past a slip on his left with two tugs tied to cleats on the quay. He drove past two more slips. In the third a small freighter was docked under a loading complex. Men were about her deck.

"This is so interesting," she said. "Look at those barges. What would they carry?"

"I don't know. Not taconite. Limestone, maybe. Timber."

They passed three more slips. They drove parallel to railroad tracks and abandoned-looking buildings, warehouses. At an unmarked dirt alleyway he turned left. They stopped at a chain-link fence. He turned off the car. They got out and stood at the fence. In the short distance they saw a minor civilization abandoned by time: train tracks sunk in the iodized soil, scrap yards tangled and twined with heaps of rusted steel, old cement silos unpainted in decades, a shack with windows of broken glass. Not far from the gate a pickup truck rounded a dirt bend. It stopped. A man opened the door and looked at them. He did not nod. He did not wave. Noah would not have needed to raise his voice to greet him, but neither did he do so. The man wore coveralls and a watchman's cap. He stepped to the back of his truck and let the gate down. A silver-and-white Siberian husky jumped from the bed and ran to the gate to sniff Noah's and Nat's shoes. They were both startled, but the dog turned as fast as it had come and walked away from them, heeling at the watchman's left. The dog had swollen teats they could see from behind, irrefutable evidence of a new shipyard progeny.

Noah said, "How would you like his job?"

Natalie was still watching man and dog walk away. "What *is* his job?"

"To guard this paradise, I guess."

Together they surveyed the vista for a few minutes more. Finally Nat said, "I could eat a horse, and I have to pee."

AFTER SCONES AND coffee—decaf for Nat—at a coffee shop in Canal Park, Noah gave her a tour of the city. He drove her past his high school and the house on High Street. He took her to Chester Park and showed her the ski jumps. He drove her around downtown and through the college campus. Finally they drove north, past the mansions along Lake Superior, and out of town.

"How long does it take to get to Misquah? I don't remember."

"A couple hours, maybe a little more," Noah said. "We're meeting Solveig and Tom at noon at the Landing. We have plenty of time."

So they drove again the Superior coast. The trees were in that instant before budding, and beautiful. The lake, when they turned upon it, churned not at all. They talked all morning of possibilities.

After their weekend at the cabin they were going back to Duluth to see if Nat could stand living there. Noah had planned it this way, hoping for a few days of kindly spring weather to trick her into loving his native city. He wanted to move back, wanted to start everything anew. Natalie, amazingly, had not rejected the idea outright, though she needed to be convinced, no doubt. Noah had a strategy. So far the weather was cooperating.

They stopped along the way at the Split Rock lighthouse, up among the trees, resting atop a cliff one hundred feet above the water. The image was fit for a tourist brochure. They stopped also at Tettegouche. They walked up the well-tended trails and marveled at the flowing water of the Illgen Falls. Noah told her about the bear and moose that drank from this river five miles upstream. She nodded, teased him about being a Boy Scout.

He slowed at the enormous loading facility at Taconite Harbor. Again great cones of taconite stood at the roadside. His father's ships had loaded here, he told her, and at countless other such harbors. She listened intently.

In Misquah they met Solveig and Tom. They lunched in the little café. Noah told Nat how he'd stood outside talking to her on the pay phone. Solveig reminisced about the taffy their mother would buy for her every time they stopped there. Natalie described stopping here before heading up to Lake Forsone. After lunch they drove to the cabin.

There were still small mounds of snow beside the shed and at the top of the hill, where the plow had piled it all winter long. The eaves trough along the front of the house had come free of the roofline and hung to the ground. Icicles, Noah thought—it had been a snowy winter—and age.

They all stood in the yard, silent for a spell.

"This is how I left it," Noah finally said.

"And you think you can fix this place up?" Solveig asked. She pointed to the gutter.

"That gutter's nothing to fix," Tom said.

"It'd be nothing for you to fix, honey."

"Hey, I'll manage," Noah said. "Don't worry."

Nat took his arm, squeezed it.

"I'm going to turn the shed into a guesthouse. I already ordered the windows. The plumber just sent me an estimate for running a water line from the well to the house. By this time next year I'll be running a four-star lodge here."

"Just show me where the hot spot is on that lake," Tom said.

The sound of birds erupted from a treetop. Ravens. They lifted into flight, arced once, and disappeared.

"Well?" Solveig said.

"No time like the present," Noah said. He stepped to the trunk of his car. Neatly packed in a canvas book bag was his mother's urn. He took the bag from the trunk and led the three of them down the path to the lake.

The last time Noah had trodden that path he'd done so with the weight of his deed as his only load. On that November afternoon he'd rowed back across the lake. The wind stiffened with each stroke of the oars so by the time he reached the dock there were whitecaps curling beyond the lee of the shore. It was as if the wind were rushing toward the deep water on the other side of the lake. As if to make it deeper still.

When he stepped onto the dock he accidentally shoved the boat. He made one grab for it but could only watch as it scudded away. He watched for a long time. Then he walked back up the hill.

Inside, he tried to conjure from the dusky heat of the stove some

vision of his father's ghost. All he found was sadness. But there resided in it a confused bliss for all that had come to pass. Their reconciliation. Late in the afternoon he trudged through the snow up to
the county road. A plow had already been through and buried the
truck. All he could see was the faded green roof. Expecting as much,
he'd brought a shovel. In the last hour of daylight he dug it out. He
drove into Misquah and called his sister.

In much the same way that she'd once orchestrated a response to
their mother's death, she began to instruct Noah. It was as if she'd
thought of nothing else since she'd left those days ago. In the background Noah heard Tom's voice. His usual gaiety was replaced with
an earnestness Noah had never suspected. Tom reminded Solveig of
details she'd forgotten in their scheme.

Noah was to report his father drowned. Man overboard trying to
net the last fish of the year. A tragedy. Noah interrupted, described
the rowboat adrift in the lake. Solveig related this to Tom, who took
the phone from Solveig. "Then it's a mystery, Noah. Call the police.
Tell them your father is missing. Tell them you saw the boat floating
empty in the middle of the lake. Tell them he'd gone fishing. It's actually more plausible this way."

Noah stood dumb in the wind. He did as he was told.

Solveig never so much as questioned Noah's undertaking, not
then, not ever.

After he'd talked to the sheriff's office, Noah called Natalie. "My
father passed away this morning," he said, looking over each shoulder
in the darkness of the vacant parking lot at the Landing. "I put him in
the water."

Natalie said nothing for a moment. Then, "You did the best thing,
Noah."

Now Noah answered her with silence.

"You did," she reiterated. "You did, and I love you. And you're braver than I thought. I'll be there tomorrow."

She would be.

It was late when the sheriff's deputy arrived. One man coming down the road on snowshoes with a flashlight's beam bouncing before him. His name was Ruutu, or so his badge said. He was a brawny Finn with a blond mustache and feathered gray hair. Noah invited him in, offered coffee. He described the false scene.

After the story, as Ruutu sipped coffee, he looked around inside. He kept licking the tip of his pencil but never marked anything in the notepad he'd taken from his shirt pocket. "Can we have a look down at the lake?" Ruutu asked.

"Of course." Noah put on his boots and coat. He took the flashlight from its spot on the shelf. They walked down to the dock.

Ruutu panned the lake with his flashlight. He shone the light up the path. In the flicker of the light Noah could see ice on the deputy's mustache. Ruutu stepped to the end of the dock. Noah joined him. The sky was luminescent with stars.

"That path down from the house is pretty well traveled," Ruutu said.

"I was up and down it a dozen times. I was frantic," Noah said, horrified at his own lie.

Ruutu nodded his head as if he understood. "Awfully damn cold to be going fishing. What was he fishing for, anyway?"

"Trout, I suppose."

"You say you saw the boat empty? That's when you came to call us?"

"That's right." Noah could not meet Ruutu's stare.

Ruutu put his pencil and notepad in his shirt pocket. "Trout season ended in September." He gave Noah a knowing look. "We can come back and search in the morning. You want us to do that?" Before Noah could respond Ruutu continued, "Listen, I knew your pop. Just a class-A man. A hell of a life he led." Now Ruutu fished a cigarette from his coat pocket. He offered one to Noah, who refused, and Ruutu lit his smoke. He exhaled over his shoulder. "We all knew he was sick. Not that he told us, but we knew. One of us would stop by of a Saturday to check on him now and again." He took another drag on the cigarette. He pinched the glowing end of it. "We'll call it an accidental drowning if that suits you. Anyone asks, I gave you the third degree. The third and the fourth." He turned to the lake. "There's some awfully deep water out there. But you probably knew that. Your pop would have made sure of that." He took a deep breath, coughed, and looked up at the stars.

"That's right, anyone asks, you tell them I asked a lot of questions. You tell them I came back tomorrow morning, that I had a look around the lake. That's how I'll write it into the report. In the meantime, I'm sorry."

MIDNIGHT HAD COME and gone by the time Noah stood again in front of the potbellied stove. The ashes radiated the last of their heat. He tried to imagine the list of necessary actions for closing the house for winter. He took the food from the refrigerator and loaded it into a garbage bag. He scrubbed the kitchen basin and counters. He swept the floor and wood box. He tidied the porch. He covered the piano with the sheet he'd been sleeping on those several days. He checked the windows and the back door to see they were locked. He packed his bags. Finally he put what dog food remained into the ice-cream bucket and set it outside for Vikar.

Satisfied, he tried to sleep on the couch. All night he listened to the wind dying. The calm settled in, the house creaked. Sometime in the middle of the night an enormous ray of white light came into the house. He startled, fearing what he could not imagine. A hum and a clattering, the light rising and falling. He sat up. He went to the window. There was Laksonenn and his plow as ordained.

Sometime toward dawn he slept for an hour. When he woke he washed his face with the last cold water. He dressed according to the temperature. It was eight degrees. He walked up to the road and dug out the rental car just as he had his father's truck the day before. He drove the Suburban down to the house and parked it for the winter.

He walked down to the lake for a last look. Though cold, the morning had risen splendidly. Overnight the skim ice had returned. It covered all of the lake. There, two hundred yards off, the rowboat sat locked in the silence, the platform still spanning the gunwales.

He waited at the Landing for his wife and sister. He was greeted as a regular, and condolences were many. People spoke to him with such solemnity in their voices, such compassion in their expressions. The proprietor bought him his coffee and cinnamon roll. That morning and the looks on those faces were as close as Olaf would ever get to a visitation, to a wake. Two days later Noah and Nat were on their way back to Boston with his mother's urn in his carry-on.

His father's obituary had appeared on the front page of the *Herald* that morning.

NOW THEY ALL stood on the dock. At the Landing that afternoon they'd been told that most of the inland lakes were still frozen, still safe to walk on. This was true of Lake Forsone. Tom stepped first off the dock. He jumped up and down three times to demonstrate its capacity. Noah stepped down next, holding both hands up to his wife and sister. Each took one and followed their husbands onto the ice. Together they walked to the rowboat. The ice had crushed it. It lay splintered, half cast in ice.

"Where is he?" Solveig asked.

Noah pointed toward the cliff, toward the deep water. "Over there," he said.

"Should we cross? Spread Mom's ashes with him?"

"I think so."

And they left the wreck of the rowboat and crossed the rest of the lake. In the shadow of the cliff, Solveig took the bag from Noah's shoulder. She removed her mother's ashes and stood facing Noah.

"Well," Noah said, "I guess we could each say something."

There was an awkward momentary pause before Tom said, "I never knew your mother, but if my wife is any testament she was a terrific woman."

"She was," Noah said.

Solveig nodded.

"And your father was kind to my children."

Solveig took Tom's arm. "He was very good to the kids. He had a lonely life, but I'll remember him every day for the rest of mine." She closed her eyes. Not to quell tears, Noah thought, but to try to remember something. "They belong together here."

"You're right," Noah said. "They do belong together." He looked at Natalie. "Do you want to say anything?"

"I love your parents even though I never really knew either of them." She smiled at Solveig, she held more tightly to Noah. "Because of them I have this family now."

Solveig stepped over to Natalie. She hugged her, then looked at Noah.

"On the day Dad died he told me to love my children better than he loved me. I said I would. I didn't realize that any capacity I had to love I owed to him. Him and Mom. That's really all that matters." He stared down at the urn. He looked out at the wilderness surrounding the lake. "They'll rest easy here."

He uncapped his mother's urn and handed it to Solveig. She spread the ashes on the ice. They were the same spectral gray.

WHEN THEY GOT back to shore Solveig and Tom walked up to the cabin under the pretense of making dinner. Noah led Natalie along the lake's edge. At the base of the ski jump's landing hill they stopped. Noah pointed up at it. He'd told her all about it.

"It's so big," she said.

Noah only smiled. They stood silently for a few minutes.

"What time is it?" she asked.

Noah removed his father's old watch from his pocket. Before he left Boston he'd had it repaired, had the escapement and jewel replaced, had a new crystal put on it. He opened it. "It's almost four."

"I can't believe I'm already hungry again," she said.

"I can," Noah said. He closed the watch but then opened it again. He read the words his mother had had engraved on the case back all those years ago, read them for the thousandth time since his father had bequeathed it to him. YOU WILL COME SAFE FROM THE SEA, it read.

He turned to face Natalie. He put his hand on her stomach, which had only recently begun to show. She held his hand where it lay.

THANKS:

To my father, for answering so many questions and offering so much advice. And to my mother, for her unfailing support.

To Laura Langlie, for her patience and counsel and fortitude.

To Greg Michalson, for his tireless work on this manuscript, it shows on every page. And for giving me a chance.

To Goran Stockenstrom, Patricia Hampl, Bill Lavender, Stuart Dybek, Richard Katrovas, Peter Blickle, Jon Robert Adams, and Jaimy Gordon, my teachers. And to Joseph Boyden especially, who has been much more than a teacher.

To Kim Barzso, my confidant in the beginning. And to Laura Jean Baker, for reading and rereading and not sparing a single thought.

To my brother, Tony, for building a beautiful website.

To Dale and Sandy Hofmann, for their support and for the use of their cabin on so many weekends. Without the quiet weekends there I might never have finished.

To Finn and Mac and Liese, my story beggars.

And to Dana, for positively everything. You inspire me in ways I'm sure I'll never understand. *No broad breaker will fall, nor waves of blue, and we will . . .*

A Note on the Type

The text of this book is
set in the typeface Bembo.

The display type is
called Koch Antiqua
and is based on forms of
old Roman writings,
chiseled in marble.